SPY GAME

SPY GAME

SUE SWIFT

FIVE STAR
A part of Gale, Cengage Learning

GALE
CENGAGE Learning™

Detroit • New York • San Francisco • New Haven, Conn • Waterville, Maine • London

GALE
CENGAGE Learning

LIBRARY OF CONGRESS CATALOGING-IN-PUBLICATION DATA

Swift, Sue. 1955–
   Spy Game / by Sue Swift. — 1st ed.
     p. cm.
   ISBN-13: 978-1-59414-658-9 (alk. paper)
   ISBN-10: 1-59414-658-6 (alk. paper)
    1. Women intelligence officers—Fiction. 2. Undercover operations—Fiction. 3. Computer software industry—Fiction. 4. Cyberterrorism—Prevention—Fiction. I. Title.
PS3619.W546S69 2008
813'.6—dc22
                                 2007036139

First Edition. First Printing: February 2008.

Published in 2008 in conjunction with Tekno Books.

Printed in the United States of America
1 2 3 4 5 6 7 12 11 10 09 08

ACKNOWLEDGMENTS

Many thanks to my longtime critique partners, Janet Shirah and Cheryl Norman.

The help of Stuart Gold, computer expert extraordinaire, was also invaluable.

This book is dedicated to my brother
Keith Swift
(1949–2006)
who liked a good spy tale.

PROLOGUE

San Francisco, California

On Saturday afternoon, Gar saw an umbrella hung in the signal tree in Golden Gate Park, so he met his contact in the Castro at midnight. To anyone watching, they'd look like two guys outside a crowded bar, sharing a smoke, but his contact passed Gar a tiny package, a package worth millions to his customers in Indonesia.

He tucked the package inside his jacket and mounted his motorcycle, heading for Potrero Hill and the shelter of a safe house. As he passed through a residential area, he slowed, and only then did he hear the growl of another motorcycle on his tail. At first he thought it was happenstance, but as he turned one corner and then the next, with the following motorcycle's roar ringing and banging in his ears, he realized he'd been tagged.

Gar tried every trick he knew to shake the tail, but nothing worked. Too late, he saw that he'd been herded toward the shore of the bay, heading too fast down a dead-end alley, with warehouses on each side and a chained metal gate in front of him.

Braking too hard, he jerked the bike into a sharp turn in front of the ten-foot-high gate. The bike slewed on the slick, mist-damp street, drawing a screeching curve to the left before crashing into the cyclone fence.

He hit hard and went down, his bike clattering on its side,

sliding out of the fog lamp's amber halo into the dark, misty night.

In a haze of pain, he lay stunned on the pavement, moving in and out of consciousness, with the bitterness of failure flooding his mouth.

The other motorcycle stopped. Gar heard the scrape of boots on asphalt. Blinking, he raised his heavy head a fraction to see an hourglass figure silhouetted against the golden light. He groaned and dropped his head back. One hand scrabbled toward the precious parcel, seeking to protect it.

The boots stopped close to his head. Too close, but nothing he could do about it. Too weak. Too much pain. Should have worn a helmet . . .

Motorcycle leathers creaked. He smelled jasmine, felt warmth, sensed she knelt beside him. He blinked again.

She had a jaunty smile and eyes that gleamed green even in the dim light. Opening his jacket, she removed the package, which contained the prototype of the computerized brain that would run some of the United States' newest, most sophisticated guided missiles.

"Thank you." She tucked the package into her jacket and walked away, her boots crunching. He heard her bike kick, catch, and roar away, its growl receding into the foggy night.

CHAPTER ONE

One week later

Ani Sharif sat across from her handler, Lewis Anglesey, in a drab office rented by the United States Security Agency tucked in a dull little strip mall in Cupertino, California. With a pang, she wondered what her deceased parents would have thought about her job with the U.S.S.A. Renée Montrueil Sharif, a French specialist in systems and organizational theory, would have taken a dim view of her daughter Ani's employment. "Only oxen were born to work in harness," she'd lecture in her accented English. "Not my child. You, Ani, were born for a grander fate."

Her father, a philosopher and writer, no doubt would have shaken his head with sorrow. Daoud al-Sharif had always picked the road less traveled. Unfortunately, his last road had led to political entanglements with the extremists plaguing his native Algeria. Ani's parents had been massacred ten years before. Ani, attending a private girls' school in Algiers, had been lucky to escape safely, first to Marseilles, where she'd stayed briefly with her French grandmother, then to the United States.

Barely age thirteen, Ani had been contacted by the U.S.S.A. almost as soon as her feet touched French soil. Already fluent in three languages—English, French, and Arabic—she was placed with a foster family in D.C. Tommy and Kate Forrester, who became her legal guardians, worked for the U.S.S.A. Since that time, the U.S.S.A. had fed Ani, clothed her, and trained

11

her, sending her to the Defense Language Institute in Monterey, California, as soon as she was judged ready. There she learned Hebrew, Greek, and Turkish, the Balkans and Middle East having been hotspots throughout history. Despite her education, she used American slang as much as she could. A spy had to fit in.

Along the way, she fell in love—with computers. Adept in the major machine languages, she could see the parallels between them and the human tongues she'd already mastered.

She knew she was the object of much curiosity within the agency. As she'd grown up and risen in the ranks, so had the Forresters; Tommy now headed the U.S.S.A., and Kate ran its domestic branch. Everyone knew Ani was their foster daughter, and she couldn't help wondering if her status had helped or hindered her career. Though she'd become one of the U.S.S.A.'s prized resources, she'd worked only as a translator, a hacker, or a courier, occasionally retrieving valuable information or commodities. Until today. Her handler had promised her she'd get her first undercover assignment.

She'd had enough of being stuck in an office while all the other agents got the cool undercover jobs. This new mission was important to her and to her future. Faking nonchalance, she stretched out her legs, then set one booted ankle on the other knee as her handler talked.

Lewis, whose short blond hair shone silvery at the temples, leaned forward over his battered, government-issue desk. "There's a spy at either Rexford.com or at a related company, CompLine. Someone's selling the Defense Department's cyber secrets, and we think it's one of the Rexfords. Have you heard of them?"

Ani straightened and set her feet onto the floor. "Of course. Thomas and Richard Rexford, father and son, are known as the Terrors of Silicon Valley. Some people call him T-Rex."

"Which one, the father or the son?"

"According to the gossip, the nickname could apply to either. But Thomas is usually called T-Rex, and Richard is referred to as Baby Rex. The rumor is that they're at each other's throats."

"Well, one of them's a traitor."

"So what? Wouldn't we normally just pull the contracts?"

"That would be unfair."

"I beg your pardon? Since when has fairness mattered in the face of national security?"

"We can't, or rather, we don't want to. The Rexfords have done good work for us. We'd rather find out who the agent is."

"How do I come in? Normally I'd break into the system, flush out the spy—"

"We've already tried that, and haven't found anything. We need someone to get close to Richard Rexford."

"How close?" Because she'd grown up in Algeria, she'd never felt comfortable with physical intimacy outside of marriage. The one time she'd acted contrary to her beliefs had been a disaster that she didn't intend to repeat.

"Close enough to hack into his laptop."

Her lip curled. "As long as it's turned on and connected to the Internet, I can hack into it from that machine right there." She nodded at the P.C. on Lewis' desk.

He shook his head. "He doesn't use it frequently, so it's not connected to the net most of the time. That's why you have to get aboard his yacht and into his home system."

"His yacht?"

"He lives on a boat at the Santa Laura Marina. I'll email his updated dossier to you."

"We could send a frogman, get on board when he's not there and steal it."

"We haven't been able to do that."

"Why not?"

"There's security in the harbor."

"Can't we infiltrate it?"

"No, we haven't been able to plant anyone. The marina is run by a small, family-owned company, and they don't hire outsiders. And we haven't been able to break in because of the neighborhood watch, so to speak."

"There's a neighborhood watch?"

"Not formally, but there's quite a community of people who live in the harbor, some for decades. You need to get a job at Rexford.com."

"What? Why should he hire me?"

"It's true that Rexford has previously employed only people he knows, mostly personnel laid off from his father's company, CompLine. But we can force him to take you on. A faked message has been sent to him via a hack through his firewalls and into his company, so it's impossible for him to let you run around loose. He can't risk one of his competitors getting hold of you."

Ani remained unconvinced. "We could rent a boat, and I could move in there temporarily, sneak over to Rexford's yacht."

"Strangers are noticed and scrutinized. Your assignment is to get that job, get friendly with Rexford, board his yacht legitimately, and let the neighbors become used to your presence. Then you can break into his laptop at any time and transmit the contents of the hard drive to us."

"What if he's not the spy?"

"We're trying to implant others to investigate that possibility, so don't worry about anyone except Richard Rexford. Your presence on Rexford's yacht, in his office, in his life, can't arouse suspicion. The Rexfords are very powerful. Maybe the father and the son don't get along, but both have Defense Department contracts and a lot of contacts in the government. We can't risk alienating either of them." He rose. "Are you sure you want this assignment?"

Ani hesitated. She didn't want to blow her chance for advancement, but . . . "Yes, sir, I do."

"Then quit questioning your orders."

She shot him a fixed stare. "I've worked with this agency for years—"

"I know. Don't try to intimidate me with your relationship with the director and the members of his family."

He's been holding me back, she realized. He's jealous. Maybe he's set me up to fail! She sent Lewis a grim smile. "I am a member of the director's family."

"If you can't handle the mission, we can find someone who will." A muscle clenched in Lewis' jaw.

"I can handle it," she said stiffly. "What's my cover?"

"We've set you up as an opportunistic cyber-pirate. You own every variant of the Rexford web address we could think of."

"That won't stop him for long. He can just go to arbitration and get it back within a month."

"Oh, but he doesn't have a month. He's already filed with the S.E.C. and is scheduled to go public within days. If his stock offering doesn't come out on time, he'll lose millions." Lewis sat down and regarded her. "Flirt with him, intrigue him, do everything you can to get his attention and get inside his company. Move in on him without arousing his suspicions. In other words, don't be too eager. He has a taste for the ladies. Let him come to you."

Menlo Park, California
Three days later

He heard her long before he saw her.

The harsh growl of a motorcycle shattered Richard Rexford's concentration as he pored over a stack of dull printouts from the Accounting Office. His focus fled as the steady vibration gentled. He guessed that the cyclist had entered the parking lot and slowed for safety.

Then, the pitch of the engine increased to a roar. Leaping out of his chair, Richard strode to the window.

At first he couldn't see anything. His office, the best his building had to offer, had a limited view of the parking lot. Instead, he could see the rolling grass lawns his architects had carefully planned.

But below, in the slice of asphalt his view included, a Harley Davidson slammed through the parking lot, slaloming through the parked Beemers and minivans as though its reckless rider were on a par course instead of the grounds of the newest, biggest, most prestigious company in Silicon Valley.

Dark hair floated from the rider's helmet, whipped by the wind into a wild cloud. He couldn't see much else, except that the cyclist wore black leather, defying the golden autumn sun.

The hog disappeared from his view, and a few moments later, silence reigned. He supposed that she'd parked near the lobby doors, out of his sight.

His gaze wandered to the far end of his "L" shaped building. The temporary sign, a tarp stretching along its topmost reaches read REXFORD.COM, the name of his new company.

The name she owned.

He imagined her entering the lobby, taking a moment to sign in with security before ascending the elevator.

Clack. Clack. Clack. Heavy shoes clattered over the hardwood floors in his outer office. Motorcycle boots?

A pause, then a buzz from the intercom. Richard pressed a button to open the connection with his secretary.

"Yes, Paul?"

"Ms. Ani Sharif is here for her appointment."

"Send her in." Standing by his desk, Richard waited.

Clack. Clack. The door opened, and there she was. He'd guessed right. She had arrived on the hog.

16

Short and trim, Ani Sharif wore black motorcycle leathers, from jacket to booted heels. Tight chaps encased faded jeans. Tousled bedroom hair, flattened at the top by the helmet, flowed curly and free over her shoulders, mysterious as midnight.

Mouth dry, he swallowed. Computer nerds tended to be an unconventional group, but this cyber-babe took eccentricity to new heights. Or depths. He couldn't decide which, but he hadn't expected a Hell's Angelette. He walked forward, extending a hand. "I'm Richard Rexford, Ms. Sharif. I'm pleased to meet you."

She grinned at him, even white teeth flashing in amber skin. Dark-fringed eyes like emeralds . . . no, jade, or perhaps peridots. He hated doing business with beautiful women. Too damn distracting.

"No, you're not." Her hand, though small and finely boned, shook his with a firm, no-nonsense grip.

He started at her touch. "I'm . . . not what?"

"You're not pleased to meet me." Her husky contralto seemed at odds with her petite stature. "You have to meet me." She set her beat-up helmet on one corner of his immaculate desk.

She was right. Not only did Ani Sharif own Rexford.com, but she'd purchased Rexford.org, Rexford.net and every form of his name that anyone in his Marketing and Legal Departments could dream up. Marketing was sure that if his famous family name wasn't in the web address, he'd lose millions.

Worse, she'd announced her ownership via email. Not a public email sent via Yahoo or Netscape or any open system. Oh, no. She'd broken into a private, guarded system. His carefully designed, heavily guarded system. If that information got out, he'd lose even more millions in Defense Department and private contracts.

The snotty little web chick had him by the short hairs, and she knew it.

She stripped off her gloves and shoved them into a pocket. Unzipping her jacket, she exposed a tie-dyed t-shirt hugging small, high breasts.

"Take a seat," he said. "Coffee?"

"Thank you. That would be very nice." Selecting the nearest side chair, she sat and stretched out her legs. "Black, please."

He went to the door to speak to his secretary. "Paul, bring me black coffee for Ms. Sharif." A moment later, Richard handed her a mug. "So how did you do it? And why?"

"I beg your pardon?" Her nose twitching, she sniffed the brew before she sipped.

Distracted by her formal speech and slight accent, he wondered if she was foreign-born, a fact that his Internet search hadn't revealed. Information about her was distressingly absent. He knew only that she was a hot young programmer whose start-up had failed, a common scenario. Shoving any personal interest in her out of his mind, he said, "My name. Why do you own my name?"

"I own numerous names." She pulled his stack of printouts closer and set her mug on top of them. "I bought your name when I heard a rumor that you wanted to leave CompLine and start your own firm. Purchasing Internet domain names is an inexpensive investment."

"You're a cyber-squatter." He sat behind his desk, opposite her.

Meeting his gaze, she smiled. Her eyes held a flirtatious twinkle. "I prefer . . . entrepreneur."

"You broke into my system. What you're doing is illegal."

"Maybe. Maybe not." She shrugged. "I'm sure neither of us wants a fight in court, or even a time-consuming arbitration. Why don't we just play 'Let's Make a Deal' ?"

He leaned back into his chair and grinned at her, recognizing a kindred spirit, someone who also loved the game. "It didn't cost you any more than, oh, five dollars to register the Rexford name, Ms. Sharif. I'll offer you five thousand."

She laughed. "I'll take Door Number Two, please. My research tells me you could lose millions. I want a proportional share."

He lifted his brows. "Shares in my company? Not a chance." He'd never tie himself to this cyber-pirate, though he had to admire her nerve and smarts.

She shook her head. "No stocks. Too speculative."

Faintly insulted, he frowned. Even in the shaky economy, insiders considered his web security company a sure thing, a great investment. Had she been living in a cave? Web chick Ani had just made her first misstep. He relaxed. "What do you want?"

"Add a zero to your payment offer and give me a programming job."

"What?" Oh, no. This woman was trouble with a capital T. Having her around daily would be a disaster. He'd never get a lick of work done, and neither would any straight male in the company.

"This is very simple. I have what you want. You have what I want: cash and a job. I know you're hiring programmers. Fifty thousand isn't unreasonable, considering your family's resources."

A gold digger. Great. "I have no idea if you're competent. According to my research, your dot com just went dot gone. Going kaput isn't a high recommendation."

Her pirate smile sped his pulse. "In six months—if I'm still around—I'll be running your programming division."

"I doubt that." He decided to call her bluff. "I'm sorry we can't reach an agreement. Contact me when you're ready to be more reasonable."

"By Monday morning I believe you'll contact me." Standing,

she picked up her helmet.

"Not likely." He chuckled at the cute little lightweight. He'd let her sweat. On Monday he'd offer her three thousand, just to teach her a lesson.

"A challenge. I like that." She turned and winked before sauntering out the door. Her chaps framed her heart-shaped backside, snug in the faded, tight jeans.

He walked to the door to close it. Scenting the exotic fragrance of jasmine, he looked through the doorway into his outer suite and saw Ani chatting to his secretary. Worse, she had a good view of Paul's computer screen, which probably showed information Richard didn't want her to see.

His dismay mushroomed. "Excuse me. I'll show you out myself." He grabbed her arm and ignored the warmth of her flesh, palpable even through the leather jacket.

Ani looked him over again as he hauled her to the double doors of his outer office. Richard Rexford, a WASP dream come true, had sea-blue eyes and unfashionably shaggy blond hair, which contrasted with the rest of his ultra-straight appearance. His athlete's body was clad in proper yuppie garb, pleated khaki pants and a starched broadcloth shirt topped by a navy blazer with corny little anchors on the brass buttons. His aftershave, slapped onto perfectly shaved cheeks, smelled like an ocean breeze.

The calluses on his manicured hands couldn't be from honest work, given his upper-class background. He probably played some silly sport like golf or billiards. Maybe he worked out, given the way he hauled her through the ritzy halls of his company.

She didn't like to be manhandled, even if the man handling her was as outright sexy as Richard Rexford. Even if his touch, strong but not rough, made her tingle down to her toes. She resisted curling them inside her boots.

A personal interest in Richard Rexford was impossible.

Ani remembered the way his eyes narrowed with contempt when she'd mentioned his family's money. She smiled. This mission was going even better than she dared hope. Who cared about Richard Rexford and his opinion? He didn't know squat.

Faster than Ani liked, Rexford sped her down the elevator and through the lobby. He deposited her out the door like an unwanted kitten, bidding her good-bye and good luck . . . even though his behavior hollered, "Good riddance!"

Ani told herself to quit letting herself get distracted by Rexford's attitude. He was a target, nothing more. She hummed a careless tune to herself as she mounted her Harley. Arrogant Richard Rexford needed a lesson, and she'd be the woman to teach him.

Chapter Two

On Monday morning, Richard clicked on his office computer and listened to its soothing hum and whir. He sipped coffee while waiting for his email program to load. Although he'd checked his messages earlier that morning, some might have arrived in the last hour.

A series of flashes, like fireworks exploding, stormed onto the screen, not his favorite screensaver, a peaceful seascape. Jolted, he leaned forward to tap the monitor's housing, even though he knew his primitive reaction wouldn't change anything. Someone had altered the programming. Computer sabotage? His nerves twanged.

Then, the cartoon figure of a woman with big hair appeared, riding a Harley across the screen. Rock and roll blared out of the speakers: the song "Born to be Wild." When the leather-clad cyclist reached the side of the monitor, she turned her head and winked at him.

She had green eyes.

Despite a weekend of Richard's hard work shoring up his firewalls, Ani Sharif had again hacked into the computer system of the most advanced web security company in the world. Swearing a blue streak, Richard peered closer at myriad tiny, shimmering rainbow characters that formed the background of the onscreen cartoon. He clicked his mouse a few times, isolating the data.

His blood chilled, then heated as rage flashed through his

veins. His source codes. The symbols merrily dancing along the screen behind the jaunty figure of Ani Sharif on her motorcycle were his source codes, the most important and secret aspect of his business—the programming that made everything run and kept everything secure. How had she found them?

Richard swore as he reached for the phone.

Ani sashayed into the Starbucks at DeAnza and Stevens Creek, pretending a cockiness she didn't feel. If Rexford didn't come through, she'd be reassigned, and she needed this job to prove herself.

She took a deep breath, inhaling the aromas of espresso, cinnamon, and money. Lots of money. Silicon Valley was still an exciting place. The fire in the valley, which had ignited a worldwide computer revolution, hadn't flamed out with the crash of 2000, but had bounced back, stronger than ever. Especially in the area of security, Richard Rexford's specialty.

If she could get aboard Rexford's yacht and into his laptop, she'd climb further up the ladder toward the highest echelons of the U.S.S.A. This job was a make-or-break deal, as far as her career was concerned.

Ani assured herself that Rexford would hire her. He had to. Not only did he need his domain name, but she'd also shown him her talent. She'd breached the defenses of his network, perhaps the most advanced web security system in the world, and found his source codes, his most closely guarded secret. She allowed herself a small, satisfied smile. She and her colleagues had stayed awake for almost thirty-six hours straight to do it, but hopefully their industry would bear fruit.

She spotted Richard Rexford standing in line behind a small woman wearing a sari and glasses. After the Indian lady ordered a mocha, Ani joined Richard, deliberately crowding him a little. She'd noticed at their meeting Friday he seemed disturbed by her physical presence. Good. Though she didn't sleep around, she wasn't above flirting to gain an advantage. She figured that since American society was sexist, she might as well play the game with all of her assets.

It sure wouldn't hurt her to flirt with Rexford, a Brad Pitt look-alike. She just needed to avoid getting too close or too involved. A romantic entanglement with a target would kill her career hopes.

Silicon Valley was a community close-knit by electronic communications. Everyone knew a lot about everyone else. If the e-gossip was to be believed, Rexford was no harmless gecko, but one of the Valley's biggest, baddest predators. Baby Rex, indeed.

Grinning to herself at the thought, she jostled him gently with her arm to get his attention. A sparkle of attraction flared when she touched him. She ignored it. This was no time to get mushy.

He wheeled, his blue eyes meeting hers. The irises darkened from aqua to indigo. Their chill would have frozen her into a human Popsicle if she weren't so determined.

She hoped her smile looked confident. "I'd like a double espresso, please. With cinnamon sprinkles." She turned and walked outside to an empty table, far from his disturbing aura.

The clear blue sky belied the approaching autumn, for inland California would stay sunny and warm into October. Two tables away, an earnest young man scribbled a systems diagram on a pad of paper. He showed it to a good-looking older fellow with iron gray hair and a Hawaiian shirt.

Rexford, carrying two coffees, stopped to greet the older guy, calling him Kenneth. On edge, Ani tapped her booted toe against her table's metal leg. Finally Richard finished his conversation and set the drinks on the table.

"Which one's mine?" Ani asked.

"Here." He pushed a cup in her direction.

"Thank you." She stuck her nose over its rim and breathed. "Um, hmm."

"Didn't have coffee yet this morning?"

"No. You didn't give me much time to get down here." She'd met with Lewis again that morning before rushing to the Starbucks to meet Rexford. She didn't like early meetings or Lewis' cheap, weak coffee. She needed this espresso.

"Eager to see me, huh?" Rexford smiled, shark-like.

Ani realized she'd made a mistake by appearing too needy. She leaned back in her chair, sipped the coffee, and smiled, delicately licking her lower lip. Richard's gaze seemed implanted on her mouth.

She said, "I wanted to know if you liked my graphics and sound."

His blue eyes narrowed. "I'm not a Steppenwolf fan."

"Then I'll be sure to play 'Magic Carpet Ride' very, very loudly while I work at your company."

"Suit yourself. I'll place you as far away from my suite as possible."

"Wherever." Ani hid her disappointment. She'd have to figure out another way to get close to Rexford. Aside from the mission, she liked sparring with him. There was something compelling about the man.

"Does this mean I have a job?" she asked.

Rexford looked as though he wanted to tear out her throat. "Yes, but there are conditions."

"Really?"

"Yes. Your preliminary screening looks clean, but you have to pass a security check through the Feds. We handle a lot of government contracts."

"No problem." She restrained her grin. There were few government secrets she couldn't access, if necessary to fulfill her mission. The U.S.S.A. would make sure she passed any security screening.

"You have to pull your weight like the rest of the crew."

"Hey, I'll earn my keep." She winked at him.

"Transfer the ownership of the Rexford.com name within ten days of today's date."

She sipped espresso to hide her immense relief. It sounded as though she'd get everything she needed. "I'll transfer ownership within ten days of receiving fifty thousand dollars." She'd been instructed to insist on the cash as part of her cover as an opportunistic cyber-pirate.

Rexford hesitated. "We have to begin creating the site immediately. Our stock offering is due for release in less than three weeks."

She smiled. "I can build your site in a couple of hours."

"I already have a design team on that project. That's baby steps for a programmer like you. I don't know of another hacker who could have breached my firewall to invade my system, not once, but twice."

She shrugged and tried to look non-threatening. If he felt threatened by her, he'd never ask her aboard his yacht. Smiling, she leaned forward. "I know we haven't started off well, but I hope that we'll have a long and . . . mutually beneficial association."

He raised his brows and cut her a sharp glance from his laser-blue eyes. "We'll see. In the meantime, I want to assign you to our newest, most important project."

"And what is that?"

He paused, then asked, "Are you aware of the cyber-war?"

"No." A lie, of course. She'd been aware of the government's battles in cyberspace since nine-eleven.

He raked long fingers through his hair. "I'm trusting your integrity now, and since you don't have much of that . . ." He shook his head. "I don't know."

She wondered what Rexford's take on the situation would be. "Tell me. This sounds interesting."

"It is, and although I hate to say it, you're the most talented hacker I've ever come across. Since they say it takes a thief to catch one, here goes." He leaned across the table. "There's a secret cyber-war going on. Attacks have been mounted against Defense Department sites, the internal systems of C.I.A. installations . . . you name it. The most recent viral attacks have come in the form of flooding."

"Flooding?"

"Hackers have been flooding the ports of military installations, causing breakdowns that have endangered national security." He narrowed his eyes. "Solve the problem and you're in. Fail, and you're toast."

Excitement zipped along Ani's synapses. Rivalries between government agencies were frequent and destructive, so neither she nor her U.S.S.A. colleagues had been allowed to fight this particular battle by the Defense Department, the N.S.A., or the C.I.A., all notoriously insular organizations. She'd love to hurl a little egg onto their smug faces, and through Rexford, it seemed as though she'd be able to get her hands on this sweet little conundrum.

Her fingers twitched, wanting a keyboard. She stared at Rexford's mocking smile.

She could tell he thought she couldn't do it. She'd show him. "How much time do I have?"

"Ten days."

She controlled her mouth, which had been about to drop open. "Why ten days?"

"Can't hack the deadline?"

"I didn't say that."

Rexford stood. "Then ten days it is. Follow me over to Rexford.com, and I'll show you around and introduce you to your team leader. After that, you're on your own." He pushed in his chair, preparing to leave.

She followed. "Who's the man in the Hawaiian shirt?" she asked him as they left.

"The head of Ferocious." Rexford had lowered his voice.

As they walked, Ani leaned closer to hear him, becoming aware of his scent, a subtle essence that reminded her of the seashore breeze. "What's Ferocious?" She'd never heard of a company with that name. She prided herself on her knowledge of the techie market.

"Ferocious Funds, a new mutual fund company. If Kenneth buys my offering, we'll make a fortune."

"You already have a fortune."

His mouth twisted. Rexford didn't seem to enjoy references to his bucks. "But you don't. You want money, don't you? Ferocious could shoot your stock options through the roof."

"I don't want stock options, thank you."

A slight smile played over his lips. "Sure you do."

"I don't want stock options in some dubious start-up. I want cash," she said, playing her role as a gold digger.

"Dubious start-up? Ha. Stock options are still where it's at in Silicon Valley. You know, for a smart woman, you aren't real savvy at business."

Ani flushed. "If I'm so dumb, why am I here . . . with you?" They'd reached the Harley. She untangled the strap of her helmet from the handlebars.

"*Touché.*" He touched the tip of her nose, surprising the heck out of her. An odd warmth rushed through her body. She couldn't identify the feeling. That bothered her. She frowned.

He turned away. "I'll see you at the office," he called over his shoulder.

CHAPTER THREE

Richard prowled the halls of Rexford.com, feeling tense and unreasonable. His new venture seemed to be well on its way to sucking him dry. If he didn't get a product out soon, he'd be forced to close his doors.

He approached Ani Sharif's cubicle and peered inside, blinking. A neon sign reading *OPEN,* the kind typical of a truck stop, flashed in his eyes. Cartoons and computer-generated art decorated the walls. The plain office lamp, standard issue for Rexford.com employees, hid beneath a swath of exotically printed fabric, giving the cubicle the romantic aura of a Moroccan bazaar or pasha's harem.

In a few short days, Ani had transformed her office from a stark, spare workspace into a cyber-punk's trash heap.

Richard hated the fact that he thought about her constantly. He didn't understand why. She wasn't prettier than any of the women he dated, but she had something daring, something different. A wild little something that stopped Richard from dumping the screensaver she'd installed into his desktop. He enjoyed the clever graphic she'd created. Cute and funny, it reminded him of her.

There had been a shortage of cute and funny in Richard's life.

"Born to be Wild." Ha.

He continued his exploration of Ani's domain. Out of curiosity, he pushed the button that opened her computer's C.D.

drive. To his surprise, he saw the familiar logo of "Mega Bet," a game he'd designed. He closed the C.D. port, pleased that a talented programmer like Ani thought his work worthy of her attention.

The aromas of cinnamon-laced coffee and jasmine perfumed the air, but Ani was absent. Absent at three-thirty in the afternoon. What the hell did she think she was doing?

His gray mood darkened further. The race to develop a method to protect the government's sites would be won or lost within a few days. Weeks, at the most.

He knew the programmers remaining at CompLine, the firm owned and run by his father and uncle, were working double shifts to crack this problem. He refused to let his father win. Aside from all Richard's other grievances, dear ol' Dad had cussed Richard out good and proper for the umpteenth time when he'd jumped ship to start Rexford.com, plundering CompLine of its best personnel.

A clatter of boots on linoleum startled Richard out of his thoughts. "Where have you been? Why are you so late?"

Ani brushed past him, looking utterly unconcerned. "I always commute late to avoid traffic."

"It's mid-afternoon. We have set work hours here."

"Really? Amazing how many people stay after five p.m." She dropped her helmet and her leather jacket onto the floor. Today, she wore tight black leather pants and a tank top in a virulent shade of lime green. Silver bangles clinked on her wrists. Enameled combs pulled back her luxuriant hair, exposing a trio of silver hoops on each ear.

Damn. He should never have hired her. Beautiful women were just too distracting. "We have a project due. Most of us are willing to work late to get the job done. When are you going to complete the website clearing software?" Maybe he could fire her. The ten days were up.

"Already done." Ani bent to fumble in the inner pocket of her black jacket, giving him an eyeful of her nice round butt.

Richard couldn't see a panty line ridging the black leather. Was she naked under her clothes? Maybe she wore a black leather thong to match her pants.

She removed a compact disc, then straightened up and tossed it to him, flinging it like a Frisbee. "I do my best work at home between two and four in the morning."

He fingered the flat, silvery C.D. If she wasn't joking, the software he held could be worth millions.

"Hey, Ani." Rexford.com's head programmer appeared at her door.

"Hello, Kevin," Ani said to Kevin Wilson. "It's done. I finished last night."

"Yeah?" Kevin's eyes, weirdly magnified by his Coke-bottle glasses, lit up like the Vegas strip at midnight. "Where is it?"

She pointed at the C.D. in Richard's hands. "I present Rexford's double-A, double-V fix for website clogging."

Richard folded his arms over his chest. Gracious of Ani to have named the software for him, but he doubted she'd come up with a solution in just a few short days. He'd set the deadline tight, sure she'd fail. He needed an excuse to get rid of her. He'd avoided her for days, but Rexford.com was a small company. Contact was inevitable and unwelcome.

Kevin jabbed Richard's side with a bony elbow. "You're gonna love this, boss. This is great."

"How do you know?" Richard asked.

"I previewed it last week."

Little impressed Kevin, a gifted programmer, so Richard gloomily concluded his ploy hadn't worked.

"I was initially sidetracked by the description of the problem as a viral attack." Ani sat in front of her desktop computer. "It's not. The shutdowns of the Defense Department sites due to overload were not caused by a virus. It's a queuing problem."

"A queuing problem?" Richard moved closer, braving the snap and sizzle he felt while near Ani.

She appeared unaffected by their closeness. "The overloads occur because, after the initial break-in, thousands of phony signals reach the server at the same time. The machinery is overwhelmed by the volume, so it crashes. Our new software sorts the signals into an orderly queue for processing." She flipped a switch. Her monitor winked and flickered to life.

"That was the easy part." When Ani paused, Kevin picked up the thread. "The hard part was creating a program to allow the server to quickly distinguish between a real hit and a fake hit. Thus was born Rexford's double-A double-V fix."

Despite himself, Richard became interested. Kevin wasn't a flake, and if he thought the software was hot, it probably was. "What's the double-A double-V fix?"

"Ani's anti-virus virus," Kevin said.

"When installed into the server's computers, it allows the system to differentiate between a real and a phony hit in fractions of a second." Ani swiveled around on her chair to face him. "It rejects the fake hit and moves to the next inquiry. Even better, it works like a virus."

"How?"

"It follows the electric trail back to the origin of the fake hit and disables the sender's Internet software, thus stopping the attack."

"What about the breaches in their firewalls?" Richard asked.

"That will require analysis of each site, because every firewall is different," Ani said.

"But that's all right. It's another opportunity for Rexford-.com to earn money." Richard decided that his company just might make it.

"This software is designed to control the damage once they're in, and to disable the attacker's systems. It's a revolutionary new approach to the problem," Kevin said, "and one that will do the trick."

"I'm working on a tracing feature that will enable the hacker's computer to be identified via its electronic signature," Ani said. "I'll have that done next week."

"Rexford's double-A, double-V fix." Richard couldn't help grinning. "Every major server on the Internet is gonna want this program. This is going to make a mint. Still glad you rejected stock options, Ani?"

She shrugged. "Money isn't everything."

"What happened to the woman who wanted only cash and a job?"

"Still sitting right here." She arched a brow at him. "I'm a simple girl with simple needs. Give me a decent salary and a hot software problem, and I'm happy."

"And a good cup of espresso." Richard's bleak mood had evaporated. He flipped the C.D. through his fingers. "How long do you estimate it'll take to get a working version ready?"

"Sheez, who knows? But we can finish the debug by Friday." Kevin grinned at Richard. "Party Friday night."

"We're on."

Each evening an encrypted message from her handler warned Ani that if she didn't make some progress toward her goals, she'd be pulled, and another mole substituted. Stuck, she didn't know what to do to jumpstart this mission. She didn't want to let anyone in authority at the agency know she was floundering through her first undercover assignment, so she couldn't call the Forresters. So she met with the one person she could trust, her foster sister.

Both orphaned refugees, Linda Wing and Ani Sharif had been fostered by the Forresters. The two teenage girls had fought bitterly until they'd matured enough to realize that their conflicts had arisen from jealousy and insecurity. Then they'd stuck together like peanut-buttered teeth. Both had studied in the Monterey area at the same time, with Linda attending nearby colleges to learn Japanese, Vietnamese, and several Chinese dialects.

With their educations completed, they'd decided they wanted to stay in northern California and had wrangled agency jobs in the San Francisco bay area. Linda, three years Ani's senior, nevertheless didn't have her capacity for computers, and Ani didn't have femme fatale Linda's capacity for couture style.

The morning after she'd delivered the C.D. to Richard, Ani sat with Linda drinking coffee. "I feel sure he's attracted to me," Ani said.

Linda looked around the coffeehouse. Situated near her home in San Francisco's Richmond district, the shop's mellow jazz would cover their quiet conversation. Communicating with another agent in this way was actually safer than email or encrypted message, both of which could be intercepted and deciphered. To any casual observer, she and Ani were just two singles discussing dating.

"Girls have been mistaken before about Baby Rex," Linda said. "He has quite a reputation."

"Granted I don't have a lot of experience—"

"That's closer to no experience."

"I have to wonder why I'm there."

Linda shrugged. "There's no doubt that you're ready for the next level. You have the cyber skills."

"But I'm no Mata Hari." Ani gnawed a fingernail. "Lewis doesn't really like me. Perhaps he gave me this mission betting I'll fail."

"Maybe you fit a profile of women Rexford has had." A slow smile spread across Linda's lips. "I wouldn't put it past Anglesey to have checked on that."

"I don't know why he didn't send you."

Linda tried not to preen, instead checking the fit of a golden anklet she wore on her right leg, the twin to Ani's. The clasps concealed a sophisticated transmitter. "I'm busy. They've implanted me into the law firm that handles CompLine's business. We think they're selling more than patents to the Chinese and North Koreans."

"How can I snare Rexford and bring him in without being too obvious?"

"Do the traditional girl thing." Linda tossed her long black hair over one shoulder. "Drop a hanky, bend over, and show him the goods."

"Did that."

"You might try dressing differently." Linda examined Ani's faded jeans and sweater. "When will you start looking like an adult?"

"Hey, I wear the same clothes that every other kid my age does. Besides, I don't know if Richard Rexford is into Chanel."

Linda adjusted the boxy jacket of her classic red suit, insuring that the shuriken tucked in its sleeve remained out of sight. Another throwing star was sewn loosely into her hemline. "This outfit was quite a find. There's a consignment store in the Castro that has the most gorgeous vintage clothes—"

"He can't seem to take his eyes off me when I'm wearing leather. Aside from its other benefits." Ani winked.

Linda grinned. She knew that Ani's motorcycle jacket, chaps, and boots hid an array of concealed weapons. Both women were walking arsenals, their weapons made of a high-tech ceramic, which defied metal detectors.

"Okay, then," Linda said. "Your cover is still the dance classes, right?"

"Yeah."

"Get him to come to you." Linda sipped her latte, enjoying its sensual variety, with the bitterness of espresso topped by the froth of the creamy, full-fat milk she'd specified.

"Allow a target into my home?" Ani frowned.

"Clear it with Lewis," Linda said. " 'Cause when Baby Rex sees you dancing in that see-through outfit, he'll be all yours."

CHAPTER FOUR

"Hello? Is anyone there?" Ani Sharif's voice crackled through Richard's speakerphone. Far from her usual sexy contralto, her voice sounded high, anxious, and concerned.

His pulse jumped. Contact with Ani still ruffled his nerves. He tamed his voice into evenness. "What can I do for you, Ms. Sharif?"

"Oh, uh, hello. Are you the only one in the building?"

She never called him by name. Not Richard and certainly not Mr. Rexford. What was that about? "It's seven-thirty Thursday night, Ms. Sharif," he said. "Everyone else is home."

"I know. I called around. No one is left in programming." Now she seemed panicky.

"What's the problem?"

"I left the office without a copy of the fix. We are supposed to finish the debug tomorrow. I'm not quite done."

"What's Kevin doing?"

"Kevin is working on triple-P."

Triple-P, the password protection project, was the programming department's next assignment. Richard paused to think. He didn't want contact with Ani, but he needed the debug on time. "I can drop a copy of the C.D. by your home. Where do you live?"

"It's rather far. Don't concern yourself. I'll come in early tomorrow."

"No. If you do your best work at home, you need it now.

Where can I find the C.D. and where do you live?"

"Umm, all right. The version I was working on is in my desktop C.D. port. I live at 2730 Skyline, off of Highway 17. It's in the hills above Santa Laura. Are you sure? It's quite a drive—"

"Oh, that's fine," he said. "You're on my way home. I also live in Santa Laura."

"You do?" Surprise lifted her tone by several registers.

He knew why. Santa Laura, a beachside town, had long been a counter-cultural haven as well as a tourist trap. It boasted innumerable coffeehouses, bookstores, an alternative college, and a marina. Everyone in his life had been startled when he'd settled there, he reflected as he concluded the conversation and clicked off the phone. Ani Sharif was merely one of a long line of people who didn't know him. Which was fine. He wasn't her business.

On the other hand, he wasn't surprised by her choice of neighborhood. The mountains dividing Santa Laura from Silicon Valley were populated by an eclectic mix of survivalists, hippies, and artists. He bet Ani fit right in with the weirdoes on Skyline Drive.

Forty minutes later, Richard turned off the highway onto Skyline. The wooded, two-lane road wound up a hill past a playground and a park. A swing set and a jungle gym were nearly invisible in the night, lit only by a few dim streetlamps. At the lane's crest a row of mailboxes sat, with a whimsical stuffed or carved animal perched atop each. A wooden bird with brightly painted, outstretched wings roosted on the box marked #2730.

He parked his Corvette at 2730 Skyline in front of a house that screamed "hippie heaven." Surrounded by trees, its redwood siding had weathered into a soft silver-gray. Hanging plants and bird feeders festooned the front veranda. A punching bag was suspended from a heavy chain at the covered porch's far end, its presence striking an incongruous note.

When he approached the door, the gentle clatter of wooden wind chimes interspersed with exotic drumming filled his ears. The drums seemed to emanate from inside the house.

Richard tensed, his imagination conjuring up wild rituals performed during the dark of night in the mountains. He'd heard witchcraft enjoyed a resurgence in the area. Did Ani belong to a coven?

Great. He had a blackmailing programmer who could put a hex on him.

Drawing in a deep breath, he tapped on the stained glass insert decorating the door. The etched design featured a bird, like the mailbox.

Nothing happened, so he tapped harder, using his gold ring to create a harsh rap he hoped would be heard.

The door swung open, releasing the steamy, tempting scents of cinnamon, patchouli, and jasmine, mingled into a heady olfactory broth. Golden light framed the petite young lady who'd opened the door, a formally attired version of Ani. Her sister?

"Ms. Sharif?"

She flicked a switch. An overhead light illuminated her delicate, Asiatic features. "No," she said.

"Uh, clearly not." Richard felt like a fool. Though she superficially resembled Ani—petite, mid-twenties, with honey-toned skin and long black hair—he'd never again confuse the two.

The female who'd answered the door wore a red tailored suit, pearls, and a polished sophistication as visible as her perfectly applied make-up. From the top of her styled coif to the soles of her stiletto heels, this woman radiated a feminine assurance that Ani lacked. Ani was a beautiful, sensual girl, but she had an air of youthful innocence. This woman was ripe.

Funny, Richard mused. He usually preferred a sophisticated, experienced woman, but this Asian doll left him unmoved.

"I'm Linda. Ani doesn't have blood relatives." Linda's English was flavored by a light, unrecognizable accent. She extended a hand decorated by long, manicured nails. "You must be Richard Rexford. Ani's expecting you."

He shook her hand with only a polite pressure, hoping to avoid her talons. Her smile broadening, she looked him up and down as though he was a prize calf at the county fair. Was she coming on to him? Maybe she was just curious. He supposed he should feel flattered by her scrutiny, but all he really wanted was to go home, kick off his shoes, and crack open a beer. Disengaging from her grasp, he eased a finger into his tight collar to stretch his neck.

A burst of excited female giggles floated out over the drumming. He peered over Linda's shoulder into a kitchen. A brass, Arabian-style coffee urn dominated a wooden table. Nearby sat a crowd of gold-rimmed demitasse cups and a tray of pastries, sticky with honey. Cut imperfectly, the small, triangular cakes looked homemade.

Ruffled cushions padded the chair seats. Their flowered pattern matched the stack of cloth napkins on the table. Everything combined to give the room a feminine, homey air his galley never would attain. It made him uncomfortable, but he didn't know why. He swallowed, fingering the C.D. in his jacket pocket.

"I'm looking for Ani Sharif." He didn't want to give the programming to anyone but Ani. Although this attractive young lady was a friend of hers, he wouldn't take any chances with his precious software.

"Sure. Come on in." Linda moved away from the door, holding it open in an inviting manner. She cocked a hip, setting one high-heeled foot behind the other, displaying herself as though she were a runway model.

Once inside, he could see more of the cottage. The windowsill above the sink bore a row of flowerpots with green, fringed plants in them. Herbs, he supposed. To the left, a doorway curtained by strings of multicolored glass beads divided the kitchen from the rest of the house. The giggles of several women came from behind the beads.

"Come." With a flip of her head and a twitch of her trim bottom, Linda led the way through the gently swinging beads. Interspersed with bells, they chimed in her wake.

Richard stepped into a caliph's soukh or sultana's bower. Women jammed the room. Clad in exotic harem-girl costumes or form-fitting leotards, they shimmied their hips to the drumbeat. Incense scented the warm, humid air. Plants draped every available surface. Patterned fabrics, in shades of red and gold, dominated the decor.

He'd walked through a magic portal into an alternative universe. This was the stuff of fantasies . . . at least, his.

"Oh! You're here." Ani left the group and approached, wearing a see-through belly-dancing outfit and a big, relieved smile.

Richard forgot about Linda and ignored every other woman in the room. Ani had grabbed his attention yet again, and he had a feeling she'd never let go.

But what was this? I Dream of Jeannie meets Computer Geek meets Motorcycle Mama. His glance strayed over her breasts, pushed high by her satiny pink bra. Filmy pants with a tiny, golden girdle covering her privates didn't conceal her excellent figure, her belly ring, or the tattoo on her left hip. Wild child. Oh Lord, was she ever. He loosened his tie.

Another golden ring adorned her baby toe. Her slender ankle was chained with gold links.

Ani in chains . . . His heartbeat went nuts.

"Uh, uh, hi." He lifted his gaze, instead focusing on her face. She glowed with a slight sheen of perspiration, from the dancing, no doubt. "Umm, Ani, may I ask what's going on here?"

Her garments swirling, she sauntered past him into the kitchen. "Class."

"What?" He followed, unfastening the top button of his dress shirt.

"Belly dancing class." She poured coffee into a tiny demitasse cup and offered it to him.

"Espresso?"

"Turkish coffee."

He sipped the rich, bitter, satisfying brew. "I'll be up all night." *Dreaming about you in golden chains.*

She poured for herself, bracelets jingling. "So will I. But I'll finish the debug."

"After belly dancing class?"

She nodded, green eyes sparkling like sunshine on spring leaves. "After my dot com went dot gone, as you put it, I had to do something."

"Ah." Richard cast his mind back to the remarks Ani had made about his family's fortune. Maybe she'd truly needed the cash he'd paid her for the Rexford.com name.

And where was her family? But Linda had said that Ani didn't have blood relatives. Did that mean that Ani's parents, her entire family, were dead?

Something flipped around inside his mind, and in a flash, he didn't regret a penny he'd paid her. Even a small cottage in the Santa Laura Mountains didn't come cheap. Maybe Ani rode a motorcycle because she couldn't afford a car. His respect for her skyrocketed.

Then he realized that he felt stifled, even confined, by her home and its overly feminine, sultry atmosphere. He couldn't breathe. His lungs craving fresh ocean air, he tugged at his collar again. He couldn't wait to get out.

"Baklava?" She held out the plate.

After Richard left, Ani ended the belly dancing class, eager to get some downtime with Linda to discuss Richard's visit. She twitched with impatience while the dance students ate their snacks and departed.

She changed into jeans and a Sharks hockey sweatshirt, then walked with Linda along the lane to the park. Linda's heels clattered on the street while Ani's cross-trainers whispered and squeaked on the damp asphalt underfoot.

Fingers of mist wove between the jungle gym's bars, leaving a film of moisture on the swing set. Ani rubbed her sweatshirt's loose sleeve on the swing's seat before fitting her butt into its curve. She pushed a toe against the dew-laden grass to get herself going, loving the wind's rush through her hair. Like a great ride on the hog, it made her feel free, in contrast to her cover as wage slave of the great T-Rex, terror of Silicon Valley.

"Well, I did it all." Linda kicked off her stilettos and plopped onto a swing, apparently unmindful of the dampness marring the skirt of her suit. She swung her legs out as she flew up and bent them in on the descent, working up a good high swing. "The hair flip, the eye twinkle, the smile . . . and nothing. But he's really interested in you."

"I'm not sure," Ani said. "Why's he so hostile? He just gave me the C.D. and ran out as though I was Typhoid Mary."

Linda chuckled. "He wants you so bad he can't stand it. Trust me on this. I saw him checking you out."

"Why doesn't he just—"

"Powerful men are like that," Linda said. "I've seen it before. They have to control everything, especially their feelings. Even their lust."

"Hmm. But he hasn't been able to control me. The way I got

into his company—"

"Exactly. He resents that. He's conflicted, which is good. You've tempted him, and he wants you. I bet he feels as though he has something to prove. It's a guy thing. He has to capture you."

"What an image. Like a hunter setting a snare. As though I'm prey." Though Ani shivered, a thin coil of heat began to unfurl deep in her belly, an almost sexual excitement.

She squelched the feeling. She couldn't be attracted to him. He was too different and too old for her. Besides, he was a target, the object of an agency investigation.

"That's the cool part." The chains supporting Linda's swing squeaked. "He thinks you're prey, and he's the big bad T-Rex, when in reality, you're the one stalking him."

"This . . . this could be, uh, interesting." Maybe even a little too interesting.

Linda laughed, a full-throated sound that left no doubt in Ani's mind that Linda loved the hunt, the chase, the capture.

Ani said, "But I feel like I'm playing with fire."

Linda slid Ani a glance. "Sexy Rexy sure is hot. That's what makes it fun."

"Hot? He's chilly as an iceberg. Did you see those eyes? He reminds me of a WASP android."

"You think so?"

"Probably makes love like a computer, too."

Shrieking with laughter, Ani and her sister swung higher into the night sky.

CHAPTER FIVE

The rich aromas of beer, garlic, and pepperoni greeted Ani when she opened the door of Pizza Polly's, the sports bar patronized by many Rexford.com employees. Now, after work on Friday, the darkened room was lit by the glow of several big-screen T.V.s hung on the walls. Tuned to the sports stations, they showed ice hockey, baseball, and a recap of the previous weekend's football. Ani caught sight of a neon sign with a cute frog, advertising both Bud and the Oakland Raiders. She liked its campiness. If she could get one, it would be a cool addition to her cubicle at Rexford.com.

Glass pitchers of beer clunked onto high, round wooden tables in the back of the room. There, Ani saw several Rexford employees, including Baby Rex himself, clashing their beer mugs together in macho display. Would they next pound on their chests?

She took a long-legged stool at a table occupied by a couple of women from Human Resources.

Evelyn Kehoe, a cool, classy blonde, glanced at Ani. "Are you sure you found the right table?" Her tone was flat and neutral.

Bitch, Ani thought. "I think so. Is there a problem?" She signaled a waitress for a beer.

"The programmers are over there." Redheaded and plump, Karen Leonhart jerked her head to the left. She indicated a table of software engineers, including Kevin Wilson, who were having a loud, drunken discussion of the relative merits of Intel versus A.M.D. processors.

Ani shuddered. "No, thank you. I avoid groups of males when beer is their only nourishment."

"Can't say I blame you. Let's get everyone some appetizers and pizza before the party gets out of hand." Evelyn waved to a waitress and ordered.

"Do Rexford's parties become rowdy?" Ani asked while they waited for their food.

"Not when I'm around." A smirk crossed Evelyn's patrician features.

Ani had heard a rumor that Evelyn was related to the Rexfords. Perhaps that made her a natural disciplinarian. "Good. Perhaps I'll leave when you go."

"Hey, don't worry. I've had some good times with the boys after hours." Karen chuckled. Her laughter made her fleshy breasts jiggle. Remembering that Lewis Anglesey had told her not to chase Rexford, Ani hoped that her own stretchy, pink velour top didn't expose too much. On the other hand, Linda had advised her to show off the goods. Ani eyed Karen's sweater, wondering if Rexford liked red ribbed knit.

Evelyn arched perfect brows at Ani. "Karen adds new meaning to the term, 'Human Relations Department.' "

Ani blinked. "Really?" She resolved to keep an eye on Karen. Maybe she'd learn something.

"You'd be surprised how hot those byteheads get if you punch the right buttons on their keyboards." Karen winked and gulped her beer.

A curious little devil inside Ani wanted to ask about Richard Rexford, but she didn't dare. She moistened her lips. "So who's hot and who's not?"

"Kevin Wilson was a pretty hot property till Delia Chavez in Accounting snared him."

"Kevin? Mr. Pocket Protector himself?" Ani asked. "Kevin is

a great programmer, but I have a hard time imagining—"

"Me, too," Karen said. "But Delia's been looking very satisfied. Vern Maxwell in Accounting . . . yum. And then, there's always talk about Sexy Rexy."

"Richard Rexford?" This is too easy, Ani thought.

"Karen, stop it." Evelyn stood. "This conversation reminds me that we need to set up a sexual harassment seminar for Rexford.com employees." Heels clicking, she left the restaurant. Ani noticed that Rexford's head didn't turn at her departure.

Karen laughed. "She can be a total bitch sometimes."

"I'm glad it's not just me. Does Evelyn have a, uh, thing for Rexford?" With one foot on a lower rung, Ani swung her swivel chair back and forth.

"Every woman alive has a thing for Sexy Rexy. Don't you?"

Ani shrugged her shoulders, wondering what to say. This undercover stuff was harder than she'd anticipated. "He hates me and he's really not my type. He seems so rigid and uptight."

"I like 'em rigid." Karen giggled. "Anyway, Evelyn and Richard are related. Second cousins, I think. That's how she got this job. Rumor is that she's been gunning for Sexy Rexy for years. Thought she had a chance when his fiancée dumped him."

"He got dumped? How long was he engaged?"

"Not very."

"No wonder he seems so . . . tense."

The appetizers arrived. Ani crunched a French fry.

"Yeah," Karen said. "He hasn't dated anyone at Rexford-.com. And who else does he see?"

"So poor Baby Rex is all coiled up in knots." Ani grinned and sipped her beer, realizing that if Richard had been celibate, his condition would make the job of tempting him easier.

The dim light had dilated Karen's pupils to dark pits. "Richard Rexford doesn't like to get his pocket picked. The way you did."

"No pity here. The software I helped write will earn Rexford plenty. I earn my keep." Ani took another healthy swallow of beer. The salty appetizers had given her a thirst.

"Hey, ladies, why don't you join us?" Kevin Wilson sidled between Karen and Ani. "The pizzas have arrived, and you're almost out of beer."

Ani allowed Kevin to lead her to the big table occupied by Rexford and several others. Kevin introduced her to Vern from Accounting and Mark Rexford from Legal. She figured the two Rexfords were related, though Lewis Anglesey hadn't briefed her on Mark. Besides, she couldn't see a resemblance between Richard and husky, dark-haired Mark. She'd already met the programmers who joined them: Daksha Goswami, a tiny Indian woman in a purple sari, and Harvey Reynolds, a reedy, balding fellow.

Ani had finished her second slice of pizza when she heard Richard Rexford mention her name and belly dancing in the same sentence. She glanced at him, wishing she were a thousand miles away. He wore a silly, half-soused grin and a roguish glint in his slitted eyes. No, she'd rather be a million miles away, even if that meant she lived on Mars. She skewered him with what she hoped was a mean stare. A very mean stare, meant to knock him into sobriety.

She hadn't the slightest idea what to do in this situation. No one had told her how to handle the moment when her cover stories clashed.

"Come on, Ani." Rexford's tone sounded reckless and a little harsh. "Show us what you've got."

Again focusing on her food, Ani chewed and swallowed one last slice of pepperoni that had fallen off the pizza onto her plate. "No, thank you."

"Why not? You scared?" His voice taunted. His blue eyes gleamed laser-bright, laser-hot.

Her back stiffened, but she kept her voice low and calm. "Of you?" She forced a laugh.

"So do it."

"Yeah, Ani," Karen chimed in. "I've heard that belly dancing is feminine and beautiful. Why not?"

Ixzit, Ani thought. Damn. How had she gotten into this situation? She tried to logically analyze her choices. She could stay and get teased all night. She could leave without dancing, which might cause bad feelings among her "co-workers." Or she could give them a brief show.

How would Linda handle the dilemma? Cool and unflappable, she'd never have gotten into this mess. But if she had, Ani bet that Linda would brazen it out.

Why couldn't she? Ani felt loose, but not drunk. She could do this without embarrassing herself or, worse, blowing her cover.

Show him the goods, Linda had said. Well, this was an opportunity. She had to take advantage of it.

Ani stood, circling around her stool. She needed room. She locked her eyes with Richard Rexford's electric gaze. She lifted her chin.

His eyes widened, glinting in the dim light.

She raised her hands above her head. Her bracelets clattered and tinkled. She shook her arms and shimmied to the music they created, letting her hips flutter back and forth.

Karen tapped her beer mug against the table in a drum-like rhythm. The others joined in, giving Ani a beat to follow.

Still claiming Richard's total attention, Ani swayed and wove her fingers through the air as though she played finger cymbals.

She gave him an inviting smile, letting her tongue poke through her teeth just a fraction.

His mouth dropped open.

His eyes glazed over.

A wild flame of feminine power pulsed through her body, a flowing energy like a solar flare in space. It streamed to the tips of her fingers and down to her toes as she undulated to the music she conjured inside her mind. She tossed her head, feeling the sensual brush of her hair on her neck and cheek.

She let herself drown in the intoxicating blue of Richard's gaze. Her body heated, but not from the dance; his stare kindled a blaze of female desire, as hot and untamed as the desert wind.

Her glance dropped to his lips. His smile told of moonlit nights and rowdy sex, bodies twisted together in erotic bliss. A carnal shudder ran through her body, blending with the sensual dance, making her hotter.

Ani slid her hands into her hair and lifted it off her neck, letting air cool her nape. It didn't stop the heat sweeping her body as she swayed toward him. He turned his head to watch her when she rounded the table.

The closer she came to Richard, the brighter the flame inside her burned. The beat grew louder and louder, filling her with images of jungle drums and primitive, savage drives. Sweat trickled down the side of her neck, then between her breasts, tickling the sensitive skin.

Erotic lightning streaked through Ani's body, igniting her core. She grabbed the back of Richard's chair and spun him around to face her. Their knees knocked. She stumbled, but he seized her arms, holding her upright.

Clutching his shoulders, Ani surrendered to impulse and shimmied between his spread thighs. She bent forward so her breasts brushed his chest, her hair feathering his nose, her lips just a fraction of an inch away from his. She inhaled his scent, a unique, tantalizing fragrance that spoke of sunwashed seas and windswept shores.

Richard's blue eyes held an intimate promise of ecstasy. She couldn't drag her gaze away from his. His hands slid down her body, trailing a sizzling heat, until he cupped her bottom. Big, warm, and strong, his fingers flexed, bringing her closer. Contact, hard and hot, scalded through her jeans and panties. What was it?

Oh, God, Rexford had a hard-on that blazed right through the denim covering her mound.

Ani snapped back to reality in a lightning flash. *This has gone far enough.*

She pulled away and danced out the door.

He'd forgotten to breathe.

Hell, he'd forgotten *how* to breathe.

Richard finally managed to suck in a deep, desperate gasp. He tugged at the knot on his tie, then jerked at his shirt's top button. It popped off, landing with a ping on the tabletop. He tore off two more buttons before downing a hearty swig of cold beer.

Several of his employees followed Ani outside, with Karen Leonhart declaring, "I want to learn how to do that, too!"

Richard shut out them and everything else in favor of reliving Ani's dance. He'd never seen anyone move as erotically, as wickedly, as Ani Sharif. He'd known he was playing catch with a hot potato when he challenged her to dance. He was sure she'd never resist his dare. A dare was one thing Ani couldn't pass by.

She lit something daring in him, a spark he thought he'd lost. She danced as though she rode bareback on a wild mustang, with a savage, untamed grace. Her exotic perfume intensified with the heat of her sinuous movements, going straight to his head, then dropping, hardening him to an almost painful degree. Her pink shirt, velvety and clinging, had outlined her lithe, elegant curves and called for his caress. Her open leather jacket hadn't concealed her nipples, which had pointed with arousal

51

when she danced. He'd wanted to lean forward and lick the trickle of feminine sweat that had slid down her chest to nestle in the seductive hollow between her breasts.

She radiated passion the way the sun flamed, the way a sandy beach scorched his soles on a hot summer day before he plunged into the sea.

Only plunging into Ani could quench his burn.

He sucked in another breath and collected himself, glancing at his remaining companions. Most had left when the pizza ran out, before the impromptu dance recital.

His cousin Mark still sat nearby, sipping the dregs of his beer. Kevin Wilson, his head programmer, moodily tore a napkin into tiny shreds. Otherwise, the big round table was bereft of partiers, though littered with the remains of their meal.

"You know," Kevin broke the silence. "It's depressing to realize that I'll never have a chance with a woman like Ani Sharif."

"Why not?" Mark asked. "The two of you work together. It's a perfect opportunity to get into her pants."

"Heck, no," Kevin said. "Delia would kill me."

"You engaged?" Richard asked.

"No, but she seems to think—"

"Think what?" Mark demanded.

"I mean . . . Well, why not?" Kevin asked of no one in particular. "Why shouldn't I go after Ani Sharif?"

"Sexual harassment," Richard said. When he realized how stupid he'd been, a nauseating weight settled in his stomach. Asking her to belly dance . . . oh man, was that dumb, or what? Ani probably was dialing her attorney's phone number right this minute. He eyed Mark. "It's not sexual harassment if she says yes, is it?"

"I'm not sure." A line appeared between Mark's brows. "I think so."

His uncle Sundeen's second son, Mark had graduated from

Harvard, so why didn't he know? Richard had stripped Comp-Line of many of its best employees, so out of guilt, he'd put an unemployed Mark in his in-house legal department, figuring his cousin couldn't do much damage there. Some Harvard grad, Richard thought.

"Bet I'll nail her first." Mark poured the last inch of beer from a nearby pitcher into his glass.

"The hell you will," Richard said, surprising himself. He frowned. From where had that possessive urge sprung?

A sneer twisted Mark's thick lips. "You think you'll bed the lovely lady before either of us, cousin?"

Richard couldn't stop his derisive laugh. He hoped he wasn't vain about women, but the sultry heat that had emanated from Ani when she'd pushed against his rod belonged to him, and no one else. He'd bet his company on it. He couldn't forget her alluring smile and the glimmer in her eyes when she'd danced . . . for him.

He moistened his dry mouth with a swallow of beer.

He could be wrong. Women were untrustworthy, a naturally manipulative breed.

But among the three of them—Mark, Kevin, and himself—no contest. "Yeah, I'd bet on me to, uh, win the race to Ani Sharif."

"You're on," Mark said.

"Sheesh, I don't have a chance. You're a lawyer." Kevin nodded at Mark before turning to Richard. "And all the women call you Sexy Rexy."

"You're kidding," Richard said. He knew about Baby Rex and enjoyed the nickname, hoping every day he'd seize his father's persona, T-Rex. But Sexy Rexy? Ha.

"Sure they do. You should hear them in the break room. It gets downright embarrassing." Kevin wiped his mouth with a napkin. "I'm a bytehead programmer. I don't stand a chance."

"Ani's also a bytehead programmer. You work with her. You

probably understand her better than any of us," Mark said.

"That's true." Kevin looked from Richard to Mark and back again. He thumped his beer glass on the table. "You're on!"

"We need to bet something important. Make it worthwhile." Mark cocked his head in Richard's direction. "Does Rexford-.com own Forty-Niners' season tickets?"

Richard shook his head. A wave of dizziness assaulted him. Too many beers.

"If Kevin or I win the bet, you have to buy a pair of season tickets to Niner football games and the winner takes all."

"What do I get if I win?" Richard wanted to know.

"Umm, let's do it this way. The losers pay for the seats, and the winner gets them."

Richard nodded slowly. Seemed reasonable to him. But the real payoff would be having Ani Sharif. His heartbeat kicked into a rapid gallop at the thought.

Okay, he'd had a beer or two. Maybe that affected his thinking, but the erotic potential of Ani . . . Oh, Lord, was she sexy. Richard drifted off into another fantasy of Ani, naked except for her chaps, with that big, vibrating Harley between her legs. He wanted to drag her off the Harley and suck her toe ring, grab her by that sexy, suggestive anklet and chain her to his bed.

Somewhere inside his mind, his good sense piped up. A little voice in his head told him that the bet was sleazy, foolhardy, dangerous . . . what if she sued? But the fantasy of taking Ani, stroking her slender, sensual curves, overwhelmed him. He had to taste her, know her, have her.

Even if he didn't participate in the bet, nothing prevented Kevin and Mark from going for her, he rationalized. He couldn't allow that. She'd danced for him alone. She was Arabian nights, hot sex on cool sheets, and everything he'd ever wanted in a lover.

She was his.

"You're on." Richard raised his glass. "Here's to Ani Sharif."

CHAPTER SIX

"I can't believe I did that!" Ani covered her face with both hands. Her silver rings pressed cool into her burning cheeks as she slouched deeper into Linda's cushy red brocade sofa.

Carrying a loaded tea tray from the kitchen, Linda howled with laughter. "I can't believe it either, except that I know that you never lie. Prissy Ani Sharif, performing the mother of all belly dances in front of a bunch of horny males—"

"I am not prissy!"

"No, I guess you're not." Linda controlled her giggles and set the tray onto her inlaid table. She poured two fragrant cups of jasmine tea. "Drink up, calm down and tell big sister all about it."

"I made a total fool of myself." Ani moaned. "How could I have done something so cheap and slutty?"

"There's nothing cheap and slutty about belly dancing." Linda blew on her tea's steamy surface. "It's a wonderful expression of your cultural heritage."

"I used to think that," Ani said, "before last Friday night. Now I realize it's—it's—"

"What?"

"It's . . . intimate. Seductive. The kind of private dance a woman performs for her man."

Linda cocked a brow at Ani. "Is Richard Rexford your man?"

"Obviously not, since he hasn't called or contacted me in days." Ani sank into the sofa, shoulders slumping.

"Ah, so that's what's really bothering you."

"I'm blowing this assignment."

"And you're not blowing Richard."

"Linda!"

Linda laughed. "Face it, at this point your feminine ego is what's injured, not your career prospects. What did Lewis say about the dancing?"

"I haven't told him about—about that part of it."

"You reported in, didn't you?"

"Of course. I told him that Richard and I attended the same staff party and, umm, flirted a little. He said he thinks I'm making satisfactory progress."

Linda couldn't stop more raucous laughter. "If a lap dance is progress. How were the tips?"

Ani glared, so Linda calmed herself and said, "Look, I'm sure there's nothing to be upset about. You've thrown out the lures, now just let him come to you."

"I don't know what I'm getting into." Ani's voice had dropped to a whisper.

"You sound . . . overwhelmed."

"I am. I never felt this way before."

"What about Michael?"

Ani winced. "I don't want to think about Michael." Another U.S.S.A. agent, Michael had attended the same weekend training camp as Ani had, two years before. During the day, they'd refined their defensive skills; on Saturday night, they'd practiced lovemaking. But Ani, shy about her inexperience, hadn't told him she'd been a virgin. The sex had been awful, and she'd never heard from him again.

"But how is Rexford different from what you felt about Michael?"

"With Michael, it was about curiosity. And seduction," she added bitterly. She'd been nothing more than a quickie for the older agent. She continued, "Now it's . . . like I'm so needy. So turned on. So sexy."

"Sexy is good, especially for a mission like this one."

"He's a target, and he could be a traitor. Oh, God . . . Will I have to sleep with him?"

"I don't think it's necessary to complete the mission. But you can, if you want to. Do you want to?"

The memory of the heat in Richard's blue eyes warmed Ani. "I think I might. But this can't be the right thing!"

"Why not?"

"Make love with a target?"

"Have sex with a target," Linda said. "If you move from sex into love, that's when you get into trouble."

"Huh." Ani turned the thought over in her mind. "But being with Michael taught me that I don't enjoy sex without some feelings."

Linda rose and went to the window of her flat. Outside, San Francisco on a Saturday night bustled and rocked. Jags and Beemers piloted by yuppies zoomed by; couples, their arms around each other's waists, strolled along the sidewalks in the unusually balmy evening.

"Some feelings are okay, but anything more? No. Not for us," she said without turning around. "We're spies. We have to keep secrets, and secrets will kill love, every time."

"I want it all," Ani said firmly. "But Richard is very determined. He wants me, and I don't think I can resist him if he decides to come after me."

Linda turned. "Then don't resist."

"Rexford can't be the right man for me, not for my first serious relationship. He's too . . . too . . . everything."

"Too much of a man?"

"Well, yeah. He's my boss at this company. It's a weird position to be in."

"Rexford.com is not your job. Now, if it were Lewis . . ." Linda wriggled her hips as she returned to the sofa.

Ani eyed her, wondering what that wriggle meant. Did Linda have a thing for Lewis? "That would be weird. He's at least forty. But Rexford's older than me by, oh, maybe ten years."

"So what? You want some clumsy fool messing with you again?"

"No."

"He's a very sexy man," Linda said.

"I thought he looked like an android. Amazing how he looks so uptight and he's so . . . not. But I can't stand some of his attitudes." Ani remembered what she'd heard about his relationships. If the rumors were true, he'd never married or had a lasting romance. He'd been dumped by his fiancée, who probably had good reasons.

"Keep in mind that we're talking about only a night or two, not a lifelong commitment."

Ani winced. "He thinks I'm a gold digger. He's never treated me with respect. I can't stand that. He'd use me and toss me aside like yesterday's newspaper." She stared at Linda. "I'd be Rexford's fish wrap."

"If you let him." Linda took Ani by the shoulders. "Just remember what you're doing. You're using him. You're the one who knows the score, not Richard Rexford."

Tensing her jaw, Ani peeked into the Rexford.com conference room, but didn't see her target. Chairs surrounded an oval teak table large enough to seat the programming staff. She'd heard that Marketing, Accounting, and Legal had attended separate lectures earlier in the day; perhaps Rexford had attended one of the prior workshops. The memo from Human Resources had demanded the attendance of every employee. Apparently sexual harassment, the subject of the Tuesday afternoon seminar, had become a problem at Rexford.com. Small wonder, if the boss wanted female employees to dance at parties.

All the chairs were filled except two next to each other, at the far side of the room.

Ani wondered if anyone in Programming had heard about her performance. Afraid she'd encounter a number of speculative glances, she steeled herself and entered the room, striding toward the empty seats.

She passed Kevin Wilson on her way. He winked at her before bending studiously over his laptop. Jolted, Ani let her stride falter. Was Kevin blushing? That dance had repercussions she hadn't anticipated. She'd fixated on Rexford, forgetting that several others had been present. She hoped she wouldn't have to field passes from everyone who'd seen or heard about Friday night. She needed Rexford to come after her, not Kevin or anyone else.

She'd finally reached her destination: the empty chairs. A mug and a laptop computer sat on the table in front of one, so she took the other. Ani frowned at the mug. It looked familiar. Could it be . . . ?

Richard Rexford slid into the chair next to hers.

"We meet again, Ms. Sharif." Rexford smiled at her, blue eyes twinkling with mirth. Though he must have understood the awkwardness of the situation, Baby Rex appeared to be enjoying himself.

Enjoying himself at her expense, the wretch.

Ani's temper, as well as her cheeks, began a slow burn. She drew a breath, hoping to calm down. If Rexford could brazen his way through this mess, so could she.

The mission, she reminded herself. The mission.

She arched back her neck, straightened her shoulders, and gave him her most confident smile. "Good afternoon, Mr. Rexford."

"Oh, call me Richard, please." His gaze dropped to her chest.

Perfect. Ask me out, she prayed. "Richard, please," she parroted.

His grin widened. "Especially since I came to this meeting just to see you."

"Really? I thought it was compulsory for everyone."

"It is. But I could have attended any of the workshops. I felt sure that you'd prefer the late afternoon seminar." Irony laced his tone.

"You guessed correctly. This was the one scheduled for the programmers, right?"

"Planned just for you. I'm aware of your daily routine. Can I get you some coffee?"

"Shouldn't I be serving you, sir? After all, you're the boss." Would he understand her mockery? She'd never fetch his coffee, not even if serving him shot her to the top of the U.S.S.A.

"Not at all," he said, standing. "We helpless males are always at the mercy of a beautiful woman."

Beautiful woman . . . yeah, right. Ani refused to be conned. Skinny as a fawn and way too unsophisticated, she knew she wasn't a match for a mover and shaker like Richard Rexford. She still didn't understand how she'd drawn this assignment. Lewis must hate me, she thought.

Before she had a chance to contradict Rexford, he'd stalked away to get her coffee. His fingers brushed hers when he handed her a mug. The contact sparked. Startled, she let the coffee slip through her grasp.

It landed with a splash in her leather-clad lap. She jumped up with a screech. The mug hit the carpet. Heads turned.

She sank into her chair, burying her face in her hands. Could her luck get worse? Men weren't attracted to klutzes. They wanted women like Linda, women who were smooth, graceful, assured. I need Linda lessons, she thought. I need training to become a Bond girl. A Bond girl with brains.

Something caressed her thighs through her coffee-warmed leather pants. She looked down. Rexford had whipped out a monogrammed handkerchief and was swabbing the mess.

Yes, Lady Luck could indeed act the harpy. "Stop it, please," Ani said.

His gaze met hers. As usual, she found herself drawn by his directness. He was blatant, his interest and desire clear. Maybe this would be okay, though she'd never heard of seduction via spilled coffee. She swallowed. The sizzling heat in her body had nothing to do with the hot liquid splashing it.

"Do you want coffee in your lap?" Richard continued rubbing her pants with his now-damp hanky.

"N-no."

"So?" His strokes grew slower, almost languorous, as his busy hand approached her crotch.

Dear heavens, but he was bold. His recklessness called to a secret, wild part of her, a hidden self that she hadn't fully explored. She wanted to wiggle toward his touch . . . would that be too much for the mission?

Maybe. Maybe not, and she didn't want to cause a scene. Surveying the room, she saw that the rest of the programming staff had apparently lost interest. People had settled into their seats with coffee. Now they opened laptops or rustled notes. Kevin eyed her with an odd look on his face. What was that about? She smiled at him and again, he turned away, his face reddening.

What on earth was going on? Was her cover blown?

Ani leaned toward Richard to whisper. "I don't think my boss should have his hands near my, uh . . ."

"Near your . . . what?" His hanky made lazy circles on her inner thigh. His hands felt good . . . too good. Warm and tingly. How would his fingers feel on her bare skin?

This was no time for her English, normally fluent, to desert her. She wouldn't let her hormones take command of her life. Ani pulled herself together. "You sh-should not touch me at all."

His hands stilled. "You touched me first."

"I did not."

"Did too. What about that one-woman Arabian girlie show you put on at Pizza Polly's?" He tossed the handkerchief onto the table.

She gasped. Her mind went blank. Her pulse jerked, and blood thundered in her ears while the warmth in her cheeks spiked into a blaze. "How dare you?" she hissed. She'd never humiliated herself so totally in her life, and now he saw fit to bring it up in public.

"How dare I?" Leaning back, he raised a blond brow. "Frankly, I wondered how you dared."

"You—you—challenged me."

He grinned. "And you rose to the bait like a big, fat fish."

Ixzit. She was the one who was supposed to be baiting the hook, not Rexford.

On the other hand . . . if he was trying to snare her, the mission was advancing in exactly the way Linda had predicted: *He thinks you're prey, and he's the big bad T-Rex, when in reality, you're the one stalking him.*

Ani sneaked a glance at Richard out of the corner of her eye, wondering how to push the mission further along. But it was hard to plot when he flustered her so much that she couldn't plan her way out of a wet paper bag.

Then Evelyn Kehoe from Human Resources whacked a spoon on a glass several times, apparently to signal the beginning of the lecture. She introduced a gray-looking man in a gray suit as an attorney who specialized in sexual harassment, and the workshop began.

Ani didn't hear a word of it. She remained acutely aware of Richard. His nearness made her body tingle and hum, each cell yearning to touch him.

Her reaction astounded her. For twenty-three years, she'd remained largely unmoved by the male gender. As a teenager, her circumstances separated her from her peers. The Forresters allowed Linda and Ani to socialize, but always in groups. Ani, motivated by the murders of her parents, had focused on her education and training at a time when most other girls obsessed about boys.

Then she'd fallen in love with computers. Most software engineers looked like geeky Bill Gates clones. Though she might admire their work, none kindled her interest as a woman.

She rarely socialized with other members of the U.S.S.A., save Linda. Agency policy was to separate operatives for security reasons. The one night stand she'd shared with her fellow agent wasn't something she cared to repeat or even think about . . . besides, Michael couldn't hold a candle to the man sitting next to her.

Richard was as different from the men she knew as a diamond differs from coal. Though she tried to keep her eyes on the speaker and her ears tuned to the lecture, Ani couldn't ignore him.

She couldn't stop her nostrils from filling with Richard's scent. What kind of aftershave did he wear? She'd never smelled anything like it. Oceanic, but not fishy, his aroma made her think of exotic ports of call and wild adventure.

When he turned and met her gaze, smiling, her synapses cheered and her pulse raced, raising her temperature to a fever pitch. In any other situation, she'd suspect the flu, but she had to acknowledge her desire for Richard. She wanted to climb on him like a tree, taste his flesh, open herself to a man in a way she'd never before dared.

The dam was broken. The gate had opened, and she knew she'd never be the same.

The speaker paused to sip from a water glass, and Richard edged closer to her. "You didn't bring a laptop or a pen for notes," he whispered.

Her heartbeat skittered. "I left my laptop at home. There aren't any pens in my office. They aren't standard issue here."

He frowned. Even his frown was sexy. How was that possible? The mission, she reminded herself. The mission.

"I'll make sure you get pens. Meanwhile, I'll take notes for both of us. This is a very important topic." He raised his brows at her, then turned back to the speaker.

Richard didn't want to stare, but he found it tough to keep his glance from straying to Ani. Even when he didn't look at her, she distracted him. Her leather pants, damp with coffee, exuded an earthy aroma that blended with her jasmine perfume, nudging at his senses until he thought he'd go out of his mind. He reminded himself that he was the boss, and he couldn't flee screaming out the door, no matter what he felt about his newest, youngest, sexiest employee.

He didn't want to want her. For one thing, she was too young. Young women didn't know the rules of the game and always became emotionally involved. He preferred brief encounters with women who didn't want to leave a toothbrush in his bathroom or clothes in his closet, sophisticated women whose self-possession matched his own.

But Ani had a sweet little body and a wild child tattoo on her hip. Girls grew up fast these days. As far as he knew, she could have taken the entire Giants baseball team last weekend without batting an eyelash.

And there was that bet. With three males gunning for her, Ani would soon become someone's bedmate. Maybe she already had a lover. But Richard wasn't worried about any competition. She didn't wear anyone else's ring, so she was fair game.

His jaw tightened. He'd have her, but not because of the bet. She'd seized a part of his soul and wouldn't let go. When they came together, theirs wouldn't be a casual coupling. He didn't know how long they'd be together, but he needed to exorcise the playful demon that kept him entranced by Ani Sharif.

The lecture couldn't hold his attention, not with Ani sitting so near, fragrant with promise. He closed the file in which he'd been taking notes and, in desperation, clicked over to a games program and started playing three-dimensional chess with his computer.

Over time, he'd worked his way up to the most complex level. Hopefully the difficult game would keep him occupied until the lecture ended. Pawn to queen's level three . . .

"Pardon me." A throaty whisper intruded upon his concentration. Soft, curly hair brushed his wrist as Ani leaned closer, her gaze on his laptop's screen.

"Shouldn't you be paying attention?" Her green eyes twinkled.

Damn. She'd caught him.

"After all, you're the boss. Shouldn't you set an example for the rest of us?"

To hell with sexual harassment lawsuits. He wouldn't be manipulated by this half-pint, sexy djinn. She'd twisted him around her little finger from day one, and he was damn tired of it.

Richard let his foot, shod in a soft leather loafer, ease toward her leg. He stroked up Ani's calf.

She stiffened and jerked upright. Her mouth dropped open.

He wanted to kiss her seductive, parted lips and slip his tongue inside to taste her. But in public, he contented himself with whispering, "Pay attention, now. I'm sure this is very important stuff for you to know." He rubbed his toe up and down her leg.

Ani drew in a deep breath. Richard watched her chest, clothed today in an Apple t-shirt, rise and fall. With a quick, nervous motion, she gathered her hair up off her nape, lifting it.

Ha. She needed to cool off.

He'd gotten to her. Richard smiled.

Chapter Seven

After the lecture, Richard saw Ani bolt for the door like a lamb pursued by a legion of wolves. Hell, maybe she was. Kevin Wilson followed in the direction of her cubicle.

Richard knew what women liked: presents. He went to a supply closet and armed himself with several boxes of pens. Ready, he neared the door of her cubicle to hear voices emanating from Ani's workspace. He stopped a foot or two away from his destination to listen.

"I want to know why I've suddenly turned into, how would you say it? Ms. Guy Magnet." Ani's voice rang clear and firm.

"I, uh, uh . . ." In contrast, Kevin floundered and stuttered.

Richard figured he'd better intervene before she completely castrated Kevin . . . emotionally, of course. Richard hoped she wouldn't do anything more drastic. But what if Kevin, flustered, admitted the bet? They'd all be in deep shit.

"Hey there, anybody home?" He hoped he sounded casual. He walked into the cubicle, rattling the boxes of pens, like an explorer waving beads as a signal of peaceful intentions.

"I was just leaving." Kevin dashed for the door, shoving past Richard in his haste. Small, white cardboard boxes scattered, bursting open to strew their contents over Ani's floor.

Pens pinged off the floor, bouncing against her boots. She raised her brows. "Thank you for the office supplies." She bent to gather a handful, then heaped them on her desk in piles sorted by color.

"Boy, are you compulsive." Richard grinned. At least she was deflected from her concerns about becoming a "guy magnet."

"I'm not compulsive. It's simply less confusing. And if the pen has the same ink color as the cover, then you know what you're going to get."

"What if the covers aren't the same color as the ink?"

Concern flitted over her expressive features. Selecting a blue pen, she scribbled on a nearby tablet. "This is bad. This pen doesn't match. See?"

"It doesn't?" He stooped to collect more pens.

"No, this is a black pen, but it has a blue cover." She cocked a hip against the side of her desk, leaning on it. "Pens should match. But don't worry about it. I'll buy them myself."

He tossed the pens onto her desk. "So it would rock your little world if I came in here sometime and replaced all your neatly color-coded pens with, say, green-ink pens in red covers, or black in red?" He laughed, trying to ignore how sexy she looked with her butt half-parked on the corner of her desk.

"I don't expect you to come in here at all." Her nose twitched, in an appealing, rabbity way.

No, not rabbity. Like a cute little bunny.

She twitched again. Definitely like a bunny. Richard couldn't resist. He leaned over her, trapping her against the desk with one hand on each side of her body.

Kissing her would be too much, too soon, and too obvious, so when his lips had moved to less than an inch from hers, he changed the angle of his approach and whispered in her ear, "Have dinner with me."

She murmured, "Isn't this sexual harassment?"

"Only if you don't want to go out with me." He slid his mouth along the tender skin of her throat, not touching her, just breathing.

The tiny hairs on her neck lifted, and her body undulated

against his, soft and sexy. She'd be easy. Fun, even. And he'd win that bet.

"Is that so?" she murmured into his ear. "All right, I'll have dinner with you, and . . . we'll see."

By Saturday morning, Ani had whipped herself into a frenzy over the contents of her closet . . . or, rather, the lack of appropriate apparel for her dinner with Baby Rex. What on earth does one wear for a date with a predator? she wondered for the thousandth time.

But not just any predator. This was Richard Rexford, a.k.a. Sexy Rexy, a lady killer with the reputation of a woman-eating shark and, doubtless, the morals to match.

He's not your type, she told herself. The only reason you accepted this date is to get closer to him, so maybe, someday soon, you'll get onto his boat.

So why was she stressing over her clothes?

Ani threw herself onto her bed with a groan. She owned jeans and tops. A sweater or two. Her leathers, which protected her in case she fell off the hog and concealed a blade or two . . . or five.

She could raid Linda's closet. That might work. Ani's foster sister owned a couture collection that rivaled any fashionista's.

An hour later, Ani sat cross-legged on the polished wood floor of Linda's apartment. Linda's laptop was open and balanced on Ani's knees.

Linda fluttered like an anxious pheasant guarding her young. "I got the senior partner's email address list, but it's encoded. I don't know how to figure out who's who without actually sending messages to each one."

"And that would arouse suspicion and possibly blow your cover," Ani said. "I understand."

"On top of that, I couldn't use someone else's computer to

send the emails, because then the responses might go to their machine. I wouldn't find anything out, and if the responses came to me, I'd get caught."

Ani chuckled. "This system is pretty simple, so this really isn't hard." Her fingers clicked busily over the keys.

"Not for you, perhaps." Linda sulked.

"I'm a programmer. I'm used to more complex tasks and more complex computers. This is easy, a piece of cake." Ani glanced at Linda. "That's okay. You're good at other things. To pay me back, you can dress me for tonight."

"That's not payback, that's a pleasure." Linda's eyes gleamed. "I've wanted to get my hands on you for years."

"Got anything I could wear?"

"Yes, but I want to go shopping. It's more fun."

"Here's a couple of CompLine email addies, which we expected . . ." Ani clicked some more. "Ooh, this is interesting. Is there any reason why your boss has the email addresses of the Chinese consulate and their overseas attaché?"

"If he's selling them secrets, he has plenty of reasons," Linda said. "On the other hand, this firm has many Pacific Rim business contacts. The senior partner travels to Beijing a couple of times every year. Their transactions could be perfectly innocent."

"Want to find out?"

After Ani had finished hacking into the Chinese consulate's computer system, downloading its email address books and files, they went to lunch, fortifying themselves for an afternoon of shopping. Linda took Ani to the Castro District, which abounded with secondhand and consignment stores.

"Why here?" Ani asked. "Why not Nordy's?"

"Nordy's is dull." Linda tossed her head, letting her sheet of black hair catch the thin afternoon sun. "Rexford doesn't want dull, he wants daring."

"I don't feel very daring."

"You need to develop more confidence for the kind of work we do." Linda frowned at Ani. "Learn to let your inner goddess free. Nordy's won't help you do that." She reached into a rack of designer gowns and pulled out a backless apple-green sheath, embroidered with exotic flowers. "Galanos will let your goddess shine."

"Wow." Ani stared at the gown, transfixed. "Why does that dress look so familiar to me?"

"Nicole Kidman wore a similar Galanos to the Oscars a few years back. Hers was more of a chartreuse color, not very flattering, I think. I prefer this shade of green, especially with your eyes. We'll try it on."

"What about shoes?"

"We'll get shoes, or you can borrow mine," Linda said. "We're still the same size, aren't we?"

"I like this dress, but I think it's too much for a simple first-date dinner."

"You're probably right, but let's take it anyway, if it fits. You can't go shopping every time someone asks you out."

"What about basic black?" Ani found a high-necked, calf-length knit.

Linda examined it, turning back the collar to expose a Y.S.L. label. "Yes, this might do. Quite demure, but the knit will cling to your assets. And finding accessories will be easier than with the green."

After borrowing shoes and an evening bag from Linda to match the black dress, Ani stowed her new outfits in the panniers of her motorcycle after folding them carefully. She wondered if it was time for her to invest in a car, though she hated to be tied down. Her cottage's lease was bad enough.

Before returning home, she walked down the street in search of an espresso, figuring she'd need it to stay alert during her date with Richard Rexford. Not that he'd bore her to sleep, but she wanted that extra edge that a good cup of java would give.

Even without the extra caffeine, her nerves thrummed. She was another step closer to her goals.

She bought a cappuccino from a street vendor on Clement, then turned to go to her motorcycle, parked outside Linda's building. As she passed an alley, something slammed into her back, smacking her hard against a graffiti-splashed wall inside the narrow passageway. Her arms flung wide, Ani and her coffee parted company, with the cappuccino spraying the area.

Her attacker cursed, evidently catching a face full of hot coffee. Ani sucked in a breath, turned, then laughed upon seeing the squirrel who'd accosted her. He was the same wimp she'd relieved of a very valuable package just a few weeks before. Small and wiry, dressed in an olive-green tank top and baggy cargo pants, he didn't look like much of a threat. In fact, he could be a welcome distraction.

"Come back for more fun and games?" She set a hand on her hip and smirked at him.

"You cost me a lot of money, bitch, and it's payback time." He pulled a jackknife, snapping it open with a snick. The blade caught the late afternoon light with an evil wink.

He moved in on her fast, but she sidestepped and helped him into the wall behind her. Hitting the bricks with a shoulder, he bounced and, using his momentum, came at her again. Slapping his hand aside, she got inside his guard while slipping a blade out from her left cuff. She slashed it under his wrist, feeling it catch on bare flesh.

"Bleed too long and you'll croak," Ani said. "You've got maybe forty-five seconds at the most before you will lose consciousness."

Dropping his knife, he staggered out of the alley, swearing as he went. She let him go, instead finding one of the napkins she'd taken from the coffee vendor. She used it to pick up his weapon by the blade. She'd drop it off at the U.S.S.A. office on her way. She didn't know what clues the forensics lab could find from the knife, but one never knew.

Finally home, she worked out with the punching bag for twenty strenuous minutes, hitting and kicking away her overload of nervous energy. Though Lewis had told her not to worry, she was troubled by the incident outside Linda's building. How had her attacker known where to find her? Had he tailed her from her home?

Ani was almost dead certain her cottage was secure. She daily walked her neighborhood to ensure that she wasn't watched, and she knew that Lewis also took measures to protect his operatives.

Was someone onto Linda? Had they been watched since her arrival at Linda's place, surveilled the entire day?

Ani pushed that set of concerns out of her mind in favor of worrying about the date with Rexford. She secreted a blade in the hem of her new dress before showering, then frowned into the bathroom mirror. She usually wore only a little mascara and lip gloss, but tonight seemed to call for a more elaborate look. Fortunately, Linda knew everything there was to know about make up, and had taught Ani how to make up her face for a dinner date.

Jewelry. She had to wear more formal jewelry, she supposed, than her silver rings, earrings, toe ring and anklet. After searching a small box she kept on her bedside table, she removed a locket.

Ani didn't have many mementoes of her parents. She'd fled Algeria with literally the clothes on her back and very little else.

She'd been lucky to get out. Others hadn't been so fortunate.

Opening the locket, Ani spent a few minutes contemplating the photographs of her parents. Her father had been a languid, slender man with amber skin and a dark, clipped beard. Kindness radiated from his gentle eyes and smile. He'd always been wreathed in smoke, a pipe in one hand, a pen in the other, with a book tucked under one arm. Her mother, in contrast, had sharp green eyes and a brisk demeanor. High heels clicking and hands waving, ebullient Renée always had seemed to be moving, a bustling presence orbiting the more laconic Daoud.

Ani's love and pain rose in her chest, threatening to burst out of her control. She pressed a hand to her heart, willing her tears away. Grieving over her long-dead parents wouldn't bring them back and would only ruin her make-up.

Richard knocked. The door to Ani's cottage opened, revealing an elegant stranger who bore little resemblance to Motorcycle Mama Ani.

Ani's black knitted dress clung to her breasts and waist, then fell in graceful folds. The dress covered her from throat to shins, but the armholes were cut high toward the stand-up collar, showing off her shoulders and arms. Sheathed in satiny, golden skin, they looked shapely and strong, maybe from controlling her big bike.

Her tousled, bedroom hair had been tamed into a restrained chignon at her nape. A filigreed gold locket gleamed softly against her black dress.

She took his breath away. Refined and sophisticated, she had transformed into a woman he could take anywhere, including to his bed. Despite her youth, maybe she could handle a brief, no-strings-attached affair. She certainly looked the part.

Richard had figured she'd dress casually, so he hadn't gone to any special effort. He wished he had. He'd worked on a software problem until the wee hours of the morning. After catching some winks he'd awakened at first light to spend all day doing the scrub, spit, and polish routine on the boat.

He'd wanted his home to look good for his guest, but he'd neglected his appearance. In cutoff shorts, battered deck shoes, and a worn dress shirt with ripped-off sleeves, open to the waist, he knew he presented a slovenly contrast to Ani's beauty.

How could he make it up to her? Richard mulled over the problem as he drove Ani down the hill to the Santa Laura Marina. He had plenty of time to think about it, since the drive was very quiet. Embarrassed by his sweat-ball appearance, he didn't know what to say, and he couldn't divine her thoughts. Her shadowed, composed face revealed nothing.

After the achingly tense drive, he reached their destination. Richard parked the Corvette, then dashed to Ani's door to open it.

Looking surprised, she exited. "Thank you." Her voice was muted, husky.

He led her to a nearby metal gate, which guarded access to the boat slips. Unlocking it, he ushered her through.

"We're not going there?" She pointed over the water to Estrella's, a wooden-sided, busy seafood restaurant on the far side of the marina.

"No, I have something else planned. Something special." Cupping her elbow, Richard escorted her down the length of the dock to where *Trophy Wife* was anchored in its slip. Ani's bare skin felt smooth and warm.

"Your shoes, please." He held out his hand.

"I beg your pardon?"

He could tell he'd startled her. He liked that. "Take off your shoes. They're the wrong kind for this decking. You'll slip and fall." He didn't want to sound callous, so he decided not to mention that her heels might scuff the freshly varnished wood.

She kicked off her shoes, exposing purple-painted toes and that toe ring. "What should I do with them?" Her golden anklet gleamed in the subdued lighting.

His libido went on full alert. "Umm, you can leave them on the dock. Nobody will take them, not around here. Let me help you aboard."

She looked the boat up and down. "The *Trophy Wife?*" She put her hand in his, allowing him to help her.

Squeezing her hand, he grinned. "My father and my uncle used to pester me to get a trophy wife. So I did." A cuddly handful, her slight weight didn't challenge him. He easily hoisted her into the boat.

She laughed at his joke, but her giggle sounded forced and uncomfortable rather than happy and amused. Damn. This would be the world's worst dinner date if she didn't loosen up.

"She's lovely." Ani tilted her head back to scan the wheel-house.

"Thanks." Richard couldn't restrain the pride in his voice. "Yeah, this is my baby." He patted a polished teak railing. He'd spent hours that day freshening everything up, without regretting a single second, or the many dollars he'd paid for expensive marine varnish.

He waved at a table and two chairs he'd set out. "Have a seat, and drink some wine while I clean up. I spent the day swabbing the decks. Give me a few minutes, okay? I also want to check my emails."

"Are you expecting an important message?"

He poured straw-colored liquid into a crystal wine glass for her. "No, I just like to check."

Ani hid her smile behind her glass. So Richard did, indeed, have a computer aboard his boat. Better, it seemed as though the date would take place here, on the *Trophy Wife,* which would give her plenty of opportunities to discover where he kept his laptop. On the other hand, why did he want to check his emails on Saturday evening? That was odd. And he'd had the gall to label her compulsive.

Perhaps he was a traitor, and was expecting an important communication. She'd better stay on her toes.

Richard flicked sun-bleached blond hair out of his eyes and disappeared through an oddly shaped door, closing it behind him. She wondered if she could peek after him, see where he kept his computer without being found out.

She chewed on her lower lip. Though he'd be taking a shower—or so he said—maybe she should play it cool for now and ask for a tour of the boat later. That wouldn't be suspicious, would it? She'd need to use the toilet at some point. That might give her the opportunity to carry out her mission.

Happy that she'd figured out a plan to complete her assignment, she heaved a relieved sigh. But she wondered what was going on in his head. Why had he shown up at her door looking and smelling like a seadog? Was it some sort of subtle insult? Perhaps, but instead, she'd been floored by his masculine appeal. His shirt, open halfway to the waist, exposed a tanned chest roped with muscle and dusted by an appealing golden fleece. Worn cutoff jeans bared brawny thighs.

When they'd met, she'd guessed that an athletic body hid beneath his proper executive's garb. Now she knew, and the reality far surpassed her raunchiest fantasies.

It was tough to feel slighted now that she could see he'd prepared for their evening together. A dark bottle, damp with condensation, sat on the table next to a tray of canapés, which were covered by cheesecloth. To keep away bugs, she supposed. She recognized the wine's famous label before sipping the tart Chardonnay he'd poured.

The munchies seemed appetizing, with an awkward look that signaled "homemade." She appreciated that. She selected a square of smoked salmon on a cracker, topped with cucumber and a dollop of sour cream and bit into it. The cuke tasted fresh and crunchy, as did the cracker. Richard must have put them together just before he'd left Santa Laura to pick her up.

Taking her glass and another canapé, she started to explore Richard's boat.

Chapter Eight

Everything sparkled. The wooden decks and railings appeared newly washed. All the brass trim and fittings had been recently polished, perhaps that same day. Richard had worked hard to impress her.

Ani regretted that she'd been so cold and quiet in the car. Trapped in the Corvette with Richard, she hadn't known what to say. Angry and embarrassed, she concluded that she'd placed more emphasis than he on the evening, which put the mission in doubt. Hoping to somehow resurrect the date, she'd decided to keep her mouth shut rather than let loose a tirade.

Then she'd noticed his hair, his scent, and his chest. His square, strong hands on the wheel, capably handling the gearshift, made her wonder how he'd touch her body. She liked him more now that she knew his muscles came from working on his boat rather than from something phony like weight lifting.

Ixzit. She had it bad for this man.

Determined not to lose control of herself and of her assignment, Ani drew a steadying breath, filling her lungs with the sharp scent of the sea. The breeze clattered the rigging of nearby sailboats against their masts with a metallic melody that blended with the seabirds' cries.

Nibbling on her canapé, she walked to the front of the boat—the prow, wasn't it?—and stared over the harbor. Outside the breakwater, the golden rays of the setting sun lit a fiery path toward the horizon. Within the marina, she could see other couples on the decks of yachts and sailboats toasting the sunset with lifted goblets and unrestrained laughter. Their voices drifted over the water to her.

She lifted the cover from a bench seat, finding a rough storage compartment inside with a pile of orange life jackets dumped in an untidy heap. No laptop, and she concluded that the laptop wouldn't be hidden in the topside storage units. Too great a possibility of water damage.

From the deck of a nearby sailboat, an older fellow in a striped t-shirt and battered jeans scrutinized her with blatant curiosity. Oops. Had the guy caught her snooping? Though embarrassed, Ani smiled and waved, faking nonchalance. Without any suspicion on his face, the man waved back before disappearing belowdecks.

Whew. She'd gotten away with that bit of curiosity. Even better, a neighbor had taken note of her. After she met a few more of the locals, she'd be able to walk openly onto Richard's boat instead of sneaking aboard, if such an action became necessary. To reward herself, she fetched another munchie and topped off her wine glass.

A pelican swooped out of the sky to land on the *Trophy Wife*'s railing, less than ten feet away from Ani. Cocking its head, it stared with undisguised eagerness at the canapé in her hand.

"Ooh, look at you." She didn't want to spook him, so she approached the big, brown bird with caution. The pelican extended its wings and opened its beak, exposing its deep gullet in obvious invitation. She flipped the appetizer into the bird's open mouth.

"Hey!" Richard appeared in a doorway. "Don't do that!"

She turned, and her breath stuck in her throat.

Damp, freshly washed hair lay neatly on his tanned forehead. His Hawaiian shirt, flamboyantly flowered in blue, hung loose and open over khaki shorts, showing off a broad, tanned chest gently furred with blond curls. They glistened in the setting sun's ruddy light.

The mission. She shut her eyes for a brief moment, searching for her focus. *The mission.*

She blinked, smiled, and said, "What's wrong with feeding the birds?"

"They crap all over the place." Flapping his arms, he advanced toward the pelican, which remained oblivious. "Scat!" he yelled. "Go over there!"

Seizing a canapé from the table, Richard pitched it over the railing toward the neighboring sailboat's deck. The pelican stretched its wings, gave a little hop, and dropped down to the other boat, snagging the appetizer with a quick, sideways snap of its beak.

She chuckled. "Don't you like your neighbors?"

"We get along fine. We watch out for each other's boats if someone's out of town."

"Interesting way to watch out for their boat."

He grinned. "We've also been known to play a practical joke or two on each other."

"Like what?" Perhaps a break-in could be disguised as a prank.

"Well, one time Lizzy and Doug filled my refrigerator with ping-pong balls. I got back at them by putting a pair of snapping turtles in their john. Stuff like that."

He picked up a glass of wine and looked relaxed and happy and very, very sexy, though she couldn't understand why. Perhaps it was the difference between his easy demeanor here, on his boat, as compared to the C.E.O. act he'd put on when they'd met.

She tried to keep her breathing even, when she really wanted to pant with lust. Afraid she'd let her glass slip through her fingers, she tightened her grip.

He reached for her free hand. "Let me give you a tour before we cast off."

This evening was going better than she'd dared to hope. Maybe he'd inadvertently show her where he kept his laptop. Hiding her triumph, she said, "Cast off?" She followed him belowdecks, letting him lead, enjoying the clasp of his hand.

"I thought we'd go for a spin before dinner."

"Sounds fun."

"Here's the galley. The kitchen, as you landlubbers would say." It consisted of a long, narrow room on one side of a hall running down the middle of the boat. Compact and miniaturized, the galley fascinated her.

"Will we cook dinner here later?" Ani wanted to spend some time in this room, exploring its mysteries. There were plenty of hiding places that might conceal her goal.

He smiled at her again. "I will fix dinner while you'll relax like a pampered guest."

She tipped her head to one side. "Pampered. I like the sound of that." She hoped her disappointment didn't show.

He laughed and guided her down the hall. "The head's through here." He pushed her inside a bedroom.

Richard's bedroom. It had to be. Paneled with teak, the room looked distinctly masculine and smelled exactly like him.

With, heaven help her, his bed, clothed in soft, well-worn sheets with faded blue and white stripes. They looked as though they'd been ordered from J. Crew or Eddie Bauer decades before. How like Richard. He even had WASP-y sheets.

She'd never been in a man's bedroom before, save that of her parents, and that didn't count. For a moment, she thought she'd swoon, like a maiden in a clichéd medieval romance. She tried to inhale a few precious molecules of oxygen. Where was the air on this boat? Didn't it have windows?

Ani forced herself to relax. This room doesn't matter, she told herself. You'll never sleep on those sheets, in that bed. More importantly, there was no desk, and no place to set up a laptop. Though he could keep it stowed anywhere, she realized, and use it while seated on his bed. That she had a legitimate reason to explore his bedroom both frightened and thrilled her.

Richard walked through the bedroom, at ease in his domain, and showed her the tiny head and how to operate the peculiar toilet. Then, tugging on her hand—why? she wondered—he led her back on deck and cast off while she watched him unwind the beautiful, intricate knots securing the boat to the dock.

He showed her the wheelhouse, and her heart jumped at the sight of a laptop computer on the built-in desk. Hiding her glee, she watched him flick switches and turn levers to start the big boat. The rumble of the engines cloaked the gulls' screeching as the *Trophy Wife* chugged through the breakwater toward the open ocean.

He'd tried to impress her, and he'd succeeded. She wanted to ask about the computer, but didn't want to be obvious. So she said, "This is terrific, really special. Thank you."

"I'm glad you're pleased. I'm sorry for showing up looking like a dirtball." His voice was quiet as he handled the big, wooden wheel.

She tentatively touched his arm, sinewy and strong. "It's all right. I can see you worked hard today."

"I did." His crooked smile spoke of his awkwardness. Surprising, she thought. She'd always viewed Richard Rexford as sophisticated and suave. Now, he showed an unexpected, vulnerable side. He continued, "I haven't brought a lady home for a long time."

Hmm. Perhaps his reputation was exaggerated. Making conversation, she asked, "So you live here all the time? On this boat?" When they left the sheltered water of the marina, she felt the sea lift and swell beneath the boat with a slight rolling motion.

"Sure do. Makes me feel free."

She liked that. He reminded her of the reason she rode a motorcycle instead of stuffing herself into a car. "Where did you get your experience with boats?"

"I ran away to sea."

She laughed. "Like in *Captains Courageous?*"

"Not quite. Harvey fell off an ocean liner, remember? I left."

She was astounded. She'd expected him to talk about a family yacht. "Why?"

His eyes narrowed as he navigated the boat past a lighted buoy. "My dad had my life planned out for me, and it sounded boring. St. Jude's, then the University of San Francisco . . . yuck. Too much parochial school for this sinner."

"How long did you travel, and where?" She knew the contents of his U.S.S.A. dossier, but she wanted to hear what Richard had to say, see if the information matched.

"A couple of years . . . pretty much all around the world."

"That sounds great." She guessed. Her escape from Algeria had been a scary flight in the dark of night. She loved America. America meant safety.

"How about you, Ani Sharif? With that name and your accent, I bet you're not an ordinary California girl."

"I don't sound normal?" Damn. She'd spent years in language schools, trying to get rid of her accent so she'd blend in. Spies couldn't stand out. Anonymity was essential.

"You're not a freak," he hastened to reassure her. "But you do have an accent. And the way you talk—"

"Oh. Well, um, I'm Algerian. I got out about ten years ago, after the trouble there started."

"And your family?"

"They didn't make it." Ani loathed talking about this.

"Sorry. I don't mean to hurt you. I do want to know about you, though. How about playing 'Let's Make a Deal,' again?"

She couldn't help smiling at his reference to their first meeting. Nice that he had a sense of humor about it. "All right."

"You answer my questions, I'll answer yours."

"Sounds very . . . what would you say? Like an interrogation. What if I don't have anything in particular to ask?" Other than, are you a traitor?

"What if I do?" He impaled her with a cool blue glance.

A funny fluttering started in the pit of her stomach, the same odd feeling she had when she looked at his chest, or his bed, or his . . . anything. Anything about him.

She shrugged it off. "All right, ask away." She figured she could fake it, then probe for anything she could use to fulfill her mission.

"Where'd you get the green eyes and the name Ani?"

"My mother's French. Ani is a typical French name. I'm named for my grandmother, who lives in Marseilles." Ani thought about grand-mère Anny, her lavender scent, and her flat, full of heavy dark furniture and antique art. "Her home was the first place I stayed after leaving Algiers."

"Ten years ago." He sounded thoughtful. "Hey, let me put on the autopilot and show you something." He flipped several switches, then grabbed her hand to guide her toward the wheelhouse door.

Ani grew nervous. "Where's the boat going?" She resisted his pull.

"Nowhere in particular." He grinned. "We're far from the shipping lanes, and it's a big ocean."

"Won't we get lost? How will we get back?"

He raised a sandy brow. "You don't have much confidence in my navigational abilities. Trust me, Ani, when we want to go home, we will. Chances are that when I turn the boat eastward we'll hit California."

"Oh, of course." She flushed.

"So come on." He tugged her hand, taking her back to the hall below the main deck.

Ani reflected that Richard had the oddest tendency to grab her and drag her along in his wake, rather like a tugboat hauling a barge. She remembered that she'd resented it when they'd met. Now, she found she didn't mind, especially since she was getting the information she needed to complete her assignment. Besides, he seemed so intent upon pleasing her.

He stopped in front of one of the framed photographs lining the paneled hall. He took the photo off its hook and handed it to her. "Look familiar?"

It depicted a misty harbor, perhaps at dawn, she guessed. White yachts, nestled in their berths, floated in neat rows. Fishing boats chugged out to sea, and birds soared through a pearly sky lit with the distinctive luminescence of early morning.

Recognition struck. "Yes! This is Marseilles harbor, exactly as I remember it. Grand-mère's flat is there, I believe." She pointed at a square, peach-colored building in the background.

Richard's eyes shone. "I took this photograph in Marseilles ten years ago."

Her mouth fell open. "You were there then?"

He nodded.

"That . . . that is amazing."

"Yeah. Just think, we were at the same place at the same time."

"Hmm." She'd been sure they had nothing in common. Now she realized they shared more than she'd understood.

But she didn't want to share anything with Baby T-Rex. Did she?

Of course not. She just wanted to do her job and get out.

CHAPTER NINE

Richard found himself showing each and every photograph on his walls to Ani Sharif while babbling faster than a talk-show host on uppers. He hadn't wanted to impress a woman so much since he was thirteen. What was going on?

Whatever it was, it felt good. By the time they hit the galley to fix dinner, both were talking a mile a minute.

He opened the galley's small fridge and removed a wooden bowl full of salad. "Take this on deck, okay?" He handed it to her.

She peered through a porthole. "It's quite dark outside now."

"Here." He flicked the switch that lit the exterior lights, then checked them to ensure none glared onto the table. He didn't want harsh illumination to ruin the romantic mood he'd struggled to create. He followed her out with rolls and silverware. After seating her, he tossed the salad with olive oil, cracked pepper, and lemon.

"You must love the ocean, to want to live on it always. And you obviously love to travel. Why did you return to California?" She broke apart a roll, sniffed the steam rising from it, and nibbled.

He fiddled with his wineglass. Having sipped a glass of Chardonnay, he felt pretty good. He hated to shatter his mood by talking about his family. But she'd asked, and he couldn't be rude twice in one night. Once had been stupid enough. Besides, they'd made a deal.

"My uncle contacted me, saying that my father was undergoing heart surgery and might die. The story turned out to be, uh, a tad exaggerated."

"What actually happened?" She stabbed a leaf of radicchio with her fork.

"As you probably know, CompLine had been under attack by the Justice Department for alleged monopolistic practices."

" 'Alleged monopolistic practices?' " She gave a wry laugh. "Everyone knows your father, the original T-Rex, squeezed the competition without mercy."

"True." He chewed and swallowed a bitter piece of chicory. "But at the time, I was working aboard a container ship in Southeast Asia and didn't know what was going on."

"Your father wasn't sick?"

"He had to undergo routine cardiac tests, treadmill and the like. He wasn't anywhere near death. My father and uncle hoodwinked me good." Richard stacked the now-empty salad plates.

Ani followed him into the galley. "They're quite a pair, hmm?"

"Sure are. They faked total helplessness so they could step aside and shove me into the hot seat." He lifted the lid off a pot of bouillabaisse. It released a steamy cloud redolent of tomato, fish, lemon, and herbs.

She sniffed, looking appreciative. He liked the endearing way her nose twitched when she inhaled. He wondered if the distinctive aroma reminded her of Provence, as it did him.

"What was wrong with your uncle?" she asked, leaning against a counter.

"His fourth wife dumped him and the divorce was brutal. Both Dad and Uncle Sundeen claimed that I had to handle the situation with the Justice Department." He ladled the fish stew into two blue earthenware bowls.

"So?" She took her plate.

"So, it went on record that Richard Rexford presided over the breakup of CompLine. Then, dear ol' Dad, miraculously recovered, exercised an obscure clause in the corporate charter, walked back in, and seized control of CompLine Software, the biggest and most valuable of the remaining companies." He gestured for her to exit the galley ahead of him.

"And you were . . ."

"Out in the cold with a tiny division specializing in games. That was when I wrote 'Mega Bet.' " He reseated her at the dining table, then took his own chair.

Ani smiled at him, her green eyes twinkling. "Wishful thinking or personal experience? You were taking quite a risk." She put a spoon to the stew, then sniffed it, with her nose doing its bunny twitch. As she sampled the soup, her delicate pink tongue poked from between her lips. Her very lush lips.

Richard's mouth went dry at the sight. He managed a chuckle. "Both, I guess. But I wasn't a total novice when it came to computers. Modern seagoing craft have a variety of machines on board. Over the years, I'd learned how to use, program, and repair all of them."

"What happened next?" She dug into the stew with her spoon. Despite her eagerness to eat, she seemed flatteringly intent on his tale.

"I was pretty angry when I found out what they'd done. So I got even."

"How?" She squeezed a lemon wedge over some fish.

"I looked ahead. With nine-eleven, I figured that web security would be an enormous business, but I didn't tell Dad or Uncle Sundeen. Instead, I fed them contrary information. As I'd intended, they decided that network and web security would be an unprofitable dead end. They dumped CompLine's web security division and all its personnel, throwing twenty people out of work." He paused to fork up a piece of the sole he'd added to the bouillabaisse. Flaky and delicate, it melted in his mouth.

"Didn't CompLine provide severance pay?" She dipped a piece of roll into her stew, chewed, and swallowed.

"Ha. My father has a heart like an overcooked shrimp—small and hard. The programmers and engineers would get jobs immediately, but the secretaries and gofers . . ." He shrugged. "I took 'em all. More, actually. A lot of CompLine's best jumped ship. Dad and Sundeen had burned a lot of bridges."

She looked at him with undisguised admiration. Too much admiration.

Damn. He didn't want Ani Sharif imagining he was a wild-eyed, softhearted philanthropist. "Hey, they were good employees. It would have been stupid to lose them." He stood and collected the stew bowls. "I'll get the desserts."

Ani followed Richard into the galley and watched him rummage in the refrigerator. She couldn't figure him out. He'd arrived at her house looking like a vagrant, but kept an immaculate boat. He'd taunted her at the pizza parlor, but tonight, treated her as though she were a duchess. He'd opened doors, pulled out her chair, and served her a perfectly prepared meal.

He tried to act like a vicious T-Rex but had gone to the trouble of fixing the mess his father had made, not once but twice.

As hard as she tried, she couldn't label the evening a disaster, especially since she now knew where he kept his computer. On top of that, she and Richard had a lot in common. A love of freedom, for one thing. Computers, for another. Maybe she'd see him after she'd completed her assignment. Maybe.

Richard straightened up and smiled at her, each hand holding a dessert plate filled with a pile of sliced strawberries atop shortcake. His laser-blue eyes glinted.

Their gleam hit her like an electric shock, zapping her back into reality. What was she thinking? He wasn't a cute little guppy. This was Richard Rexford, one of the biggest, baddest great white sharks around.

No doubt his father had a completely different story of the start-up of Richard's firm. Gossip said that Richard had ruthlessly stolen every talented programmer in the place, leaving CompLine reeling. Rumors still abounded; apparently Thomas and Sundeen plotted to destroy Richard for his alleged crimes against the family firm.

He was her target, maybe even a traitor. Get with the program, Ani, she reminded herself.

She swallowed, her mouth parched. She was definitely in over her head. Thinking that she could play games with Richard Rexford was crazy. She needed to get to his laptop computer and get out. She wasn't sure how to do it, but hoped to figure that out before the end of the night. She had to minimize contact with Rexford. Another date would be insane.

She cleared her throat, which felt thick and dry. "I don't want to like you too much."

"You're right." He put the desserts onto a counter and crossed the galley to stand in front of her, mere inches away. "So why don't we stop this right now?"

His heat radiated, igniting every cell in her body. The raw sexual tension between them, thicker than the stew she'd eaten, unnerved her. That dangerous flutter started again, but this time it made her tingle from head to toes.

She couldn't speak. She couldn't move. She couldn't look away from his unfathomable blue eyes.

Taking her chin in his hand, he brushed her lips with his. He didn't break eye contact, and neither did she. The intimacy created was unbearable, as though he'd reached inside her and caressed her soul with the gentlest of touches.

The brief kiss wasn't nearly enough, but sharpened her appetite for him. She wanted more and took it, grabbing his shirt front and dragging him closer so she could flick her tongue over his lips, deliberately enticing him.

He pulled her into his arms, drawing her to his male heat. He dipped his head again to kiss her and this time, he didn't hold back. He slid his tongue between her lips, making love to her mouth with an insistent rhythm. Desire pounded at her in waves, intense and powerful as a high tide. Her body throbbed with passionate hunger.

"It's going to be very good between us, you know that?" he whispered into her ear.

"Mmmm, yeah." Too good, maybe. She'd never experienced anything like Richard's kiss. Hot and deep and all encompassing, like a desert whirlwind, he threatened to sweep her away.

But she couldn't let herself be swept away. She couldn't take what he offered, no matter how much she wanted it. Linda might be able to have sex with a target without hesitation or regrets, but Ani didn't think she was built the same way as was her sister.

Allowing caution to assert itself, Ani sighed and pulled away from him.

As if reading her mind, Richard said, "Look, I'm in no rush. I just had to know how you'd feel and, umm, taste." He looked at the floor. A lock of blond hair fell across his forehead.

Ani wanted to stroke it, play with it . . . and with the rest of him. Every inch. Instead, she somehow managed to lift her brows. "Like really good fish soup, I bet."

"Yeah, really good."

"Even if you do say so yourself."

They both laughed.

"But now that the first kiss is over, we can relax and enjoy the night, okay?" Richard picked up the desserts and carried them outside.

Enjoy the night. Ri-ight. How on earth was she to get into the wheelhouse without him? Biting her lower lip, she followed him on deck, then said, "I want to see the view from up top. I bet you can see a lot of stars."

"Good idea. Maybe after dessert." He set down the plates and smiled at her.

Damn, damn, damn. How was she going to get up there alone?

If she couldn't maneuver it tonight, she'd have to see him again. But if this mission wasn't over in one or two dates, she could be in a lot of trouble, not only with Lewis, but in her heart.

During the drive back to her cottage, Richard took her hand and placed it on his thigh. She rubbed her palm across his muscles, enjoying the texture of the golden down on his leg. No conversation, but the silence wasn't strained, at least as far as Rexford was concerned. Ani herself was tight as Britney Spears' jeans. She was pretty sure he'd want to see her again, and made a mental note to make sure of his feelings before the night was over.

He shifted his weight, and she wondered if he'd tired of her touch. She clasped her hands together around her knee and wondered how best to renew his interest. This seductress act was harder than she'd anticipated. Her respect for Linda rose.

After turning onto Skyline Drive, he again reached for her hand. "Bored with me already?" His glance caught hers in the mirror. His eyes twinkled.

"Ummm . . . just a little."

Tires screeched as he pulled over at the park and stopped the car. "Well, I'll have to take care of that." Reaching for her, he dug his hands into her hair, brought her close, and kissed her. Closing her eyes, she met him halfway, rubbing her tongue against his. The erotic contact made her sizzle all over. She heard a click, then suddenly, he came closer still, wrapping her in his warm embrace. She guessed he'd unlocked his seat belt, so she followed suit, wondering into whose stomach the gearshift would poke.

One of Richard's hands cupped her breast, and Ani decided she didn't care about the gearshift. He gently squeezed her. Every thought fled, replaced by a scorching flood of want that swept aside all caution. Even so, she gasped with shock when his other hand slid beneath her skirt and up between her thighs. His tongue slipped deeper as his fingers stroked her higher and higher, nearing her feminine warmth.

This was too much. After that dance, Ani didn't want Richard Rexford to conclude she was easy. A one-nighter was out of the question. She had to lengthen the relationship so she could get on his boat again to find that computer. But she had quite a job ahead of her. He'd wound around her like a giant squid devouring prey. She had a tight grip on the front of his Hawaiian shirt, keeping him close while they played wet, sloppy tonsil hockey. She didn't intend to give it up in the front seat of his car on the first date. She didn't intend to give it up at all, not if the mission could be completed without such a radical step.

Ani loosened her grasp on his shirt, smoothing it with shaky fingers. Easing her tongue out of his mouth, she gave his lips one last, satisfied flick as she drew away.

Richard's eyes slowly opened. They'd glazed over. She tried not to feel smug, but she couldn't help enjoying a heady surge of feminine power. She could bring Sexy Rexy to heel with just a kiss.

She smiled. "Want to play?"

"I thought we were." He gave her a slumberous, sexy look from beneath heavy lids. Bedroom eyes. That's what Richard had, bedroom eyes, eyes that made her dream of rolling around on his WASP-y bed with him, naked and panting.

She gathered the remains of her composure. "No, really." She escaped from the car and trotted over to the swings.

Following her, Richard tried hard to figure out how the seductive siren he'd held in his arms a moment before had abruptly transformed into a giggly kid.

Ani kicked off her shoes and swung high. Her hair whipped behind her as she rose and fell.

Oh, what the hell. He took the swing next to hers. "Bet I can go higher than you."

"There's no way."

"Can, too. I'm heavier than you."

"You're out of practice." But she pushed harder at the ground when she dipped.

He shot high into the misty night sky. The chains creaked. "Whoa. I'd better not break this thing." He scuffed his deck shoe along the ground to slow down.

"I win! I win!" Ani sang.

She jumped off her swing in mid-flight, and he grabbed her around the waist. They tumbled together onto the soft grass.

He kissed the tip of her nose. "Have a good time tonight?"

"Yeah!"

"Me, too. How about getting together on Saturday?"

She frowned, her dark brows meeting in a straight line. "Okay, but you have to let me help."

"It's a deal."

"Another deal?"

He laughed. "I guess it's in the blood." He stood and offered her a hand. "And next time, you don't need to dress up."

"Don't I look all right?" She stood, using his hand for leverage.

"You look wonderful." He stroked her face. "You're absolutely the most exciting woman I've ever met."

She gave another slight, delicate gasp. "Really." Her voice held a sarcastic edge.

"Yeah, really. Learn how to accept compliments. Say, thank you, Richard, darling." He slid his arms around her.

"Thank you, Richard, darling." The sarcasm was heavier.

He grinned at her, loving the game. "Very good. Do what I say and we'll get along fine."

She huffed and tried to pull away.

He didn't let her.

She narrowed her eyes at him, and he couldn't resist kissing her nose again. "On Saturday, I might take you fishing. You want to gut fish in that beautiful dress?"

"N-no. Are we going to fish on your boat?"

"Maybe. Or we can go to the pier and buy some fish there."

"Ooh, the pier! I love the pier! Can we go to the boardwalk, too?"

"Sure. And on the roller coaster."

"You like the roller coaster?" She looked astounded for what might have been the twentieth time that night.

"Of course I do. Who doesn't? Look, Ani, I'm just an ordinary guy."

She scoffed. "Yeah, right. Richard Rexford, Mr. Average American."

CHAPTER TEN

Ani mulled over Richard's words as she lay in bed that night. *Just an ordinary guy.* If Richard Rexford was ordinary, then frogs could become princes.

He'd turned her inside out with his kisses. And when he'd caressed her breast . . . remembering his tender, experienced touch, her nipples hardened, rubbing gently against her soft, worn sheets.

He seemed to know how she'd react and to anticipate her response, stoking the fire with his mouth, his hands. *Just an ordinary guy.* But there wasn't anything ordinary about how she felt in his arms.

She wondered where this strange new relationship would go and what she wanted from it. Part of her, the sane part, knew she was in way over her head. But her wild streak overpowered rational thought, especially when he kissed her.

How could this relationship be okay? He was nothing more than the object of her mission. But according to Linda, having pleasurable sex without love was possible, even with a target. How could that be right for her? Ani was Algerian, and although she'd lived in America for a decade, her background wouldn't let her play the field with an untroubled conscience. The encounter with Michael had taught her that.

She stirred restlessly in her bed. Her narrow bed. A memory of Richard's wide bed, with its worn, comfortable-looking sheets, crossed her mind. How would it feel, to stretch out with

Richard in that big bed? Her body tingled and she rolled over, clutching her pillow to her chest.

Ani pushed her fantasies away, reminding herself of her agenda. She'd get into his laptop and out of his life before either of them got too involved. Their next date would definitely be the last.

On Monday morning, Ani faced Lewis Anglesey across his gray, nondescript desk in the unassuming office from which the U.S.S.A. conducted its northern California operations.

Her handler didn't look happy, and if Lewis wasn't happy, Ani felt threatened. "What's wrong?" she asked. "I got onto Rexford's boat, found his laptop in the wheelhouse, and have another date Saturday. This is perfect. If everything goes right, I'll be done with this assignment in less than a week."

Lewis frowned. "I'm not sure that the computer in the wheelhouse of his yacht is the one we're looking for."

Her heart sank. "Why not?"

"Most modern craft have pre-installed computers," he said. "The laptop at the helm of his yacht is more likely to be used for navigation, global positioning, that sort of thing. They come preprogrammed and have a specific electronic signature."

"Why couldn't he use the same machine for both tasks?"

"Maybe he could, but we know he's not."

"How?" Ani swirled the dregs of her coffee around in a cheap Styrofoam cup, hating the bitter brew, hating Lewis, and hating this assignment. Her guts were telling her that Richard Rexford wasn't a traitor.

But this was her first undercover mission. She had ignorant, inexperienced guts, and she wouldn't tell Lewis what she thought. He already disliked her and was probably jealous of her. She didn't want to say anything that would remind him of her initial reluctance to take this job. So she kept quiet about her feelings, with mounting guilt. Even without her attraction to Richard Rexford, she believed he was a nice guy who deserved better from her than deception.

"We are aware that he used his laptop early yesterday morning," Lewis said. "The communication we intercepted didn't have the electronic signature matching the wheelhouse computer."

Ani clapped a hand to her cheek. "You're right. He went belowdecks when we first got onto the boat, and he said he was going to check his emails. That seemed strange. I had wondered if there was something clandestine coming in."

Lewis' frown deepened.

She continued, "I had forgotten that detail. So there has to be another computer somewhere on that yacht."

"Yes, and you have to find it."

"I am looking, but so far, when I'm on the boat, so is he. I have had limited opportunities to search, though I've eliminated several potential hiding places for the laptop." She hesitated. "I could slip something into his wine to put him out, which would allow me to search unimpeded."

"No. When all's said and done, he's still a citizen, and we can't harm him unless absolutely necessary."

"Why didn't you hack in when you had the chance yesterday?"

He looked embarrassed. "We couldn't."

"Why not?"

"Rexford's tightened his firewalls."

"I already gave you his source codes!"

"He's altered them. Can you retrieve the new ones?"

"Sure, but we're working on a program that utilizes chaos theory to continually alter firewall source codes." She gave her handler an apologetic smile. "Sorry, but Rexford.com is a web security company. I do have to maintain my cover story, don't I?"

Lewis rubbed his temples. "Yes, you do," he said heavily. "And you're doing a good job. Just keep at it. This is only your first assignment, and something you'll discover is that these missions take more time and patience than you initially anticipate. Be cautious and careful."

On Monday morning, Richard went to Ani's cubicle and found it deserted. He'd figured as much, given her oddball work habits. When he returned to his office, he asked Paul to contact Kevin Wilson and Mark Rexford. Richard wanted to see them at eleven a.m.

Each arrived with similar looks of trepidation. Richard rarely called his employees on the carpet. Any necessary reprimands came from the team leaders. If a termination took place, Human Resources took care of the matter. When he wanted direct input into a project, he preferred to talk with employees on their own ground where they'd feel comfortable. This time, though, he'd pull rank to get what he wanted.

Kevin slouched in one of the small side chairs. Maybe he didn't understand the interpersonal dynamics of placing himself in a physically inferior position. More likely, he didn't care. Mark, who remained standing, obviously did. His body language radiated tension. He knew something was up.

Richard allowed his lips to curl into a smile as he took his large chair behind the desk, the power position in the room. The window behind him shadowed his face while revealing the expressions of his visitors.

"Mark, please sit down." Richard gestured, knowing his tone of voice turned the request into a command. He waited while his cousin slowly complied, and let silence dominate the room until he chose to speak.

"A couple of weeks ago the three of us made a wager concerning another employee of this company." He steepled his hands and looked at Kevin, then at Mark. "At this time, I have decided that this bet is morally reprehensible and legally unwise. I'm calling it off."

"Calling it off? What do you mean, calling it off?" Mark was on his feet again, glaring at Richard. "We made a deal."

Mark's overheated response surprised Richard, but he wouldn't be deterred. Ani was special, but he wouldn't tell his employees about their date. That was private. "We made a deal that could subject this firm to thousands of dollars in liability. You should have been the first person to advise against it." Richard remembered that Ani had broken through his firewall and installed her own programming onto his desktop computer, while locating his source codes. "Ani Sharif is too talented an employee to antagonize. In compensation, I'll buy the Niner tickets, and the two of you can have first choice."

A crafty expression entered Mark's slitted eyes. "You care that much about her?"

"What are you talking about?" Richard asked.

"I know you took her out Saturday night."

Richard's temper spiked, but he avoided reacting. His relationships were none of Mark's business. "How did you find that out?"

Mark shrugged. "I drove by her place. By the way, nice 'Vette."

"You were watching us?" Richard jumped out of his chair.

"It wasn't as though I stalked you. I happened by her house in the early evening, and there you were."

"Did Ani give you her address?" Richard wanted to put his fist through the wall at the possibility that Ani was seeing Mark on the side.

"No. I got it from her personnel file."

Richard's blood began to boil . . . no, vaporize. "Using confidential files for personal gain is inexcusable. You're fired."

"You can't fire me for this!"

"Watch me. Out." Richard strode to the door and held it open. "Clean out your desk and get out of here within one hour."

Mark stood for a moment, his disbelief palpable.

Richard's anger kept him from relishing the sight. "Do I need to call security?"

Mark took a deep breath, his face dark and red. "No, you don't. But you may have to get another lawyer for wrongful discharge." He stomped out.

Richard shrugged. His temper calmed, and he glanced at Kevin. "I'm sorry you had to witness that."

Kevin's mouth, which had hung partially open, now closed with an audible snap. "Are you kidding? I never thought I'd have a chance to see young T-Rex in action."

"Congratulations." Richard couldn't help the wry note in his voice. He poked his nose out the door. "Paul, contact Human Resources and tell them that Mark Rexford is no longer employed here. Make sure he's off the premises by noon."

Subject: you have received an e-card
From: greetings@e-cards.com
To: ASharif@rexford.com

On Tuesday afternoon, Ani stared at her monitor. Who had sent her an email card?

Richard. It had to be Richard. Though he was a target, not a date, who else would send her a card? She couldn't stop her heart from dancing a tango in her chest as she double-clicked on the card's electronic address. She tried to wait patiently as the card's image resolved.

A dozen red roses, their dew-laden petals velvety and soft, filled the screen. Soft violins played as a note appeared:

The silkiness of your skin rivals the loveliest roses. I can't wait to hold you again.

Richard.

Saturday. Four days until she could kiss him, touch him, hug his body to hers.

Reality intruded. *You're going to find his laptop and then dump him on Saturday, remember?*

Nevertheless, Ani leaned back in her chair and enjoyed the moment. Sweet of Richard to think of her during his workweek. Electronic or not, the virtual bouquet pleased her, sent the blood rushing to her head like bubbles on the wind.

How to respond?

Why respond at all? Maybe hard to get was a good ploy. Ani knew that Linda used it all the time.

Another part of her argued. *He made you a delicious dinner. He kisses like . . . well, better than anything you've felt before. Send something!*

She moved the mouse to reply to Richard's card with a similar one. But was that enough thanks for the wonderful evening? Leaning her chin on her hand, she pondered.

Smiling, she clicked to a site that delivered real flowers, then arranged for a bouquet to be delivered to Richard the very next day.

CHAPTER ELEVEN

Richard's stomach lurched as the old wooden roller coaster clattered and clanked. It labored to the top of its highest curve, climbing into the blue autumn sky. Then its chains and brakes loosened, plunging their car down the steep slope amid the delighted screams of its passengers.

Next to him, Ani raised her arms in the air and let loose a screech that rivaled that of a mating cat. He tickled the taut skin exposed by her midriff-baring top. She batted at his hand, squealing. He couldn't stop laughing. He hadn't had so much fun since he'd returned to California. Damn, but Ani was fine.

The roller coaster dropped to the bottom of its track, then twisted to the left in a tight, fast arc. From his seat, he could see the crowd of Saturday afternoon merrymakers on the boardwalk: young families with a kid or two, groups of sullen teens playing it cool, other couples. The boys strutted and showed off while their girls, pretending they were above it all, didn't shout or screech.

Ani fitted right in with her cutoff shorts and cute red top, which tied provocatively between her small, high breasts. She'd braided her hair and shoved it through the hole in the back of a Giants baseball cap. Its bill shadowed her face from the sunlight.

With a flash of self-consciousness, he realized he must look old in comparison to her youth. How did they appear to others? Like a well-matched couple or a father out with his teenaged daughter?

He knew that ocean and sun had wrinkled his skin. Prematurely gray hair mixed with the blond on his head. He still received an occasional admiring glance or two from women, but what was he doing with Ani? She needed someone her age, someone young.

The ride ended and Richard extended his hand to Ani, helping her off.

"Want some cotton candy?" She tugged his arm in the direction of a booth advertising corn dogs, cotton candy, and sodas. The aroma of popcorn blended with the salt breeze.

"I thought we'd go fishing or, if you're not in the mood for that, buy some seafood at Carinelli's." He nodded in the direction of the Santa Laura pier, which held a variety of shops, including fishmongers.

"We should probably go to Carinelli's. What if we went fishing and didn't catch anything?" She tucked her arm into his. She evidently wasn't plagued with any of the doubts that haunted him.

"Good point. But it's a big ocean with lots of fish in it." He squeezed her hand. He hesitated, then forged ahead. "Hey, Ani. How old are you?"

She shot him a sideways glance from beneath her impossibly thick, curly lashes as they walked down the length of the boardwalk to the pier. "Grand-mère Anny taught me that a gentleman never asks a lady that question."

"I'm not a gentleman. I'm a crusty old sailor with sand in his shoes and sea salt in his hair. How old are you? Am I dating jailbait?"

"I'm not underage," she snapped, her face growing red. "How could I work for your company if I were?"

He shrugged. "We get away with a lot in the name of national security."

"But why do you ask?"

He didn't want to talk about it. Searching for something to say, he stopped. Since their arms were still linked, she had to halt, too. She swung around to face him.

"I'm interested in everything about you," he said lamely.

She raised her brows, the irritation on her face fading. "I'm twenty-three. And you?"

"Thirty-four. Eleven years older."

"I can subtract, you know."

"I know that." He should have said, anything between us won't last very long . . . Eleven years is too big a gap. But, selfish pig that he was, he shut up. He wanted her. He didn't want to imperil their fragile new romance. He regretted raising the issue, but he had to know. And after he'd berated Mark about peeking into her file for personal advantage, Richard couldn't honestly do the same thing. So he'd asked, and now he knew he had eleven long years on her.

Richard's deck shoe pulled up slowly from the boardwalk with a sticky, sucking sound. He swore.

Ani snickered. He hopped on one foot, trying to get a glimpse of the sole of the other. Strings of pink bubble gum kept him stuck to the boardwalk. She continued to giggle while he hobbled down to the beach to coat the gum with sand. She joined him, her red high-tops sinking into the loose sand.

He scraped the sole of his shoe on a piling. "Am I too old for you?"

She leaned against the pier. "Perhaps. Am I too young for you?"

"Not a chance. I like 'em young and tender." He leered at her, hoping to disguise his distress at her answer. *Perhaps.*

Ouch.

"Let's go to Carinelli's and get some young and tender shrimp." She climbed onto the pier.

★ ★ ★ ★ ★

By the time they'd discussed the menu, bought dinner, and returned to the boat, the sun had dipped toward the horizon. The sky had started to streak pink and coral amid the blue.

Richard remained on deck to fool around with a tiny hibachi while Ani headed below to the galley. After tossing her hat onto the counter, she washed her hands, then began to thread prawns and pineapple onto skewers.

She'd had a great time until he'd raised the age issue. Why couldn't he have left well enough alone? She picked up a chef's knife and savagely hacked at a pineapple wedge.

His fears amplified hers. She reminded herself that she did not intend to become involved with him. But they had so much in common. And now they shared something else. Doubts. He worried about the age difference, and she had additional factors to add to the mix. Big factors. Her cultural background. Her job with the U.S.S.A., and their suspicions about Richard's patriotism. She didn't insist that anyone she was with be a rabid supporter of whatever administration occupied the White House, but she couldn't love a traitor.

Because she was alone, she took the opportunity to poke through every cupboard and cranny of the galley, even inspecting the clever, space-saving table and bench that pulled out of the back wall. Folding it back into place, she sighed. Nothing. The laptop had to be hidden somewhere else belowdecks.

Returning to her tasks, which were chopping pineapple and peeling shrimp, she mentally reviewed the differences between herself and Richard Rexford. Could she stay with him, assuming that her gut was right, and he wasn't betraying the country she'd come to love?

He was adventurous, and she'd had enough adventure when she'd left Algeria to last her a lifetime. On the other hand, was she deluding herself? Despite her previous focus on translation and computers, she was now a spy on her first undercover mission. If she didn't like excitement and adventure, she wouldn't have craved this opportunity for advancement in the U.S.S.A.

He was a workaholic who'd checked his emails during their last dinner date. How much of his time could she expect to enjoy, given his obsession with Rexford.com? But she also liked to toy with a software problem all night. The earliest hours of the morning, when the world was quiet and still, were her most productive.

No, she couldn't fault him for his work habits since she shared them.

However, none of this mattered, because he sounded as though he had misgivings. So her decision to stop seeing him was correct. She wouldn't be upset, she decided, if he didn't ask her out again after she'd completed the mission.

Richard walked into the galley. Like a big, golden lion crammed into a too-small cage, he dominated the room with his masculine presence, banishing her doubts. How could this be wrong, when it felt so very right?

He came up behind her and slid his arms around her waist, bared by her cropped top. He smelled of sea and smoke and hot, sexy male. His hands warmed her naked skin, sending a scorching, sensual heat to her femininity. It sure didn't seem as though he was having second thoughts, and her resolve to resist him melted like a sno-cone left on the boardwalk in the sun.

Ani tipped back her head and feathered a row of tiny kisses along his jaw. He tasted salty, like the ocean. She rubbed her tongue along his light stubble, enjoying the slight raspy sensation.

He turned her around and gave her a deep soul kiss, slipping in his tongue to suck on hers. The sense of being taken overwhelmed her and she moaned, pressing her body against him, seeking his hardness. He withdrew, tugging on her lower lip with his teeth, his blue gaze boring into hers. Desire stole her breath.

"The hibachi's ready. How are we doing here?" Caressing her breast, he nodded at the skewers.

She inhaled, regaining her composure. His question, along with his casual tone of voice, told her that he wasn't as involved as she. She strove for nonchalance. "Just about done." She handed him a plate with six skewers of prawns and pineapple neatly lined in a row.

"Great." He gave her a breezy smile. "I'll put these on the grill, and then we'll open some wine and make salad."

He took the food on deck, leaving her more confused than ever.

After beating a hasty retreat from the galley, Richard arranged the skewers on the hibachi grill.

If she weren't so damn young, he wouldn't hesitate to take her to bed immediately. Hell, he was ready to do her on the floor. Her kisses were mind-numbingly sexy.

The coals in the hibachi glowed red beneath a gray shell of ash, reminding him of Ani, a passionate woman disguised as a cybergeek.

Did he dare pierce that shell to let the passion free?

The shrimp sizzled, matching his mood.

Yes, he'd dare. He wanted her, and from her reactions, she felt the same way. Though younger than the women he usually bedded, she wasn't untried, he bet. With that wild child tattoo on her upper thigh, anklet and toe ring, she looked as though she was one hot babe in the sack.

But there was more between them than desire. She was special, unique. He respected her. He remembered what he'd seen when he'd picked up Ani this afternoon.

She hadn't been quite ready. She'd poured him a tiny

demitasse cup of thick, strong coffee before settling him in her cottage's sitting room. Bookshelves lined the walls, some sagging with the weight of accumulated tomes in three different languages: French, Arabic, and English. Examining them, he found an old edition of *Alice in Wonderland* . . . in French, with childish writing identifying it as hers.

Photos of Ani and her family, tucked here and there, revealed more: A wide-eyed little girl clutching the hands of a fashionably dressed woman and a reedy, amiable-looking man. Ani and her parents at the Eiffel Tower, the Trevi Fountain, the Egyptian pyramids.

Figuring that he and Ani were friendly enough for him to snoop a little, he'd explored her house, passing through the sitting room, down a hall, to the open bedroom door. Her back to him, she fumbled in a closet. Her bed, a single, was covered with a swath of tasseled paisley fabric, feminine yet exotic. Matching curtains edged the window.

On her bed, a laptop sat, its screen glowing. He walked into the room to check it out.

Turning, she gasped. "What are you doing in here?"

Aware he'd intruded, he backed off. "Sorry. I thought we were close enough that I could see your room."

She relaxed fractionally, shrugging, but he'd sensed her lingering tension. What the hell? Her reaction seemed exaggerated for the situation.

He sat on the bed, jiggling the mattress. The cover of the laptop fell closed with a click. "What are you working on?" he asked.

She went red. Without a word, she tapped the tiny button that opened the C.D. port.

Out came a Harry Potter game. He'd laughed at her, and she'd gotten even redder before whacking him over the head with a pillow.

He'd never met anyone quite like her. Her mixture of innocence and boldness intrigued him like no other woman ever had.

The coals popped and smoked, bringing his attention back to his task. The shrimp cooked quickly, so he carried the food back into the galley and put it on the counter. "Let's eat indoors. It's cool and misty outside."

"Okay." She jabbed salad tongs into a wooden bowl filled with greens, then looked around. "Where?"

"Watch this." He went to the far end of the galley, then tugged a padded bench seat out of the back wall. Nearby, he unlatched a table stored vertically against the side of the boat. He lowered it over the bench.

"Wow." Her eyes widened. She put the salad on the table.

Those big green eyes were just so cute. Did she reflect the same wonder during sex?

Time to find out.

He squeezed her hand. "Please sit down." He retrieved the platter of shrimp and pineapple and set it on the table. "Thanks for helping with dinner."

"Oh, that was no problem. I told you last week that I wanted to help. I'm not used to being served, except in restaurants."

After pouring wine, he handed the filled goblet to her. He sat next to her, deliberately crowding close, then snaked an arm behind her head, drawing her into its curve. "It's a poor host who makes a servant out of a treasured friend." He used a fork to pull the cooked food off the skewers.

She sipped her wine. "Am I a treasured friend? That happened fast."

He ran a finger along the line of her cheekbone, turning her head so she'd have to look at him. "Sometimes it does happen fast." He pressed a piece of warm, grilled pineapple to her lips. Hot, sticky juices spilled over his fingers. Hot and juicy. Would she also taste hot and juicy?

After a moment's hesitation, she opened her lips and accepted the fruit. He kissed her, tasting the delicate flavor of her mouth mingled with the sweet pineapple and the lingering tartness of the dry white wine. She responded, shoving her fingers into his hair to bring him closer.

He pulled her onto his lap, enjoying her petite curves molding against his body. He reached for a grilled shrimp and placed one end of it in her mouth. He bit off the rest, grinning at her startled expression. Oh yeah, Ani was gonna be a lot of fun.

She took a piece of pineapple from the platter and rubbed it along his jaw, then his lips. After feeding it to him, she licked away the sticky trail she'd drawn.

He shuddered with want. He wondered if she could feel his erection, poking hard and sharp into the softness of her thigh. He kissed her lips, then along her neck as he adjusted her weight so he was nestled between her thighs, achingly near her heat.

He rubbed the skin at her waist before exploring the knot between her breasts that secured her top. Tight, it resisted his attempts to loosen it so he instead cupped one taut breast, dragging his thumb over its crown. Her beaded nipple thrust firm and high.

That he turned her on meant everything to him. He broke loose from the kiss to frame her face in both hands. "Ani," he said, his voice rough.

She touched her nose to his and asked, "Yeah?"

He smiled at her. "Let's make love. I want you very much, and I think you want me."

Her green eyes went huge and liquid, holding desire and a hint of . . . fear? Nervousness?

"All right," she whispered. "But, umm, there's something you should know."

Yeah, definitely nervousness. Why?

Maybe she needed reassurance.

"There's nothing that could make me want you less or admire you more. I care, Ani, I really do."

She gulped. "That means a lot to me because . . . I, uh, I, umm, haven't done this much before."

"What do you mean, honey?"

She squirmed. "Well, once, but . . . it didn't go very well."

He held her close. "Tell me," he murmured.

"I'm so embarrassed." Her lids dropped so he couldn't look into her eyes.

"Was it the first time?"

"Yeah." She'd reddened again.

"And it was horrible?"

"Yeah." The tiniest hint of a sob shook her voice. "It was a, uh, couple of years ago, and . . . I haven't tried since."

"Aw, Ani." He tightened his embrace. "Look at me."

She tilted her head so he could see into her eyes, bright and full. She blinked, and a single tear ran down her cheek. He kissed it away, then slid his lips to her mouth, pressing gently at first, then with growing desire, even a little anger at the jerk who'd spoiled this gorgeous girl. She returned his kiss with mounting wantonness, showing him that her need was as great as his, perhaps greater.

Lust wiped his mind blank. On fire, he kissed her passionately, sucking at her lips, her tongue. His blood rushed southward. Though his shorts weren't snug, they tightened when he swelled.

Despite one bad experience, this beautiful little siren had chosen him to lead her into full womanhood. He might not be her first, but he'd be her best and maybe, her last.

From where had that crazy thought come? He shoved it away. She was too young to consider tying herself down, and he wasn't inclined. But regardless of what the future might hold, he'd make sure she always remembered him.

He whispered, "Don't worry. I'm glad you told me. I'm gonna make this perfect for you." He hugged her tight and kissed her on the lips. Sliding off the bench, he took her hand and led her to his bed.

CHAPTER TWELVE

Richard entered his bedroom ahead of Ani and switched on a lamp set on a bedside table. The soft glow allowed her to see him without a glaring light destroying her mood.

She sat on his bed and reached for the knot between her breasts.

His gaze pinned to her chest, his attention seemed almost comically exaggerated. She'd heard men were ruled by their joysticks. She hadn't known that this *Cosmo*-type truism applied to the T-Rexes of the world, but perhaps it did.

She fumbled with the knot, and he knelt before her. "Let me." Leaning forward between her open thighs, he set his teeth into the tight, red fabric and tugged. Her shirt rubbed her nipples, bringing a heady rush of pleasure. With every cell aglow, heat centered in her female core.

Richard held her hips, perhaps to steady himself. The warmth of his hands, so near her pelvis, made her tremble with want. She grabbed his shoulders to stay upright.

Another jerk at that stubborn knot and the cloth fell away, displaying her too-small breasts to his ardent stare. He didn't seem to object to their size, but immediately took one nipple into his mouth and cupped the other breast with a free hand. Warmth enveloped her.

He laved one, then the other, sucking hard. A frantic, intense pleasure shot from her breasts to her delta. She let out a little scream and fell back on the bed, hauling Richard with her.

Laughing, he dropped on top of her, squashing her into the mattress. When she squeaked a protest, he laughed harder, then kissed her on the mouth. Not deeply but hard on the lips, pushing them into her teeth, letting her feel his strength.

He rolled over and pulled her on top of him. He licked her breasts again as he unfastened the top button of her cutoffs. One . . . two . . . three . . . four opened.

"Ani, you're gorgeous." His smile radiated lust. "Take your clothes off, baby. I want to see you naked."

Passion zipped across every synapse. She'd never stripped for anyone, but . . . "Uh, how about you?" she asked.

"Okay." Richard toed off his deck shoes and kicked them away.

Standing, Ani did the same with her high-tops.

He grinned. "That's the way it's gonna be, huh? That's all right." He sat up and unbuttoned his shirt, his gaze never leaving her. He peeled it away, leaving his sun-browned torso bare and exposed to her gaze.

His body showed the hours of sailing and working on his boat. Rippling muscle roped broad shoulders, tapering to a narrow waist. Golden curls dusted solid, sculptured pecs. In his prime, Richard Rexford epitomized masculine perfection.

He smiled at her. "It's your turn."

She remembered he'd already seen her chest and, bless him, proclaimed her gorgeous. She closed her eyes and, hoping he didn't lie, eased her shirt off her shoulders and dropped it to the floor.

He audibly sucked in a breath.

She blinked.

Challenge in his eyes, he stood and unzipped his khaki shorts. The rasp of the metal teeth separating echoed in the quiet room.

She shoved her denim cutoffs down over her hips. Now he could see her stupid, childish white cotton underpants. Moaning inwardly, she wondered, why didn't I wear something sexy and sophisticated?? Another part of her head reminded her, That's because you weren't going to do this, stupid!

She looked at him. His boxers, decorated with yellow smiley faces, were too silly to be believed. Laughter bubbled forth. She dropped onto the bed, giggling. Impossible to stay embarrassed by her panties when twenty smiley faces leered at her from the vicinity of Richard's crotch.

He promptly jumped atop her. "You even have virginal underwear," he muttered, snapping the elastic band around her waist. "Do you realize how much you turn me on?"

"I do?"

"Oh, yeah. That red shirt you wore today. It reminded me of hot salsa. I had to know if you tasted as spicy."

"Do I?" she asked with disbelief. She'd never had such a strange conversation.

He nipped at one dark-peaked breast. "Yes, you do. And your body . . . Oh, honey. Dusky nipples." He tweaked hers. "Olive skin." He stroked down her side to her hip. "You're every harem fantasy I ever had." He kissed her mouth again, lingering over every stroke of their dancing tongues. Each nibble of his teeth on her lips made her hotter for him. She tingled as though fireworks exploded along her flesh.

He stroked down her body again and slipped his hand inside her undies. Each press of his fingers drove her higher and higher with an intense, prickling heat she'd never felt before. "You're wet and ready, darling." He tugged at her elastic waistband. "May I take this off?"

"Yes," she whispered, her body growing taut.

Richard dragged her panties down over her feet, then tickled her arch. "I love your sexy toe ring." He turned it, then sucked lightly on her toe. He dawdled and played as he explored.

She experienced a flash of anxiety as he toyed with her anklet.

What if he broke the clasp? A cadre of U.S.S.A. operatives would descend upon the *Trophy Wife* within minutes. That would certainly spoil the mood, she thought, grinning.

"What's funny?" he asked.

"You're tickling a little, but it's okay."

"Good," he murmured. "I want this to be good for you. I want this to be great." After licking and caressing his way up her legs, he arrived at her inner thighs. Spreading her knees, he burrowed his nose into her curls. "Umm, hmm."

Ani covered her face with her hands. She'd read about oral sex somewhere, and it had struck her as an odd concept. Now she discovered that this was the strangest, most embarrassing thing she'd ever done.

He kissed her, using his thumbs to open and expose her. To her shock and surprise, she burned, hot all over with a flaming bliss unlike anything she'd felt before. Richard rubbed his tongue against her, and ecstasy rolled through her body, unstoppable as the wind. He did it again and again.

She forgot how to breathe. Opening her mouth, she managed only short pants as the pleasure built.

Something foreign entered her. She looked down and saw Richard slowly sliding a long finger into her body. That felt weird at first. Invasive. Then he licked her at the same time he thrust inside and the anxiety transmuted into amazement, a sparkling, exploding rapture beyond anything she'd ever felt or even thought of. It went on and on, making her cry out again.

He feathered his fingers up and down her body, lingering at her breasts. Little quivering flickers of the same sweet flame danced over her skin, diminishing into a tingling joy that encompassed her with a sense of peace and completion.

She sighed and turned her head to look at Richard.

He smiled at her.

"Wow," she managed.

Leaning over, he kissed her. "And that's not even the main event."

"I don't know if I can handle much more."

His grin widened. "Better get ready, sweetheart." He sat up and pulled off his boxers.

"Oh, my." She couldn't help staring at his erection, which jutted from a nest of blond curls. Though he was tanned all over, with no pale areas or lines, his manhood glowed darker than his suntan. "You're, uh, big."

He chuckled. "You're very kind, honey, but I'm just average."

She poked it with a hesitant finger.

He groaned, and she reached for him with eagerness. First she stroked his length, surprised by the feel of his organ. Hard and soft at the same time, it reminded her of steel cloaked in the finest silk.

He groaned, so she rubbed harder, using her palm to take all of him at the same time. He gasped, a high, sharp sound.

"Oh, baby, that was great. You can do that any time." His voice went low and husky. "But I want to slow down a little. This will help." He reached inside a drawer of his bedside table, took out a square packet and ripped it open.

"What's that for? I don't need that."

He arched his brows. "Of course you do. Do you want to get pregnant?"

"Hey, I'm not stupid. I won't get pregnant this time of the month. And you're healthy, aren't you?"

"Of course I'm clean. I tested at the end of my last relationship."

She breathed easier.

He continued, "But counting days is a very unreliable method of contraception. Do you know what the doctor told the woman using the rhythm method?"

She rolled her eyes. "No, what?"

"Congratulations. You're gonna have a baby."

She pushed out her lower lip. "It's my first time with you. I want to feel you inside me. Is that so bad?" She'd heard men hated condoms. Why was Richard so pushy?

"I don't want you to worry, honey. I don't want us to have to count days and wait for your next period and, and have all that stress." He caught her arms and leaned in close, whispering. "I want this to be perfect for you. Please trust me."

She rolled away from him, feeling sulky and unreasonable.

He sighed. "Let's compromise. I'll give you a stroke or two without this." He tossed the condom onto the table. "But when I stop to put it on, no arguments, okay?"

Ani nodded, looking happier. Good. Richard hated to argue with her. Talk about getting lucky. Ani Sharif in his bed made SuperLotto into pocket change.

"Come here." He opened his arms.

She snuggled into his chest and licked the hollow at the base of his throat. His pulse drummed. Blood roared in his ears, a wild tide of want. He slid his hands up the satin smoothness of her back to finger her braid. He tugged off the band securing the end, then separated the strands of her beautiful bedroom hair. Sexy, fragrant, and wild, it draped seductively over her naked shoulders.

Dizzy from her jasmine perfume, he buried his face in the dark, scented mass while his hands sought her breasts again. Weighing them in his palms, he reveled in their dainty fullness. He wrapped her hair around one fist and gently pulled her head back to expose her throat. She arched her back, thrusting her breasts high. Her nipples, hard little points, beckoned him again. He wanted to feast on those dark pearls, roll them in his lips and tongue.

He took their invitation, suckling until she moaned and cried out something incomprehensible in Arabic. Pressing her back onto his pillows, he spread her thighs and set his hips inside hers, grinding back and forth against her wetness. Two or three strokes, and she cried out again.

He bucked into her, slowly easing in the rounded tip. She was narrow and tight and oh, so hot and wet. She panted, allowing him to fill her mouth with his tongue. He thrust into her long and slow, focusing on her pleasure. He had to. If he let himself go, he'd finish too fast and leave her behind.

Her response was flattering, sexy little gasps and cries of delight that made him swell with pride. He generally liked to make sure his bedmates were happy, but Ani was special. He wanted to love her better. She deserved his best.

He slid out, then in again three or four times, taking it as easy as he could. Tearing her mouth away from his, she screamed, writhing and twisting. He somehow yanked himself away. Scrabbling for the condom packet with shaky fingers, he managed to rip it open and sheathe himself.

Marginally calmer, he looked down at Ani. Her glowing face and body, flushed with passion. He stroked her lower lips with the tip of one finger, spurring another moan. She seemed ready for more so he fitted his covered shaft to her luscious opening. He took her slowly, no more than a half inch at a time.

He wanted her to beg, and she did, sobbing something in Arabic before reaching for his hips and gripping hard. She dug her nails into his butt to urge him inside. The slight jab of her fingers combined with the encompassing ecstasy of her threw him over the edge into forever. He tumbled into a sea of bliss so deep and powerful that he felt like a child's toy tossed upon its glittering waves.

He came back to consciousness with a soft, squirming mass under him, struggling to escape from beneath his weight. Ani.

"God, I'm so sorry." Richard freed himself from her velvet clutch and staggered to the head. Sweaty from lovemaking, he turned on the shower. He stuck his head out the door and regarded Ani, still sprawled across his bed, legs spread-eagled, looking like a sumptuous banquet of hot female flesh. His sumptuous banquet.

"Hey, sweetheart. Want to do it in the shower?"

CHAPTER THIRTEEN

Ani tugged the tangled, stifling sheets away from her throat and chest. Blinking herself awake, she stared at the unfamiliar surroundings.

The wood-paneled room sported masculine teak furnishings. A vase holding a bouquet of red roses sat atop a chest of drawers. A narrow shaft of sunlight arced through a round porthole to her right, hitting the middle of her body. No wonder she felt hot and sticky.

Recognition flashed across her sex-befuddled brain.

She was in Sexy Rexy's bed, and next to her was Richard, slumbering by her side like a great golden bear deep in hibernation.

She peeled away the bedclothes and tiptoed to the bathroom, hoping Richard wouldn't mind if she took another shower. Was there a limit on the fresh water the boat carried? He'd never mentioned anything about that. Perhaps the boat was hooked up to a land-based water source.

With a stab of guilt, she realized that she hadn't given a thought to her mission all night long. Instead, she and Richard had made love, napped, then awakened to play some more.

What had happened to her? The U.S.S.A. had been her life for ten years. How could she have been so careless?

Turning on the shower, she poked through the two tiny cupboards in the head below the sink while waiting for the water to heat. Again, nothing, but she really hadn't expected

Richard to keep a laptop where steam and water could damage it.

She stuck a hand into the shower, testing the water, then stepped in, worrying about Richard, the U.S.S.A., her life, and everything. What was she going to do? You're a failure, she told herself. Forgetting about a mission—that was bad. She ought to resign at once.

But Linda, an operative with three years more experience, would probably say that nothing was wrong.

Ani let the warm water sluicing down her body relax her. She had plenty of time to complete the mission, so everything was okay. If Richard was still asleep after her shower, she'd look around for the laptop. Already, she could truthfully tell Lewis that the laptop wasn't in the galley or the bathroom, and that was good. She had something to report.

When she left the bathroom, rubbing her wet hair with a towel, Richard had sat up in bed. He gave her a sleepy, satisfied smile. She hoped she wore an equally smug expression, though inside she felt a little irritable. She wanted to find his laptop, send its contents to the U.S.S.A., and finish this job so she could enjoy Richard without guilt.

"Hi," she said, awkwardness taking over. Awakening with a target was another new experience. Was she supposed to kiss Richard hello?

"Hi, yourself." Adorably blond and tousled, he swung his legs over the side of the bed and came toward her, blue eyes glinting in the morning light. He wrapped a big, warm arm around her shoulders. "How about breakfast?"

Estrella's, the restaurant at the mouth of the marina, was jammed with happy, chattering patrons waiting for tables, so Ani figured that the place must serve great Sunday brunches. After talking to the hostess, Richard, looking regretful, returned to Ani, who'd waited in the crowded foyer. "I'm sorry, honey, but they can't seat us here for an hour, unless you want to eat at the bar."

"The bar's fine with me. I'm very hungry this morning." She inhaled the mouthwatering aromas of bacon and eggs that pervaded the restaurant.

"You were a busy woman last night," he murmured into her ear.

She feigned a shiver. "Yes, someone kept attacking me."

"Umm-hmm." He nuzzled her lobe.

His public display of affection brought a rush of emotions. Lust, first and foremost. And . . . pride. Yes, pride. He didn't hesitate to claim her as his in front of the world.

He took her hand with a seductive caress of his fingers, then led her through knots of people over to the long, polished wood bar. He guided her to two empty seats. She picked the captain's style wooden chair next to the window, which provided a view of the breakwater and the ocean beyond.

He stroked her shoulder as he sat.

"That feels good, but . . . do we want to go public at work?" she asked.

"Why not?" He set a hand on her thigh. Her bare thigh.

A quiver ran through her body at his touch. "What about that lecture on sexual harassment? And I don't want to be the subject of gossip." How could she sneak around if people were talking about her, watching her?

He raised a brow. "That's a problem. You know about the rumor mill in Silicon Valley. People are gonna talk."

"Not if we keep quiet." She toyed with the wrinkled lapel of his Hawaiian shirt.

"Baby, last night was incredible and I want to shout with joy from the rooftops." He tickled her side.

She giggled. "I do too, but not at work."

"You're wacko. You can't keep your hands off me and we're in a public place."

With a flush of embarrassment, Ani dropped her wayward hand, which had strayed from Richard's shirt to his chest. "Work is different."

"You bet it is. I'm the boss." He leered at her.

"That's not fair!"

"Life ain't fair, baby cakes. I'll tell you what. Let's make a deal."

"Another deal?"

"Yeah. Why not? Let's agree to keep our hands off each other at work and in public. First one to break pays the price. And I bet it's you."

"As if." She narrowed her eyes. "What price?"

"Twenty-four hours."

"Twenty-four hours of what?"

"Of whatever I want, wherever I want it."

She hesitated. Did she trust him? Could she?

"Why not? Do you think you'll be the first to break?" That familiar, taunting note had returned to his voice.

Ani shook her head. "Of course not. I can control myself."

"But how great if you didn't." He smiled at her. "Being completely out of control might be a lot of fun."

"Have you ever been completely out of control, in . . . in bed?" She hoped she wasn't a prude, but Richard was so much more experienced than she. Did he plan some sort of freaky bondage scene?

"No. So it would be a new experience for me, if I lose the bet. You'll break, Ani, long before I will."

"I won't. I couldn't." Letting go to that extent could endanger her assignment. What if he found one of the weapons concealed in her clothes?

"One other thing."

"What?"

"When I rub my ear, like this . . ." He tugged on his left lobe. He leaned forward to whisper in her ear. "It means I'm thinking about coming inside you."

She gasped.

"Deep and hard." Leaning back into his chair, he gave her a smile infused with pure lust.

Her body ached with a want that centered between her legs. What had he done to her? One night and she'd become a marshmallow, eager to bow to his every whim. This wouldn't do. She hardened her attitude and stiffened her back.

Richard's eyes gleamed. "Still want to make a deal?" He enjoyed teasing her, the wretch.

Pressing her lips together, she stuck her hand out to shake. "You have a deal."

He grabbed it and nibbled on the fleshy part below the thumb. "How about we go back to the boat and I eat you for breakfast?"

"Hey, Richie," a gruff voice interrupted.

Richie? Ani looked up as the bartender, a grizzled old fellow, slapped two coasters in front of them.

"Harry, you old sea dog." Richard stood and leaned over the bar to give the barkeep a casual, masculine embrace and a slap on the shoulder. "Good to see ya. I didn't know you worked the Sunday brunch shift."

Harry shrugged. "Best tips of the week, aside from Friday and Saturday nights, and half as crazy. I can't break up bar fights any more. Too old." His gaze roamed toward Ani. "Speaking of bar fights, who's this little sparkler?"

"Harry, meet Ani Sharif. Ani, this is Harry Gaskell. He's been knocking around bars and boats for as long as I can remember."

Ani extended a hand, which Harry engulfed in his big, rough

clasp. "Nice to meetcha, Ani. You look as though you could cause a fight or two on a wild Saturday night."

She chuckled. "Not me. I'm just a mousy little programmer from Richard's company."

Harry snorted. "They're makin' mice mighty pretty these days. Welcome to Estrella's," he said in a more impersonal voice. "What can I get for you folks?"

"Champagne," Richard said promptly. "We're celebrating."

"Oh?" Harry looked interested. "What's the occasion?"

Ani speared Richard with a narrow-eyed glance. She did not want her personal business spread around to all and sundry, even if this was cozy Santa Laura. She hoped he got the message.

"Life. We're celebrating the joys of life . . . and love." Richard winked at Ani.

"Champagne it is. The good stuff?" Harry rubbed a cloth along the bar.

"Nothing but the best for Ani."

She smiled. "I shouldn't drink too much today. I have to work tomorrow. Don't want to slack off. The boss might get mad at me."

Extending an arm, Richard rubbed her between the shoulder blades. "Something tells me that you're in with the boss pretty good right now. I don't think you have to worry too much about him getting mad at you."

"Ah, so that's the way the wind blows, eh?" Harry tore off the foil from the neck of a champagne bottle, then untwisted the wire cage. Wrapping a towel around the cork, he removed it with a pop.

"Sure is." Richard leaned his elbows on the bar.

Harry poured the straw-colored, bubbly liquid into flutes. "Let me tell you something about this kid, Ani."

Richard groaned. "Oh, boy. Here it comes."

"Hush, Richie. Drink up and keep quiet." Harry pushed a glass toward Richard.

"Richie." Ani picked up her glass. "I've heard Richard called many things, from Baby T-Rex to Sexy Rexy, but Richie is not one of them."

Richard scrubbed both hands through his hair, still damp from his morning shower. "I don't think I want to hear this." Standing, he retreated toward the men's room.

"Good heavens." Ani eyed Harry. "What secrets do you have to tell me?" Meeting Harry, who appeared to know Richard very well, was a break she hadn't anticipated. She was in like Flynn, and she bet she could get onto Richard's boat any time she wanted with no questions asked. Even better, she could tell Lewis that she was getting close, not only to Richard, but to his good friends.

"Richie's a good guy, but those parents of his . . ." Harry shook his head.

"How long have you known Richard?" A little sore from last night's lovemaking, Ani squirmed on the hard wooden seat.

"Since he was just a little nipper, learning to sail his first knockabout."

"Wow. Did you teach him?"

"Sure did. There was no one else, see. Old Thomas was obsessed by his business deals. Still is, from what I hear. And Michelle was long gone."

"Who's Michelle? His mother?"

"Yeah. She left when Richard was three. Didn't he mention that?"

Ani shook her head. "He never talks about his childhood." The information had been in Richard's dossier, but she was glad to hear it supported by someone who knew Richard well.

"That's because he didn't have much of one." Harry slapped down a menu in front of her and left to attend to other customers at the crowded, noisy bar.

Ani gazed at the brunch selections with only part of her mind in gear. She'd never heard anything positive about Richard's father on a personal level, and Harry's gossip shored up her impression of Thomas Rexford as a hard, unloving man.

She shivered. On top of an uncaring, neglectful father, Richard had lacked a mother to nurture him. What would a U.S.S.A. psychologist make of Richard's background? Would it make him more, or less, inclined to disloyalty?

Poor Richard. Ani couldn't imagine growing up without the love and support of her parents. Daoud and Renée were gone now, but their affection had been the most important constant in Ani's life. Then the Forresters had taken care of her. She credited her two wonderful sets of parents for her happiness.

She had a cozy home, an exciting career, and a man she loved.

The realization that she was in love with Richard didn't startle her. At some time during the night, during the lovemaking or the cuddling or the deep, sweet kisses, her perception of herself had changed. She no longer would walk through life alone. She was now part of a unit, a couple.

Ani and Richard. She warmed at the thought. He'd been right to order champagne. Today they'd celebrate their love.

Turning her head, she watched Richard emerge from the men's room. Hands in the pockets of his denim shorts, attired in one of his flashy Hawaiian shirts, he didn't look like any fantasy man she'd ever imagined. She'd thought she'd end up with another operative, not a California beach bum masquerading as a software executive.

Richard returned, and Ani offered him the plastic-covered menu. He shook his head. "I know what they serve here, believe me." He looked at Harry, who stood nearby, with a pencil poised over a pad, apparently ready to take their order. "Exposed my deepest, darkest secrets yet?" Richard asked.

"Naw. Didn't tell her about the time you plowed the runabout into the seawall, or sank the Zodiac, or smashed the windshield of your father's Chris Craft." Harry laughed. "The kid was a wild one. Game to go out in any weather."

Richard grinned. "Just makes it more fun."

Fun. Loving fun with a special man had been the missing ingredient in the brew of her life. Until Richard.

Ani didn't know how, but she'd figure out a way to resolve her job with the U.S.S.A. with her relationship. Other agents had lovers or spouses. Why couldn't she?

CHAPTER FOURTEEN

"Yippee! The drought is over!" Linda twisted the cork off a bottle of Dom Perignon, then let it fly out the open window of her apartment's kitchen into the Sunday evening sky. "Woohoo!" She poured the bubbly into a pair of cut crystal champagne flutes.

Ani blushed. "I don't see why everyone's making such a big deal over it," she grumbled. "Richard also wanted champagne."

Linda chortled. "That's because he nailed untouchable Ani."

"He doesn't know that I'm untouchable Ani," she said. "We shagged on the second date. He probably thinks I'm a slut."

"No, he doesn't. He thinks he's lucky," Linda said with assurance. "Trust me on this. So how was it?"

Ani giggled behind one hand. "It was great! To Richard." She lifted her glass.

"To great sex any time, any place, anywhere." Linda drank deeply.

"To lovers." Ani sipped, then put down her glass and sighed. "I never thought I could feel this way."

"Whoa. Michael was that bad?"

"I guess. Or Richard is that good."

"I'm trying not to get jealous." Linda chuckled.

"Now I understand what a selfish lover Michael was," Ani said. "I know I should have been honest with him, but still . . ."

Linda gave her a searching stare. "Ani, are you in love with Richard Rexford?"

She nodded. "I am. And I'm so scared."

"Why?"

"He's a target, possibly a traitor."

"You don't believe that, do you?" Linda set her glass onto the counter.

"Not a chance. I haven't gotten into his laptop, but I think I would have seen or heard something by now."

"But you're worried that you're wrong."

"Yeah. What if I'm in love with a traitor?"

"Chances are you're not, but don't let it spoil your fun."

"It's more than fun, Lin."

She shook her head. "It can't be. Not for us."

"What if it is?"

"Again, chances are you're not really in love."

"Why do you say that? I feel that I am!"

"Sure you do. But it's your first time. You'll fall in and out of love ten thousand times before it's real."

Something about Linda's superior attitude bothered Ani, but she couldn't pin down what it was. "What if I'm not like you?"

Linda preened. "You're not. But that's all right."

Ani narrowed her eyes at her sister. "Not everyone can be so perfect."

"Sorry." Linda punched Ani lightly on the arm. "Had I turned into Ms. Condescending again?"

"Duh."

"I don't mean to be a bitch. Look, just enjoy yourself, okay?"

"I can't. I feel disloyal . . . to the agency as well as to Richard."

"You're not being disloyal to the agency," Linda said, sounding firm. "You can use your feelings for Richard to continue to lead him on and fulfill the mission. That's what it's all about."

"I thought that loving others was what it's all about."

"Not for us."

"Other agents have lovers, get married."

Linda's eyes opened wide with shock. "Get married? Has he said anything about marriage?"

"N-no."

"You're letting your emotions run away with you." She crossed her arms over her chest. "You need to keep your head, keep the mission in mind, and stop that silly daydreaming about Prince Charming coming down the pike to sweep you off your feet. It isn't going to happen."

Ani sighed. "Not in this lifetime."

Subject: you have received an e-card
From: greetings@e-cards.com
To: ASharif@rexford.com

Ani's heart thumped. It had to be from Richard. Grinning, she double-clicked on the e-address of the card.

As the image came into focus on the monitor of her office desktop, she wasn't disappointed. Pixels settled into the triangular, silver shape of one of America's favorite chocolates. A Hershey's kiss.

A message appeared.

Here's a kiss from me . . .
when may I have one from you?
How about Saturday?
Missing you,

Richard.

She missed him, too, though they'd parted less than twenty-four hours before. She should have enjoyed the moment completely, but a nagging worry intruded. When would they start to use the "L" word? And how could she reconcile her emotions with who she was?

Love. She was sure her feelings for Richard were real, but his for her remained a mystery. Her job aside, Harry's story about Richard's childhood didn't augur well for their romance. If he'd never known a loving relationship, how could he have one with her?

She sure wanted him, with a craving that had reached uncontrollable heights. Memories of their night together muddled her concentration. She'd nearly fallen off her bike that same day when she'd ridden into sight of the Rexford.com office building, because she recalled how he made her feel when he thrust into her.

Smiling, Ani clicked to a site that delivered candy. She ordered a super-sized Hershey's kiss to be delivered to Richard. Seeing even a picture of chocolate made her hungry, so she picked up her wallet. She headed for the employee break room and the bad-for-you munchies sold in the food machines there.

"Hey, Ani! Wait for me!" Karen from Personnel approached and followed Ani to the bank of coffee and snack machines lining the back wall of the stark, linoleum-floored room. Today she wore a fairly conservative outfit: a navy suit, complete with pearls. "What's up?"

"Not a lot." A total lie, but Ani wasn't going to talk about her passionate weekend with the boss.

Karen dug in her wallet for change. "That's not what I hear." She shoved coins into a slot in the snack machine, then punched buttons. A bag of potato chips rattled to the bottom of the machine.

Ani's cheeks blazed. "What did you hear?" She kept her voice calm. She had no intention of adding grist to the Silicon Valley rumor mill.

"Baby Rex called Kevin and Mark onto the carpet."

This didn't sound like anything related to her. Ani relaxed. "Yes? What did they do?" she asked, feigning interest.

"I don't know, but Mark Rexford got the full T-Rex treatment."

"Was Mark fired?"

"Well, I heard Rexford wanted to give Mark the boot, but the head of Legal begged to have him reinstated. Apparently he has some top secret information about CompLine's legal status that would really help us out."

Ani nodded. "That's a reason to keep him around. Clever of Mark to keep a bargaining chip. Why did Baby Rex want to fire him?"

"I don't know, but I heard your name was mentioned."

Ani's heart lurched. She barely knew Mark Rexford of Legal. What was going on? What had Kevin to do with the situation? How could it affect her mission? To cover her feelings, she pushed money into a machine and purchased a bottle of water.

Karen continued, "That was why Kevin was in on the meeting. He's your boss, right?"

"Yes." Ani frowned. "I wonder what this is about." As far as she knew, no one at Rexford.com was aware of her affair with Richard but Sexy Rexy himself.

Was Mark the traitor? Was he on to her? *Ixzit.* She prayed her cover wasn't blown, and made a mental note to tell Lewis about this new development.

"Maybe it had to do with the belly dance." Karen gave Ani a sly wink. "Both Kevin and Mark were there."

"So were a lot of other people," Ani said, feeling defensive.

"Yeah. It was great. Hey, will you teach me how to do that? I wanted to ask you at the time, but you left kinda fast." Karen looked reproachful.

Ani refused to feel guilty. "A friend of mine in Santa Laura teaches belly dancing. You're welcome to join her class." She didn't want Karen, or anyone else from Rexford.com, at the lessons she continued to hold at her home, preferring to keep the myriad, confusing parts of her life separate. Matters were chaotic enough.

"Hi." A deep male voice sounded from the door of the break room.

Richard. Ani's breath caught in her throat.

He sauntered into the room, his blue blazer slung casually over a shoulder. "Did I hear a discussion of belly dancing?"

Ani's temperature rose, and she sensed her face again taking on a glow like fireflies at midnight. She pressed the chilled bottle of water against her cheek.

Turning his head, Richard winked at her. She prayed Karen couldn't see.

Fortunately, Karen seemed oblivious. "Yeah, Ani says I can take lessons."

Richard's vivid stare stripped Ani to her soul. She tried to act nonchalant even though her insides were in tumult, but this was the first time she'd seen Richard since he'd dropped her off at her cottage.

If anything, her yearning for him had intensified, despite Linda's warnings. Ani had spent last night desperate for sleep while her wayward brain kept replaying scenes from their lovemaking. How he'd tasted. How he'd felt inside her. His fingers and tongue on her . . .

"Well, I can testify she's a great dancer." His tone was mild.

His mere presence made her nerve endings tingle with need. She clenched her fists around the water bottle to keep from jumping his bones on the spot. "I, uh, I . . ." She cleared her throat. "I told Karen she could take lessons sometime. A friend of mine in Santa Laura is the real expert."

He cocked one eyebrow. "I have no doubt of your expertise in everything you try." Raising one hand, Richard tugged on his left earlobe and smiled.

The mental screen in Ani's mind went blank, then filled with the erotic image of Richard's finger easing inside her. Blinking, she swayed.

He grabbed her arm. "Are you all right? Let me take you back to your cubicle." Sliding an arm around her waist, he led her down the hall to her workspace.

Ani thought she'd die from embarrassment. "What's Karen going to think about this?" Regaining her composure, she wrenched out of his grasp and sat at her desk.

He loomed over her, large and predatory, filling the small space. "I don't care what Karen thinks."

"You're very close to losing this bet."

"Not me, baby cakes. You're the fair maiden who swooned into my arms in the employee lounge when I tugged on my ear. You know what I was thinking about, don't you?"

Coming inside her. "Ye-es."

His lids dropped, shuttering that fabulous, bedroom gaze. "I have visions of my gorgeous Arab slave-girl stripped and ready to fulfill every wild fantasy."

She didn't know what she'd do with Richard if she won, but the alternative . . . what could he be planning? "Not a chance."

His eyes opened. "You're going to go back on your deal?"

"No." She swung back and forth in her swivel chair. "I'm going to win."

He leaned over her. His breath feathered the hair near her ear. Little tremors of excitement fluttered low in her belly.

Was he going to kiss her?

She'd win the bet. Her mind reeled at the thought.

Richard whispered, "We'll see about that."

CHAPTER FIFTEEN

Subject: you have received an e-card
From: greetings@e-cards.com
To: ASharif@rexford.com

Ani double-clicked. Anticipation made her heart trip and tumble in her chest. The two days that had passed had showed her how tough staying away from Richard could be. Evidently he felt the same way. A red rose had appeared on her desk yesterday, and a bag of Hershey's kisses—the real ones—greeted her this morning.

What would it be this time? And what gift would she send Richard to match his virtual present?

A painting of lovers, naked and intimately entwined, filled her screen. But they weren't in bed. The picture made it clear that this reckless pair had selected an office for their coupling.

The male had the woman bent forward over a desk, and he was gripping her hips as he enjoyed her. She didn't look too unhappy either, with her long dark hair draped over her back, her head thrown back in an attitude of complete abandonment.

Ani's sex throbbed as she stared at the erotica. She placed her palm on her mouth. Richard had trapped her neatly, or perhaps she'd trapped herself. The pattern had been set.

He sent her virtual roses; she'd sent him a dozen lovely flowers from e-bouquet.com.

Virtual chocolate had arrived; she sent him the real thing.

He'd returned the favor just this morning.

Now he evidently expected her to respond in kind. With sex. The context of the message was clear.

Sex.

In the office.

She'd lose the bet.

Ani had thought she'd defeated her childhood habit of chewing her nails. She was wrong. She pulled ragged fingertips out of her mouth, then hit a button to clear the screen. However, the naughty thoughts that filled her brain wouldn't leave so quickly.

Clicking to the file with her current assignment, she tried to lose herself in her work. She didn't want Richard to think she'd use their relationship to slack off. Triple-P, the password protection project, demanded more from her as a programmer than any task she'd previously encountered. The application of chaos theory to—

Ani's monitor went flat and blue. "Aargh!" In shock, she jerked her hands off the keyboard. Due to sheer inattentiveness, she'd crashed her system right down to the blue screen of death.

What had she done? Or, rather, what had Richard done to her?

She dashed out of her office, meaning to clear the air once and for all. No more sexy emails. No more flirting and, definitely, no more ear tugging. Ever.

She strode through the double doors to Richard's suite, past his astonished secretary.

"Uh, Ms. Sharif, shouldn't I let him know you're here?" Paul reached for his intercom.

"Don't bother. I can announce myself." Ani crashed against the half-open door to Richard's inner sanctum. She saved herself from falling on the floor by grabbing the doorknob.

Richard, seated in his high-backed desk chair, swung around

at the noise. He surveyed her. "My, you do like to make a dramatic entrance, don't you?"

"You—you—you—" Too late, Ani saw that someone else was in the room. Vern from Accounting. She briefly closed her eyes, wanting to hide beneath Richard's desk.

Rising, he smiled. "Vern, thanks for the reports. I'll get back to you in a day or two about your suggestions. Make an appointment with Paul for a meeting, say, Tuesday."

Vern shook Richard's proffered hand. "Yes, sir. Uh, hi, Ms. Sharif." With a look of relief, he gave her a half-wave as he escaped.

Richard's smile stretched wider. "Now you definitely owe me one."

Ani recovered. "What do you mean?"

"Vern's accounting report was very interesting. They're the highlight of my month, Vern's reports."

She huffed. "Really?"

"And you interrupted us. I expect payback."

"P-p-payback?" Her mouth dropped open. Man, but he played dirty. He obviously would do anything to get what he wanted.

"Ready to concede defeat?" He approached, taking a position between Ani and the door.

She sucked in a breath and tried to reclaim her composure. "You must stop this. I can't work. I can't think. It's not fair!"

"It's not fair, it's not fair." Pitching his voice high and whiny, he imitated her. "Get used to it, little girl. This is the real world. This is how adults play."

He bent so his lips were less than an inch from hers. "Life isn't fair."

She jerked her head back as if a cougar had neared. "I'm not going to lose this bet."

He closed the door. She heard the tumblers click in the suddenly quiet room when he locked it.

"This has nothing to do with the bet. This is . . . payback." His voice went low and husky. "Did you get the card I sent you?"

"Th-that's why I'm here."

"Good." He came closer, so close she could smell his scent, feel his heat. "Didn't it look fun?"

"I, I don't know. I've never done it like that before."

"So why are you here, in my office?" He trailed a finger along her cheekbone, across the seam of her trembling lips.

"You're . . . you're losing the bet."

His fingertip slipped into her mouth, massaging the sensitive flesh just inside. "Oh, no, honey. You're here. You're mine." His voice had hardened. "Don't forget it." Cupping his hand around the back of her head, he leaned forward. With his lips less than an inch from hers, he whispered, "Do you think we can come without touching?"

She involuntarily jerked at the outrageously sexy thought, her mouth feathering his, giving him the slightest butterfly kiss. The contact tingled to her toes.

Withdrawing, he smiled. "You lose. I win. Or, rather, we both win."

Ani backed away from Richard, acutely aware of Vern from Accounting and Paul the secretary in the next room. He stalked her, forcing her to retreat until a hard ridge nudged the backs of her thighs through her jeans. She glanced down. The desk.

He planted rock-hard arms on each side of her, trapping her.

"Wha—what are you doing?" A frisson of excitement rippled along her spine.

"It's payback time, honey. I'm taking what I'm owed." He swooped down to capture her mouth in a demanding kiss that seemed to presage the future of their relationship. *Whatever I want, wherever I want it.*

Oh, she could resist, ram a knee into his crotch or stomp on his skimpy loafers with her motorcycle boots. But she didn't want to deny the lure of the unknown love Richard offered.

Ani returned his kiss in full measure, letting their tongues clash in a dangerous game. He reached for the zipper of her jeans. She clawed at his belt buckle. Freeing him was easy. She clasped him in both palms, making him swell with need, glorying in his response.

He jerked and tugged at her tight denims, his fingers a fraction of an inch away from one of her concealed blades. She tensed, grabbing his hands, helping him strip her while keeping him away from her weapons. He wrapped one arm around her waist, peeling down her jeans to her thighs. The desk felt cool and hard beneath her naked backside.

Richard pried her knees apart and tried to edge between them. The heavy denim blocked his way. "Turn around for me, sweetheart."

She obeyed, her heartbeat quickening to an impossibly rapid tattoo.

He bent her over the desk.

Like the woman in the picture he'd sent her.

Ani tried to inhale, but she'd gone taut with desire. She could suck in only tiny, panting breaths.

His hand caressed her from behind, tracing her furrow. A finger entered her, then another, gliding freely inside. "So lovely and ready," he murmured. His hand withdrew, and she heard a crackle. Turning her head, she saw him take a condom packet from his pants pocket.

In an agony of suspense, Ani gripped the far edge of the desk. She didn't know how this would feel . . .

His big, warm hands massaged her bottom. The waves of rapture flowing through her from his touch dissolved any lingering resistance. Then his palms pressed the halves apart. She managed a breath, aware she was entirely open to him, offered and vulnerable.

Something larger and broader entered her soft flesh. She closed her eyes to let it happen and Richard took her, long and slow, letting her body set the pace as her muscles relaxed, accepted his length and girth. She thought she'd burst apart because it was so good. He withdrew an inch or two, then eased in again, this time sliding into her all the way. She must have gasped because he leaned over her and covered her mouth with his, as if reluctant to allow a single sound of her pleasure to escape.

Bending over her, still deeply embedded, he murmured, "I thought about this all week. Sweet Lord, you'd tempt a priest right out of his vows." He reached around her to the nest of hair concealing the seat of her pleasure. Crossing her arms, she buried her face in the crooks of her elbows to keep herself from crying out. She came with the caress of his hand. His warmth covered her shaking body.

But he wasn't done yet. He kissed her ear, then nibbled on the lobe. "Darling, I want to do this harder and faster. Can you take it?"

At that moment she would have jumped off the Eiffel Tower if he'd asked. She nodded.

His heated body withdrew. His hands skittered down her back, resting on her hips. His grip sent new tremors racing through her. He plunged into her three, four, five times . . . she lost count of the heavy, fierce thrusts before a final surge into her body made him shudder with his release.

Except for her pulsing sex, she didn't move and neither did he. They remained quietly locked together, intimately joined, breathing in tandem while the aftershocks of her orgasm faded into a gentler bliss. Finally, she sensed him reaching between them and carefully removing their protection, then moving away from her.

His zipper rasped. He picked her up and carried her to his big desk chair, cradling her in his arms. "All right, baby?" His smug tone of voice left no doubt that he certainly thought it had been all right.

"Fantastic." She rubbed her face against his chest, enjoying the slight abrasion of his starched shirt on her cheek. Did satisfaction also echo in her voice?

He chuckled. "You don't have much to compare me with."

She started to speak but he put a finger over her lips. "Please don't go there. I shouldn't tease you. I'm glad, very glad, that you're mine." His voice rumbled with male possessiveness. "I never want that to change."

Hmm. The fearsome T-Rex using words like never? As in forever?

No. Couldn't be. This was just romantic exaggeration. She'd heard that men would say anything while in the depths of passion. Why should Richard Rexford be different?

She hesitated, deliberately forcing away any thoughts of her other job. "It, umm, doesn't have to change."

"Does this mean you'll, you acknowledge you've lost the bet?"

She didn't dare look into his eyes. "Ye-es." What was she doing?

Richard's chest rose and fell, shifting her head. His heart beat faster, thrumming in her ears. He lifted and turned her so she had to look in his eyes. Their brightness was almost painful to bear.

"You'll give yourself to me . . . in any way I ask?"

She couldn't speak. She nodded.

"Because you lost the bet?"

"Because I . . . I trust you," she whispered. "I think."

Though she tried, Ani couldn't shake off her moodiness. Beset by multiple worries, she survived on coffee and very little else.

What would Richard demand of her? She knew he wouldn't be satisfied by anything less than complete submission, and how could she reconcile that with her job?

She kept a knife in her left boot heel. Another hid in a sheath strapped to her right calf. Other blades rested in her belt, in the cuffs of her leather jacket, even in the waistband of the cutoff shorts she'd stripped off for Richard the first time they'd made love.

Did his demands mean that he'd somehow seen through her? Did he know she was an agent? Richard and his father had many contacts throughout the U.S. government, and although the U.S.S.A. was a super-secret organization, it wasn't entirely unknown. It could be found, if one knew what lines in the federal budget to question, who to ask, which plain hotel rooms and anonymous strip malls to watch.

If he'd made her, if she'd blown her cover, her career as a U.S.S.A. agent was toast. After a decade of struggle, she'd have nothing.

She wouldn't even have Richard. Surely he'd view her lies and deceptions as nothing but a betrayal of the darkest sort . . . and she couldn't fault him for coming to that conclusion.

Two days later, still tortured by doubt, she followed her foster sister into the nondescript office where their handler waited. Ani told herself that, although she didn't know quite what to report, she couldn't betray any hint of uncertainty. The secret pact between her and Richard couldn't be divulged, not even to Linda.

But Linda provided a distraction. "Something strange is going on at my assignment," she told Lewis and Ani. "I think someone's on to me."

Lewis leaned forward, resting his arms on his desk. The cuffs of his pale blue, Oxford-cloth shirt were rolled up, exposing surprisingly muscular forearms.

Ani noted that Linda's gaze slid from Lewis' arms to his big hands, then to his face. Her foster sister, normally so self-assured, faltered before she spoke. "They've moved me into the senior partner's suite and given me a desk next to his executive assistant."

"Isn't that a promotion?" Lewis asked.

"Yes, and they've given me a raise. But it's peculiar, trust me. I've been there less than twelve weeks, and I don't deserve this. I've been cultivating the image of a brainless good-time girl, interested only in clothes, makeup, and men."

"Do any additional responsibilities come with the new position?" Ani asked.

"None," Linda said. Standing, she paced the length of the office, her heels clicking on the cheap linoleum. "It's as though they want to keep an eye on me."

Lewis eased back into his chair. Ani could see his considering gaze roam over Linda's body, his male interest clear.

Ani couldn't blame him. Linda, as usual, was polished as a pearl. Today she wore a snug, fitted suit with a pencil skirt and a peplum that emphasized her curves. The emerald green fabric complemented her amber skin and dark eyes.

"How close are you to completing your assignment?" Lewis asked.

"Close," Linda said, sitting in the chair beside Ani's. "I retrieved the senior partner's email address book and found his contacts with both the Chinese and CompLine. Using his email, Ani hacked into the computer system of the Chinese consulate and downloaded their email address books and files."

"That was a couple of weeks ago," Ani said. "I haven't been

able to get into CompLine yet. They have very sophisticated firewalls."

"I've had Stratton in D.C. looking everything over," Lewis said. "Either your boss at the law firm is totally innocent, or the messages are in a very complex code."

"Want me to take a look at it?" Ani asked.

"No, you have enough going on," Lewis said.

"There wasn't anything about Mark Rexford in there," Ani said. "Have you found out anything about his involvement, or the meeting he had with Richard Rexford?"

"No. As far as we know, he's clean."

"So where do I stand?" Linda fixed Lewis with a steady stare.

He tapped the eraser end of a pencil on his desk. "Wing, go back in there. We can't pass by the opportunity you've been given. You have access to your boss's correspondence as well as his Blackberry and his Rolodex, and I want you to get hold of everything as soon as possible. And copy the firm's files on CompLine. Then we'll yank you."

"I hope it's not a trap." Linda ground her spiky heel into the linoleum.

Lewis' jaw tightened. "You're equal to whatever they throw at you, but I respect your instincts. In one week, someone will phone to tell you of an urgent family crisis demanding your presence in, say, Indianapolis." He treated her to a thin smile, then turned to Ani. "What's your report, Sharif?"

Ani made a conscious effort to stay relaxed. "Another weekend, and another date with Richard Rexford. Both previous meetings have been aboard his yacht, and I believe that this one will be, also."

"Good. Find that laptop, transmit the contents, then break off the relationship." He rubbed his chin, considering. "Maybe you'll also have to go to Indianapolis . . . or wherever."

Wherever. That didn't sound good, but what could Ani say?

She couldn't tell her handler that she was in love with her target. She cleared her throat. "What did you find out about that guy who attacked me?"

"Nothing. He's nothing." Lewis dismissed the matter with a wave of his hand. "Just a messenger-boy."

"Who does he work for?"

"Everyone. He's a mercenary. A ho."

"A spy ho?" Ani asked. "I'd laugh if this weren't so serious."

"Don't worry about him." Lewis crossed his arms over his chest. "He won't be coming back."

Ani exchanged a glance with Linda, who lifted her brows.

"Yes," Lewis said. "The consequences of failure in this business are . . . severe. I suggest both of you keep that in mind."

CHAPTER SIXTEEN

Richard drove the 'Vette screaming around the curves of Skyline Drive. He couldn't get to Ani's home fast enough. This was gonna be fun. She'd promised she'd give herself to him any way he wanted for the next twenty-four hours, and he'd test her with total submission.

Their relationship had spiraled out of his control. He hoped she didn't know, but he'd fallen completely under her spell from the first moment she entered his office. Letting a woman lead him around by Mr. Dickie was a mistake. Letting her into his heart was worse. He'd learned both lessons when his mother had dumped his father and abandoned the family. Richard couldn't count the number of times his father, that old misogynist, had ranted about the unfaithfulness of women.

Though Richard didn't believe everything Thomas said, Uncle Sundeen's string of failed marriages had been instructive. Sundeen couldn't keep up with alimony and child support payments due his five wives and countless children. Hell, he didn't have a family, he had a tribe. Richard instinctively shuddered away from the horrible possibility of following the perilous course his uncle had charted.

Yeah, Richard knew he needed to take back the helm in this relationship. That wouldn't be hard. Ani had been inexperienced, and he bet he could control her through sex. He'd never let her know how much he wanted her. Needed her, actually. She'd renewed his joy in life, something he'd thought dead.

151

He knew she was scared. A wicked, sinful part of him relished her dread. He couldn't wait until her fear turned to faith in his ability to satisfy her utterly. Her need had to match his, or he'd be lost.

He brought his car to a screeching halt outside Ani's cottage. Despite the high stakes, or maybe because of them, his over-eager feet tripped as he climbed the steps to her porch.

Tomorrow he'd take her to his father's brunch. Richard imagined Thomas Rexford's shock when he spied exotic Ani Sharif. Thomas had wanted his prince of a son to marry an appropriately WASP-y princess, but neither prince nor the selected princess had cooperated. Richard wondered if his father would again play matchmaker, and if Celeste would be in attendance the next day.

He knocked at Ani's door. While he waited for her, he looked around the veranda. The wind had blown dried fallen leaves into the corners, giving the porch a forlorn, lonely look. But the punching bag suspended by a hook in one corner was shiny and clean, as though recently used. He guessed that Ani used it for exercise in addition to her dancing. A lot of women these days were into self-defense.

Ani opened the door. Wearing jeans and a snug purple sweater, she looked cozy-warm in contrast to the November weather. Though sunny, the chilly breeze carried more than a hint of the approaching winter. "Are you sure I'm dressed appropriately?" she asked.

"You're fine, but can you bring an overnight bag and a dress for tomorrow? I'm taking you somewhere special for brunch."

"Hmm. I don't have much to choose from."

"How about that beautiful dress you wore for our first dinner? That would be perfect." Perfect to knock dear 'ol Dad's socks off.

"Oh, okay. Come in while I pack." Leaving him in her

kitchen, she dashed into the interior of the house, presumably to go to her bedroom.

He wondered if he should follow her to her room to get an early start on the day's sexual festivities, but before he entered the cottage, a prickling sensation shivered up his spine. Was he being watched?

He turned in the doorway and looked around. He scanned the street and the nearby foliage looking for his scumbag cousin. Richard hadn't wanted to keep him at Rexford.com, but the firm's legal counsel had insisted, stating that Mark knew too much. If he turned, he could destroy Rexford.com. Richard surmised that Mark would do what he could to screw the company anyhow, given the situation, and had instructed Legal to neutralize Mark by giving him busywork like reviewing employee contracts.

"What's wrong?" Ani had returned and now watched him quizzically.

"Nothing." He leaned against the doorpost. "Well, for a moment, I had a funny feeling like someone was casing your place, like for a break-in, but I guess I was mistaken."

"Huh." She paused, as if digesting the information. "I guess I should take a look around. I don't want a burglary while I'm gone."

"You'll look around?" He laughed. "What if there's someone there? Is my little cybergirl going to program him out of existence?"

An odd expression flitted over her face. "That's, umm, almost insulting. I assure you I can take care of myself."

"Ani, honey, you're a very capable person, but how tall are you? Maybe five-five?"

"What about it?" Now she sounded huffy.

"If some six-foot, two-hundred-twenty-pound gorilla is out there, I don't want you to be alone." He tucked her hand firmly in his. "We'll look around together."

She bit her lip. "I can handle this."

"Remember our bet. Twenty-four hours of whatever I want. This is included."

"Well . . . all right."

"Look, I don't want you to be really afraid of what's going to happen today."

She expelled a breath and squeezed his hand as they walked down the steps and off the porch. He led her around the house.

"Yeah, I'm going to ask you to do some things you've probably never done before. But it'll be good for you. I promise." He stopped and took her by the chin, making eye contact with her. He brushed his lips across hers.

Her green eyes widened and she cleared her throat. "Okay," she murmured, her voice husky. "Okay," she repeated, in a firmer, clearer tone.

I suppose it's okay, Ani thought, as she followed Richard to the back of the cottage.

She kept the brush clear twenty feet around the building, not only to discourage prowlers but because of the fire danger. But there was a chance that someone lurked. The memory of the attack outside Linda's apartment nagged at her. She trusted Lewis, but he could be wrong.

Someone was onto her. *Ixzit!* If she didn't figure out what was going on and stop it, she'd be the U.S.S.A.'s official cyber-geek for the rest of her life. They'd never let her out of the office again.

Fortunately, the bushes around her home were populated by nothing more ominous than a few honeybees. But while they explored, she heard the choke of an engine starting out on Skyline Drive, and a hum as it drove away.

"There he went," Ani said nervously.

"Do you have a security system?"

"Of course, but I should call a, uh, neighbor and ask him to keep an eye on the house." She pulled out her cell phone as they walked to Richard's car and sent Lewis a text message.

As they drove to the marina, she put her job out of her mind to concentrate on what was going to happen. She'd dreaded this weekend for the last three days. Dreaded and anticipated with what could only be described as wet dreams. When she tossed and turned in her narrow bed at night, she'd fantasized endlessly about what Richard would demand.

Could she give him what he wanted? And how would she feel about such submission? How would it change their romance?

How would it change her?

Despite her cultural background, her parents had raised her to be independent. Ani had always imagined she'd insist upon a relationship that was free and equal.

How could she have agreed to this? What had Richard done to her?

What did he intend? He assured her that it would be good, but good was relative. How could he know what would be right for her?

They drove through the brilliant morning. Autumn was shifting into winter, bringing shorter days and the vivid blue skies so characteristic of northern California. Set against the cobalt heavens, liquidambar shot flaming spires into the sky. Birches and aspens glowed yellow against the dry, golden hills.

When Richard parked his car near the Santa Laura Marina, Ani could see that half the slips were empty. Sunlight glittered off the water, and the rigging of nearby boats clattered against their metal masts and booms. Sailboats and yachts clogged the narrow waterway out to the harbor; everyone, it seemed, was taking advantage of what could be one of the last perfect boating days in the year.

He opened the heavy metal security gate for her. It closed

behind her with a dull clang, shattering already raw nerves. She jerked, her mood jarring with the otherwise glorious day.

Warm fingers settled on her shoulder and squeezed. "Come along, darling." Taking her elbow, he led her along the dock to the *Trophy Wife*. He jumped onto the gunwale to extend a hand to her.

With his aid, she hauled herself up and over the side of the boat. Her foot slipped on the polished wooden edge, and she fell into Richard's arms.

He held her to his broad, hard chest, crushing her breasts against him. The steady beat of his heart vibrated against her, and her body tingled. His breath fluttered the hair at her temple, sending a wave of desire through her, excruciatingly hot, staggeringly sweet.

Stroking her cheekbone, he said, "Let's go below."

He guided her to his bedroom. She couldn't stop her hand from trembling in his. She wondered if he noticed.

"Any second thoughts?" he asked.

He'd noticed. She managed to press her lips together and shake her head.

"You don't have to look so nervous."

Languid and limp, she sagged down onto his bed. "I'm scared," she whispered. "I don't know what's going to happen."

He sat beside her and took her into his arms. "That's part of the fun of it. You didn't know what was going to happen last week in my office, did you?"

"N-no."

"And everything was okay, right?" He passed a palm over her nipple. It hardened against her purple sweater.

"Ummm." Leaning forward, she pushed her breast into his hand, seeking to increase the pleasure. "Oh, much better than that!"

"Okay." He stood and eased her onto the bed. At the door,

he turned and said, "When I get back, I want you naked." He closed the door behind him with a soft click.

I want you naked. Well, she could do that. She'd expected to be nude, hadn't she? But the abrupt tone of the demand left her startled. More than simple lovemaking, this was submission.

Her jaw clenched. She could leave, but she'd made a deal, hadn't she? Besides, she wanted this, had dreamed of it for days. Better, his order to get naked left her in control of her arsenal. She sat and took off her boots, tugging them hard to get them out from under the hems of her jeans, but careful not to break the delicate gold chain encircling her ankle. She ran a finger over the knife concealed in one heel, and placed the boots close to the bed, just in case.

More blades in the jeans and in the hem of the sweater. Knowing that her weapons were accessible didn't calm her nerves. That she was armed wouldn't protect her heart from Richard, or from the deal she'd made with him. She'd promised to give herself to him, and she wouldn't resist.

As she stripped, she folded her clothes over a chair, hoping the very ordinariness of the task would calm her fleeting pulse. But her excitement increased with each scrap of clothing she removed. She draped her damp panties over the back of the chair, hoping they'd dry before morning.

She heard the thrum of the *Trophy Wife*'s engines. With a bump against the dock, Ani tumbled onto Richard's bed. She rose and peeked out a porthole. They were moving, all right. Where was he taking her? And why?

The sea air flowing into the cabin was cooler than she expected. Her skin prickled. Her nipples became erect to the point of achiness. She rubbed her palms over her breasts, hoping to quell the strange sensation.

She trusted Richard. Didn't she? And now he'd show her something special, give her an experience she might never have again. She believed she was on this planet to learn. Tonight she'd learn how to trust her lover completely. She hoped time wouldn't prove she'd misplaced her trust.

After a few minutes Richard returned, bearing a tray with a bottle of champagne and two flutes. Sidestepping a cheval mirror, he put his burden onto the chest of drawers.

"Uhm, where are we going?"

He grinned. "You're such a worrywart. We're out of the harbor and in the open ocean."

The boat heaved gently with the swell, and she peered through the porthole. She didn't see any other watercraft, but asked, "How do you know we won't hit anything? I saw a lot of boats leaving the harbor."

"Most of them stick pretty close to shore, go to Santa Cruz, Monterey, wherever. We're farther out." His voice gentled. "Don't try to delay this."

She lifted her chin. "I'm not."

"You are." He pulled her into his embrace, pressing his clothed body against her nudity. His soft, worn jeans caressed the skin of her thighs, while his nubby fisherman's sweater abraded her nipples to a higher pitch of tenderness. The contrast between his clothing and her nakedness highlighted her vulnerability. She tried to pull away, but he resisted, enclosing her in an unbreakable circle with his arms and his hard, strong body. "No, honey. You're mine today, remember?"

Embarrassment swept her in hot waves. She closed her eyes.

"Look at me." His voice was calm, but insistent.

She stared into his face, trying to read the mood behind the façade. What mysteries did his boyish smile hide?

He let her go, then poured wine. Handing her a glass, he watched her sip.

The room stilled, becoming a soundless space that enclosed her entire world. She was intensely conscious of everything: the beat of her heart, so heavy she could see her breast tremble; the tiny hairs on her arms lifting with her tension; Richard's blue eyes, scrutinizing her.

He said, "Undress me."

She'd thought about him ripping off her clothes, but she'd never imagined he'd demand her obedience in this way. But it was such a simple request . . . why did this order make her hands shake?

"I'll make it easy for you." He toed off his deck shoes, then pulled his sweater over his head. Beneath it, he wore a white dress shirt. It had lots of buttons up the front.

"Come on, Ani." His voice remained soft, cajoling.

She sipped some wine, hoping the glass wouldn't slip from her hand.

"Let me know when you want another drink." He removed the flute from her unresisting fingers, setting it atop his dresser. "Now, I want you to undress me." His voice hardened. "Now."

She approached on hesitant legs, slipping between Richard and the large, oval mirror next to the dresser. She reached for the top button of his shirt, then tugged it out of the confining cloth. Then another. And another, exposing a narrow V of tanned skin. Unable to resist, she parted the fabric and stroked his chest, running her fingers through the coarse, golden curls decorating his body.

After pulling off his shirt, she knelt and ran her tongue down his midline to thrust it deep into his navel, savoring the intriguing oceanic tang she associated only with Richard. Plunging his hands into her hair, he groaned in response. His erection ridged his jeans.

She stroked that enticing bulge, eliciting another moan.

"You're killing me," he said. "Please, hurry."

Her mind in a whirl, she struggled with his jeans' thick metal buttons, wrestling them free of the heavy denim. He'd manipulated her into obedience and submission, but, somehow or somewhere, their roles had reversed.

Richard was begging.

She hauled off his pants, yanking them down his toned body. His erection poked the silk of his boxers. He looked bigger than she remembered. Her mouth went dry, all the moisture in her body seeming to flee. Her femininity throbbed as she remembered how his bigness felt inside her.

Playing with him, she snapped the elastic around his waist, then stroked down the slippery silk, caressing his backside. His buttocks flexed beneath her fingers. She liked the boxers, printed with wild zebra stripes. Nevertheless, she tore them off with one quick motion, eliciting his gasp. She smiled.

When she'd seen him before, he'd pointed straight out. Tonight his shaft aimed at his chin. Was this a sign of his heightened arousal?

"Please." Caressing her head, Richard guided her mouth toward him.

Ani sucked in a deep breath and opened her lips. He pressed in partway, then retreated before filling her mouth.

His body shook. He slid to the floor. She suckled him gladly, burying her face in his lap, enjoying his loss of control. He eased her head away from his hips. "You're too much, you know that?"

She winked at him, glad to have regained some semblance of her old self. This submissive stuff would never do. "Your slave-girl has pleased you, Master?" She gave him a saucy grin.

Shouting with laughter, he turned her over and lightly smacked her bottom.

The shock of the spank vibrated through her. "Hey!" Squirming out of his grasp, she tried to get away, but he caught her around the waist and swung her onto the bed.

He bounced down beside her to kiss her thoroughly. "You're

wonderful. You know, I probably shouldn't tell you this, but there's no one like you for me."

She eyed him, her interest sparked. "Why shouldn't you tell me?" she asked.

He evaded the question, instead toying with her nipple. "Look at us," he murmured in her ear.

Ani turned her head to see their reflection in the big, oval mirror that stood next to Richard's dresser, opposite the bed. Shocked, she realized he'd watched everything in the mirror, watched the entire time she'd undressed him and taken him in her mouth.

Her body wrenched and she instinctively tried to free herself from his grasp.

"No, darling." His hands tightened around her breasts, plucking her nipples into impossibly sensitive points.

She writhed, lost in a carnal fog. She didn't know the naked wanton in the mirror, with her head thrown back, her open, red lips panting with lust. The twist of his fingers, midway between pleasure and pain, rocked her to her foundations. She drew in a breath. Richard had reclaimed control with a simple turn of his hand on her breast.

"Time for act two," he said.

"Act two? What's that?"

He went to the closet and removed a paisley-printed robe. Patterned in red and blue, it looked like silk. After shrugging it on and belting it, he extracted something else.

Something long and silken.

Twisted silk cords, the kind she'd seen tying back heavy brocade curtains. These were a dark, metallic gray.

Like chains.

He turned. The cords dangled from his fingers. He smiled.

Her cheeky mood evaporated. Her heart thudded against her chest wall, a wild bird desperate to escape the cage. But she didn't move.

"Come with me."

She reached for her sweater.

"No," he said. "Just as you are. Naked."

"Outside? You're kidding, right?" She searched his face.

He grinned. "Outside. Come along, now."

Remembering her agreement, she gulped and followed him topside. Out on deck, Ani discovered that Richard was right. No other boats were in sight. Land was a narrow brownish strip on the eastern horizon. The only sounds were waves slapping against the boat's hull, the cries of seabirds, and his breaths, puffing warm against her nape.

Despite their isolation, she felt unbearably exposed, her naked vulnerability heightened. The spicy sea breeze stiffened Ani's nipples and slid over the tender skin inside her thighs, caressing her body with cool, flowing fingers. But the sunshine had pooled and warmed the wooden decks, including . . .

Including a padded lounge chair, draped with quilts, set in the middle of the deck.

Richard sat on the lounge and reached for her.

She resisted. "You want to—"

"Yep."

"Out . . . out here?" She gestured at the open ocean.

"You got it." He pulled her onto his lap. His erection poked out of the slit in the robe, jabbing her in the thigh. He adjusted so it slipped between her legs. She sighed and shifted, wanting him against the sweetest spot.

"This is weird," she said. "I feel as though someone could come along at any time."

"True enough. That's part of the fun of it. Anyone could come along at any time, but right now, it's just you, me, and the sea gulls."

Reaching around her, he looped one end of the cord around

162

her wrist, then pulled it behind her back. He captured the other. He tugged the silken rope tight and tied her wrists together in some elaborate manner; a sailor's knot, she supposed. He'd left plenty of rope, using it to loosely wrap her forearms together.

The position arched her back, causing her breasts to thrust out, exposed and available. He took their unspoken invitation, cupping them with skilled fingers. The heat from the sun melded with the warmth of his hands.

"I don't want anyone seeing me like this."

"I'm seeing you. Is that all right?"

"Ye-es."

"You don't sound convinced."

"I'm not."

"Too bad. You're mine now. Ever since I saw you with that chain around your ankle I wanted you this way." His whisper was husky, rough, sexy.

He nuzzled her neck, and she thought she'd come apart from want. She leaned against his silk-clad chest, trying to breathe.

Richard's big palms covered her aching breasts and she moaned, wanting him with a desperation she didn't understand. He left her breasts and grabbed fistfuls of her hair, drawing her head back so he could cover her mouth with nibbling kisses that heightened her craving for completion.

"Richard, oh, Richard, please, please . . ."

He laid a row of tiny bites along her jaw and down her neck. "What? Please, what?"

"You know what. Please."

"Tell me what you want," he growled into her throat.

"I can't say it! You know I can't." Ani's mind blanked.

"Say it."

She gabbled something in Arabic.

"In English, sweetheart." He feathered his lips along her neck, soothing where he'd savaged.

"Inside me. Please." She squirmed on his lap, seeking his entry.

With a tug, he loosened the cords binding her; they fell away, dropping onto the deck. "Turn around, honey, and face me."

Oh, no. She'd have to look into those laser-bright eyes, the ones that saw her secret desires. But she couldn't refuse, could she?

He'd untied her bonds, so she wasn't bound with anything but her word, and her love. Her commitment.

She turned around where she was, and he helped, tugging apart her ankles so she sat on his lap, straddling him. She was completely open and he took advantage of the position, probing her feminine folds with his long, clever fingers, sucking her breasts as he readied her.

Lifting her with one arm, he pulled her onto his shaft with the other. She slid fully onto him, letting gravity do the work. Seeking her pleasure, she gasped and bucked. Richard reached between them to caress her again, and the sharp sweetness spiraled toward a shattering climax. Leaning forward, she bit his shoulder, crying out. He wrapped her in a warm, silken embrace as he came, groaning his release into her ear.

Richard stared at the ocean for a long time after Ani, spent and sated, had fallen asleep. He rolled over, glancing down at her with envy. In her rest, she reflected none of his inner turmoil.

After the stunning realization he'd fallen for her, he'd needed to reassert control over her and the relationship. He'd figured a bondage game would do it, but the exercise had bound him more tightly to her. Ani constantly surprised him. Her special blend of shyness and wantonness, her eagerness to explore whatever life brought . . . Richard had never encountered anyone quite like her.

But so what? Their lives could never mesh. He couldn't see

free-spirit Ani and her hog living aboard the *Trophy Wife*. Hell would freeze over before he'd move into that ultra-feminine cottage on Skyline Drive.

He reminded himself that he was too old and too jaded for her. She deserved someone with the same fresh, young outlook about life, not a cynical old sailor. However, he wouldn't give her up. Oh, no. He couldn't recall a moment of their lovemaking without getting hard again. He was far too selfish to do the right thing. He'd never let her go.

And was she ready to settle down? Probably not. Hell, she could have a hundred men before she made her choice. Doubtless she'd dump him when she moved on.

At the thought, pain jabbed through his chest. He rubbed his breastbone, willing the twinge away. *Get over it, Rexford!*

CHAPTER SEVENTEEN

"Who am I going to meet today?" After she squeezed into Richard's sports car, Ani arranged the skirt of her black dress over her knees, shaking away a few drops of rain spattering the hem.

"Since it's a brunch at my father's house, you'll know a lot of people from the office. Oh, and, uh, there'll be a woman there named Celeste Evans."

Richard seemed uncomfortable, clumsily missing the ignition on the first try. He shoved the key home and turned it. The car roared into life.

"What about her?" Ani clicked the halves of her safety belt together.

"She's quite a character." Dressed today in full yuppie regalia, he switched on the headlights. They pierced the unexpected mid-morning drizzle. "She epitomizes the maxim that a woman can never be too rich or too thin." He glanced at Ani. "Celeste would add, or too blond. She must own stock in Revlon or Clairol. She's a little . . . different."

"Different in what way?"

He hesitated. "Let me see. Uh, she practically lives in her shrink's office. She jumps on every flavor-of-the-month New Age fad like it's the wisdom of the ages. She's both spoiled and chintzy. She once left an ashram in Oregon because she couldn't bear to live without facials. Another time, she tried to buy a new Mercedes with her charge card."

"What? Why?"

"She said she wanted her frequent flyer miles."

Ani blinked. "Why would a wealthy woman care about frequent flyer miles?"

"Rich people stay rich because they care about things like frequent flyer miles. My father never lacks for anything, but I've seen him argue at Starbucks that he deserves a discount on his coffee because he doesn't take cream."

"Oh." Ani added the fact to her store of information about Richard's father, none of which was positive. "So Celeste likes her bank balance. What else?" She hadn't heard anything that would explain Richard's anxiety, unless he simply didn't want to see his father. She could appreciate that, considering the reputation of the original T-Rex. But nothing in the U.S.S.A. dossier explained Richard's odd behavior.

"I, uh, used to be engaged to her."

Ani leaned back into her seat, feeling too poor, too fat, too dark, and too foreign. Not fiancée material. Spies were never fiancée material. "Ah. That's why you're so nervous."

"I'm not nervous. Only wimps get nervous." He fiddled with the leather-covered wheel.

"Oh, please. Everyone can get nervous, and you're nervous right now."

"I have no reason to be nervous. There's nothing between us any more."

"Who broke it off and why?"

"Uh, well, she did. Said I was emotionally unavailable."

"Are you?" Ani thought it very likely. Even after the crazy sex yesterday, she hadn't heard the "L" word . . . also, there was the information from Harry, which shored up the conclusion.

Silence reigned.

"Maybe," Richard finally said. "Look, my mother skipped out when I was, uh, two or three. Then she and her boyfriend were killed in a car wreck. I was raised by my father and my uncle. I admit I don't always relate to women well."

She said, "I think you're being a little hard on yourself. You can do or be whatever you choose. If you want to be emotionally available, you will be. I just hope you'll let me know what you intend."

He pulled over and cut off the car's motor. "Ani, I care about you very much." He clasped her hand. "I intend to treat you with honesty and respect." He started the car again.

Not the words she'd wanted to hear. A sudden pain constricted her throat. She reminded herself of the mission, forcing herself to believe that his emotional shell would let her break off their romance without guilt when the time came.

"Thank you," she said calmly, though her heart felt like a silicon chip: thin, fragile, and highly breakable. "I can't ask for more than that."

But she wanted more. She wanted everything. Yesterday had proven she could trust Richard to treat her kindly. Even when he wielded ultimate power over her, he'd given her an earth-shattering orgasm. After they'd napped, he'd pampered her with a full body massage, which had culminated in prolonged, gentle lovemaking.

Yes, he could be trusted with her body, but she still fretted about the future of her heart, especially since it no longer belonged to her. Willingly giving herself to him in the ways he'd demanded had broadened her emotions about him, adding trust to a list that included desire, love, and respect. But he hadn't exposed his feelings except, of course, for lust. She knew he wanted her. She figured he had to respect someone who could trash his security firewall at a moment's notice. As for love . . . from what Richard himself said, perhaps he wasn't capable of loving her or any other woman.

A strange heaviness made a home in her chest, crowding her heart. She swallowed and set her jaw, refusing to embarrass herself by weeping. Had she been wise to start an affair with Richard Rexford? She wasn't sure that making love with him had brought her closer to completing her assignment. On top of that, she'd never experienced such a maddening blend of pleasure and tension. *Perhaps I'm just not suited for love.* The tidy world of bits and bytes, keyboards and programs, had never been as exasperating as romance. Even her job with the agency had always been clear-cut and without emotional confusion.

The added stress of her secret life had become an unbearable burden. Occupied by Richard all day and all night, she'd neglected to look for his laptop. She'd barely managed to read the text message Lewis had sent to reassure her that her cottage was secure.

After brunch, she and Richard would return to the boat, and then she'd have to strike. In the meantime, she'd figure out a way to distract him. Matters couldn't go on as they were.

With Richard at the wheel, they rapidly descended the Santa Laura Hills. The drizzle diminished as they approached the chi-chi suburb of Atherton, home of the original T-Rex. He turned off El Camino Real, the main boulevard that linked the cities of Silicon Valley, onto a narrower street. Leafy trees arching over the avenue created a lush setting for opulent estates. Hedges, electric gates, and fences with thick plantings provided privacy for the wealthy. The white-on-brown street signs tended to display faux British or Spanish names: Encinitas, Winchester, Darlington.

On Darlington Lane, a name Ani considered unbearably precious, Richard turned left into a wide driveway. He stopped at a gatehouse guarding an enormous property dominated by a mansion with, of all things, a metal mansard roof. Scores of well-tended rose bushes bordered the home. To her left, a glass-walled greenhouse stood, surrounded by flowerbeds. On her right, tennis courts divided extensive, verdant lawns.

"*Hola,* Diego!" Richard jumped out of the car to greet a thin, white-haired man. *"Como está usted?"*

Ani zeroed in on the fact that Richard had used the honorific *"usted,"* rather than the more casual Spanish form *"tú,"* used with equals.

The men slapped each other on the back, then Richard led Diego to the car. "Diego, this is Ani Sharif. Ani, Diego and his wife, Herminia, practically raised me from, I guess, age ten, right?" Richard appealed to Diego.

"*Sí, Señor* Richie. You were just a leetle tyke." Diego, who wore khakis and a green polo shirt, gestured about three feet off the ground. He clicked a button on a small box clipped to his belt, opening the big iron gate. " 'Allo, Ani. You go on in now. Herminia and *tú padre,* they await you with the other guests. You are late as usual, *Señor* Richie."

After climbing into the car, Richard grimaced. "Late for the command performance. Woe is me."

"If you do not wish to do this, why are we here?"

"Annual, unavoidable gathering for family, friends, and business associates." Richard's mouth tightened. "Actually, I think I attend because I still hope that my family will, somehow, manage to put the 'fun' back into dysfunctional." He winked at her.

She laughed.

"At least you're here. You'll make the day bearable."

"Only bearable? Really? How flattering you are."

Chuckling, he drove through the open gates, then past the banks of Mercedeses, Rollses, and Beemers littering the driveway. He parked behind the mansion in what she assumed were the family parking spaces, his Corvette dwarfed by a Land Rover and a limo.

Eager to check out the home in which Richard had grown up, Ani didn't wait for him to open the door for her.

"I know I should take you in through the front entrance, but

I want to say hi to Herminia. Is that okay?" He opened a back door for Ani and led her into the kitchen.

"All right."

Larger than her cottage, the kitchen sported industrial-sized appliances. Crowded with tuxedoed staff, it bustled with waiters bearing silver salvers loaded with appetizers and flutes of champagne. Presiding over it all, snapping orders in Spanish and English, stood a woman who'd make two of skinny little Diego at the gatehouse.

Without saying anything, Richard swooped in and grabbed the lady around her white-coated waist.

She gave a little shriek. "Ricardo, you devil!"

He planted a big one on her cheek. "*Hola,* queen of my heart."

"You are a silver tongued liar." She pushed him playfully. "Diego, he has already called to tell me of your friend." Shrewd dark eyes scanned Ani. "*Hola,* Ani, and welcome. You will have coffee, yes?"

"Yes, please." Ani's spirits lifted. It seemed that WASP-y Richard was on good terms with his foreign-born staff. Her parents had often told her to judge a person by the way he or she handled those economically inferior to him. No doubt Richard could buy and sell twenty Diegos, but he treated the elderly gatekeeper and his wife with respect and affection.

Herminia poured. "*Señorita* Celeste, she is here."

He groaned.

Herminia handed Ani a cup of coffee. "Hush, you bad boy. And do not worry. She has brought, what do you say?" Herminia's dark eyes held a teasing gleam.

"What?" Richard sipped his coffee.

Herminia stuck her round button of a nose into the air. "You have been so bad, I shall not tell. Celeste has brought . . . a secret."

Ani's interest was piqued. "Is it a good secret or a bad

secret?" She slid her cup and saucer onto the marble counter.

Herminia laughed. "For *Señorita* Celeste, it is a very good secret, I think! Now go." She gave Richard's arm a gentle push. "Go see *tú padre.*"

"Might as well get it over with." Setting down his cup and saucer, Richard headed out of the kitchen through swinging double doors. "Come on, Ani."

She trailed in his wake as he shouldered his way through a crowd of Silicon Valley denizens. They ran the gamut from fish-out-of-water byteheads in rumpled khakis to Sikhs wearing turbans or saris, to San Francisco society figures dressed in designer fashions. Ani thought she recognized a Chanel that could have come straight out of Linda's closet.

Standing on the elevated slate hearth dominating the enormous living room, Thomas Rexford loomed, larger than life. A three-inch height advantage will do that every time, Ani mused. She wasn't fooled, and it appeared that Richard wasn't, either; he hopped blithely onto the stonework beside his father, then reached for Ani's elbow.

"Well, Pop." Richard gave his father a falsely hearty slap on the shoulder.

Thomas tried to look down his nose at his son, a difficult feat considering Richard had several inches on him. "Richie."

Evelyn Kehoe tittered. "I haven't heard that one in years."

Richard glanced at her. "Since only my oldest friends call me that, it's unlikely you ever will again, cousin Evvie."

Ani winced for the woman. Richard wasn't usually so rough with people. What was going on? Perhaps Evelyn, who Ani remembered from Pizza Polly's, had made another play for Richard. Seeking to defuse the situation, she cast around for something, anything to say. "Uh, should I call you that?"

His gaze gentled as he bent toward her. "I don't care what you call me, honey, just as long as you call me," he whispered.

Ani jumped, startled. She remembered she'd lost the bet, and he could now flaunt their romance as he pleased. She tensed. What would Richard do next? Beneath his strait-laced exterior, he hid an iconoclastic flair.

He kept hold of her arm. "Dad, I want you to meet Ani Sharif. She's—"

"One of your most talented programmers," Thomas Rexford rumbled. "I've heard great things about you, young lady. Apparently you skunked us on the problem the Defense Department presented."

Despite pride in her work, she tried not to preen. Instead, she shrugged modestly. "At Rexford.com, everything is a team effort."

"Not according to Kevin Wilson." The senior Rexford gulped what looked like Scotch, glittering in a cut crystal tumbler.

"Do you know Kevin?" she asked.

"Certainly I do." Thomas beetled silver-gray brows at Richard. "He was formerly head programmer at CompLine."

"Oh, boy, here it comes again," Richard muttered into her ear.

"You ought to come to work for us at CompLine. I'd offer you higher pay and better benefits than this rascal, here." Thomas punched his son's arm.

The circle of onlookers chuckled appreciatively.

Red flagged Richard's tanned cheeks. "She signed a non-competition agreement."

"I did?" she asked.

"It was in your employment contract."

"Was it somewhere in the pile of paper that personnel gave me to sign?" She hadn't really cared, and still didn't. The agency took care of the details for her.

"Exactly." He tugged on his ear. His arch smile reminded her of a dolphin at play.

A carnal heat flushed her body. I'm lost, she thought, as she remembered him filling her. Hoping to conceal her randy mood, she shrugged again. "That's, umm, all right. I'm happy at Rexford.com, sir," she said to Richard's father.

Thomas harrumphed. "There isn't a non-competition clause ever written that I can't break. You just keep that in mind, young lady."

"Uh, thank you, sir." Ani, reminded of silverback gorillas beating their chests in leadership displays, wanted to escape the bizarre conversation. She didn't like being the center of attention, so she eased her arm out of Richard's hand. "Excuse me." She softened her voice. "Where's, umm, the women's room?"

When she emerged from the bathroom, located off the entrance foyer, she couldn't help noticing a tall, thin woman more exotic than any of Ani's Algerian relatives. Nothing about her appeared to be natural. Her chin-length, bobbed hair, an artificial shade of ash blonde, spoke of a passion for peroxide. Her tanning-booth-brown skin contrasted with too-white, too-square teeth that resembled peppermint Chiclets. She wore an elegant black and gold caftan, leopard print heels, and a boy toy draped on her arm.

Anyone with style and aplomb enough to wear inch-long false lashes and leopard-print pumps to a formal brunch at the Rexfords' stuffy Atherton mansion fascinated Ani, who wanted to meet her.

"Hi, I'm Ani Sharif."

"Ani Sharif." The blonde had a lovely, husky voice. She stroked her boyfriend's arm. "And who is Ani Sharif?"

"A, uh, friend of Richard's."

She threw back her head and laughed. "Old T-Rex is trumped again!"

"I beg your pardon?"

The woman quieted. "I'm Celeste Evans. Old T-Rex—

Thomas Rexford, Richard's father—has been trying to persuade Richard and me to marry for decades. He likes my family's money, you see."

Ani rolled her eyes. "He has that reputation."

"So every time Richard and I are forced to attend one of these gatherings, we bring dates." She grinned at Ani. "Can't let the old boy start planning a wedding. He has a way of getting what he wants."

Ani smiled. The instant she set eyes on Celeste, Ani knew Richard had told her the truth. She couldn't imagine a less compatible mate for him. For one thing, he'd never allow Celeste's stiletto heels to mar the perfectly polished decks of his precious boat. His bathroom was too small for the array of cosmetics Celeste had to wear to achieve her unusual persona.

Jealousy fled, replaced by a strong instinct that she'd get along fine with Celeste. Ani squinted at Celeste's arm decoration. A young man who looked familiar, he wore his baggy jeans loose, slung low over slim hips. His Oxford cloth shirt, unbuttoned to the navel, exposed a lean torso rippling with muscle. He kept a possessive arm around Celeste's waist.

"Gianni, darling," Celeste said to the boy in her husky voice, "could you fetch me some champagne? Go to the kitchen for it. Thomas always keeps the good stuff there for himself. Herminia, the cook, will know where the Dommy is." She turned her attention, and her mascaraed gaze, on Ani. "You may have seen Gianni on a billboard or two. He's Calvin's Man of the Month."

Ani regretted Richard's absence. How would he respond to the information that his former fiancée was dating an underwear model? "Yes, I thought I recognized the, uh, six-pack." She winked at Celeste, who laughed.

"So you're with Richard. Tell me, have you done it on deck yet?"

Ani's mouth dropped open. She was sure she'd burst with embarrassment, like an overfilled balloon.

"You don't have to answer." Celeste held up a hand.

Regaining her voice, Ani said, "It must be all over me."

"An interesting exercise, isn't it? Just you and the fish. And what about the handcuffs?"

"Handcuffs?"

"I tried them with Richard on the recommendation of my therapist."

Richard, naked and helpless, cuffed to a bed . . . Ani's mind reeled, spinning with the delicious possibilities. "A, uh, sex therapist?"

"Yes. It's not fun and games, you know. Bondage is about trust and control. She thought that Richard had issues, and we tried to work them out in bed."

Ani now knew much, much more about Richard and Celeste than she'd ever wanted. "Uh, Celeste—"

"You should have seen the look on Richard's face when I showed him the cuffs." Celeste's ripped-velvet voice trilled with laughter. "It was a scream."

"Oh, my God."

"Didn't work. He refused. Didn't go for the tantric sex, either." Celeste sighed. "Poor thing. He really needs primal scream therapy."

"Primal scream?"

"Of course. Just look at the relationship between Thomas and Richard. Full of repressed hostility. Haven't you noticed? They don't hug or even shake hands, they slap and punch." Celeste shook her head, a sorrowful expression on her face. "Pure passive-aggressive responses, absolutely classic."

Ani didn't know anything about passive-aggressive responses, but there was nothing repressed about the hostility between the Rexfords. She again reminded herself that she was a very lucky woman. Though her parents were gone, she couldn't recall a time when love didn't unite their family. Poor Richard.

The subject of her musings strolled to her side, sleek and handsome in pressed khakis and a navy blazer. Pride swelled in her chest. He was gorgeous, and he was hers.

Catching her eye, Celeste winked. Ani's wayward mind promptly visualized Richard nude and helpless, his muscular body arching and straining against handcuffs . . . . She started to sweat. She reached for the glass of champagne Richard carried. Perhaps it would cool her down.

Richard slipped a tense arm around Ani's waist. "How are you, Celeste?"

She inclined her head. Her arm jewelry reappeared with champagne. "Very well, thank you. Have you met Gianni?"

Richard's arm loosened, his hand becoming relaxed and casual on Ani's hip. She realized that he'd been dreading this meeting. Perhaps he feared Celeste wanted him still. The presence of her playmate appeared to have eased his concerns.

Mark Rexford, dark and sinister in navy pinstripes, approached. "Looks like you won the bet, Richie."

The hand at Ani's waist stiffened anew. "There is no bet," Richard said, his voice neutral.

Ani frowned at Richard, who evaded her gaze in favor of glaring at Mark. Richard's cousin wore a sly "I know something you don't know" smirk.

Unease snaked up Ani's spine. "You told Mark about our bet?"

Celeste glanced from face to face, grabbed her friend's elbow, and beat a hasty retreat in the direction of the buffet.

"Not that bet," Richard said.

"There's another bet?" Ani had sensed Richard holding back, but this wasn't the normal resistance of a confirmed bachelor to say the "L" word.

"Only one bet I know about." Mark snagged a canapé from the tray of a passing waiter. "The one we made after your impromptu dance recital."

Bile rose into her throat. *No. Please, no.*

"Shut up, Mark." Richard's voice was icy, his face set and furious.

Ani stared over the precipice into the abyss below. Did she really want to know about this? With an effort, she filled her lungs. She'd never evaded the truth before, and she wouldn't now. "No, Mark, please tell us. What bet?"

CHAPTER EIGHTEEN

Richard's hand shot out and grabbed Mark by the throat. Unnerved, Ani skedaddled to a refuge near the door as the two men went at it. Mark hooked a foot around Richard's ankle, tripping him. Though his hand slipped off Mark's neck, Richard managed to clutch Mark's necktie. Both men fell in a fighting, wrestling heap.

Suddenly, Kevin Wilson appeared at her side. "Are they fighting over you?"

"I don't know." She set down her glass, her mind stupefied. "They were talking about a bet."

Guilt shaded Kevin's eyes.

She resisted shaking him. "You know about this, don't you?"

Like Richard, Kevin couldn't meet her gaze. "We were . . . umm, no one meant anything bad, really, Ani—"

"What's this about?" She turned on him, determined to get the truth. She'd wring the little twerp's neck if she had to.

He gulped. "After that belly dance, well, we, uh, bet on you."

Light dawned on a horrible new day. "Bet . . . on me?" She remembered Kevin's clumsy efforts at flirtation, and the rumors that Karen Leonhart had mentioned.

Suddenly everything made sense.

The men had bet.

On her. On her body.

Kevin's story had a hideous ring of truth. Richard, a risk-taker, enjoyed bets. She and Richard had just made another

179

sexual wager, which he'd won.

That son of a stinking camel had wagered on getting her into bed.

Her voice rose with fury. "Does everyone know?"

"N-no. Just the three of us. And, Ani—"

"Thank you, Kevin." Forcing her head high and her angry tears back into their ducts, Ani stalked away to survey the site of the altercation.

The men had been separated by their respective fathers, Thomas and Sundeen. Mark's torn collar revealed red marks on his throat. A waiter was applying an ice pack to the back of Richard's head. She hoped it hurt. A lot.

She wondered what she could or should say to him, but she shied away from a public confrontation, especially with rage balling her fists and tying her tongue into knots. Dimly aware of Kevin attempting to talk with her, she shoved him aside and left the mansion.

Richard returned to his boat that evening in a mood fouler than the nasty November weather. After the fight with his cousin, Thomas and Sundeen had insisted their sons stay longer and make nice. Celeste had gotten into the act by lighting candles, dimming the lights, and insisting everyone hum "om" to align their energies.

Ani had disappeared. After searching every room in the estate as well as its extensive gardens, he'd finally discovered from Diego she'd left in a cab. With increasing desperation, Richard realized she knew about the bet, and if she had any sense, she'd never forgive him.

When he'd phoned her cottage, no one answered, but she could be screening her calls with a message machine. He stopped by on his way back to the marina, but found the cottage empty. But he'd catch up to her eventually, maybe on the boat. She'd left her toiletry bag there.

All he needed was a chance to explain. They'd shared so much, and though he realized that the bet was deeply insulting, he felt that the bond they'd created would overcome this minor obstacle.

The marina, shrouded with fog, looked dark and unwelcoming. No wind blew, so rigging and flags hung still. The place should have been quiet, but instead, he heard an unusual avian clamor, as though scores of seabirds were in a frenzy. Clattering wings and the screech of gulls pierced the dank evening air . . . and the tumult seemed to be centered on his boat.

Instead of a still, empty deck, the *Trophy Wife* teemed with seabirds. Gulls and pelicans perched on the rails, pushing and shoving, scratching his beautiful teak. Where birds didn't fight and scrap, birdshit splotched the polished wood.

"Fuck!" He sprinted toward the boat, waving his arms. "Get the hell offa there!" He climbed over the gunwale onto the deck, putting his foot onto a fat gull. It squawked and pecked at his ankle.

"Son of a bitch!" He kicked it, and when it moved, he saw that it gripped a piece of popcorn in its beak.

The full impact of the tragedy struck him. Not a square foot of his deck was empty. Every inch, in fact, was crowded by birds, splashed with poop, or scattered with popcorn.

Ani had taken her revenge.

Damned effective, too, he had to admit. But he was bloodied but unbowed. She may have won the battle, but this was just the deck. His wheelhouse and living quarters were untouched . . . weren't they?

He looked up, and his heart sank. Above him, in the wheelhouse, he could see a flickering light, as though flapping wings momentarily obscured a lamp before moving away. Shit. He distinctly remembered leaving no lights on when he and Ani departed for that disastrous brunch. He'd hoped to return long before sundown, hoping for another nice mellow afternoon of sex with her.

What had she done in the bridge?

Probably what she'd done on the deck: thrown around popcorn and then let the birds do what came naturally.

But what of his living quarters?

Hurrying toward the hatch, he lost his footing on the slimy excreta and fell on his ass, sliding toward the open door. Cursing, he managed to grab the edge of the hatch and to avoid falling inside. Which was fortunate, because he would have crushed several pelicans.

His worst fears were confirmed. The hatch leading below-decks was open, and a noisy crowd of birds flew in and out of the dark doorway, some with popcorn in their beaks.

Another fucked-up chapter in a totally fucked-up day. Swearing, Richard reached for his cell phone. He had no idea who to call to get rid of the birds and clean up the mess, but he'd figure it out.

"Well, I did it." Later that night, Ani drooped her head back, resting it on the cushions of Linda's red brocade sofa. "I got the laptop, downloaded its contents, and walked out on Richard Rexford."

Carrying a teapot from her kitchen, Linda gave her a searching stare. "You've successfully completed your first undercover assignment, but you don't seem happy about it."

"I'm not." Ani closed her eyes, trying to shut away the pain, but it didn't work. Instead, a sob wracked her chest. Tears seeped through her lashes and spilled down her cheeks.

She heard a clatter—Linda setting down the tea?—and then felt the comforting warmth of her foster sister's arm around her shoulders. She hugged Ani close. "Tell big sister all about it."

Ani burst into tears and, between sobs, told Linda what had happened at the brunch. Offering a box of tissues, Linda asked, "So what did you do?"

After blowing her nose, Ani wiped her cheeks. "I had t-to complete the mission, so I took a taxi to my place, changed and got on the hog. On the way to the marina, I stopped at a supermarket and bought a couple of those giant bags of pop-popcorn."

Linda tilted her head. "Popcorn?"

"P-popcorn," Ani said. Her voice steadied as she told her story. "When I got to the marina, I remembered the keypad code that Richard had used. After I got inside, the rest was child's play."

"Did anyone see you?"

Taking a fresh tissue, she dabbed at her eyes and wiped her nose again. "Yes, the neighbors, but they'd already noticed me around the boat with Richard. They just nodded at me and went about their business. Then I went below—his locks are ridiculous—and finally found that laptop that Lewis was sure Richard had."

"Where was it?" Linda poured tea, offered it.

Ani sniffed its fragrance. Oolong. The gentle scent helped her calm down. "In his bedroom, which I suspected. I'd prepared a meal in the galley, so I knew it wasn't in there. It wasn't on the bridge, because he uses that computer for navigation. The only other place it could be was his bedroom."

Linda winked. "But you'd already spent plenty of time there."

Ani found a rueful smile. "Yes, but Richard had been with me. I hadn't had a chance to search it properly. It was on a closet shelf with a few other office supplies. I guess he just would open it and sit on his bed when he wanted to work, since the boat isn't big enough for a real home office. After I was done, I threw around the popcorn to get the birds to come. I needed their mess to cover searching his boat."

"Well done. I don't understand why you're so upset."

Ani stared at her. "That bet. They bet on, on me! It was totally sleazy."

"Yes, it was. Completely disgusting. Now that you know what Richard Rexford is truly like, you can dump him and forget about him." Linda's tone was tough.

"But—but—"

"But nothing. Your mission is over. It's actually good that you learned about the bet. You have a perfect excuse for leaving Rexford.com."

"What'll, what'll I tell Lewis? I don't want him to know that I got so involved with Richard. It's unprofessional."

"Lewis won't ask, and you won't tell him," Linda said. "Chances are that he already knows that the info from the laptop's been transmitted. Tell him you'll submit your resignation from Rexford.com due to sexual harassment."

Ani nodded glumly. "Why not? It's the truth."

Her sister hugged her tighter. "Stay here, with me. Work on my laptop. That way if Rexford comes sniffing around your house, you won't be there."

Ani pulled herself together. "I'll go back to my place and get my laptop. I love you, big sister, but you're so technologically backward that your laptop will drive me crazy."

On Tuesday morning, when Richard turned on his desktop at work, he faced Ani's grim image, clad in black leather. He hoped at least he'd see her animated figure riding across his screen to the chords of "Born to be Wild." He sighed, figuring he was about to witness the completion of Ani's avian revenge.

"Sweet, are they not?" Ani's fingers, elegantly gloved, played with a beautiful Amazon parrot seated on her shoulder. "I hope you enjoyed my friends."

He couldn't divine her mood. Her voice was calm, her expressive eyes covered by mirrored lenses. "Obviously I cannot continue in my present position with your firm. This message constitutes my resignation. I will stop working at the end of the week to allow the personnel department time to process this change in my status."

The screen went blank and barren, matching Richard's heart. He buried his face in his hands. Like a perfectly aimed arrow, Ani had hit him right where he'd hurt the most. She'd destroyed his home, his sanctuary.

He'd been unable to contact anyone on Sunday night to come out to clean up, so he'd missed a day at work handling the mess. Worse, the popcorn had attracted rats and mice, vermin that bred faster than flies. They'd slink around for months despite the most determined eradication efforts. Because he lived on the boat, he couldn't use strong pesticides to get them out. Every scratch of their vicious claws, every splotch of bird crap on his ruined decks reminded him of Ani.

Ani, who was gone.

But he could get used to that, he told himself. He'd known the bet was sleazy and unforgivable. They'd been loving on borrowed time. Ani, a sweet, trusting girl, was better off without him. Due to the difference in their ages, she would have been on her way . . . some time. He just wished he could have kept her around a little longer.

Forever, in fact, but that was a stupid dream. Impossible, so he dismissed the fragile hope, letting ice encase his heart. He had it on good authority that he was emotionally unavailable. He didn't deserve her. She was better off without him.

He wouldn't send her sexy emails or haunt her cubicle at three in the afternoon, hoping to see her. No way.

CHAPTER NINETEEN

Tapping on her laptop in Linda's kitchen, Ani deleted yet another of Richard Rexford's emails without opening it. Perhaps one had been business related, but she didn't care. She'd arranged her departure with Human Resources and worked outside the office, electronically transferring her output to Kevin. She'd avoided contact with anyone at Rexford.com. Too humiliating.

Three days had passed since that mortifying brunch in Atherton, when her heart had unraveled like a shabby old sweater. Three long days and three even longer nights.

She tried to cheer herself up. Her assignment had gone perfectly. Soon Linda would be finished also, and they planned to vacation together in Maui before reassignment.

As for losing her lover, well, Ani would just have to get over it. Other people did. What other choice did she have? She sucked in a deep breath, trying to dispel the thick, choking cloud of sorrow that crowded her heart. *Stop it, Ani!* Maybe she'd meet someone fun in Maui.

She clicked on an email from Kevin Wilson.

Ani, I tried to tell you at the party that Richard Rexford cancelled the bet weeks ago. Mark was lying if he said the bet was on. I heard from Karen in HR that you've resigned. Please reconsider! You're an asset to this company and leaving so soon may damage your reputation and future job prospects.

Despite her pain and rage, hope, a frail flower, unfurled a

timid petal in Ani's heart. She replied:

*Career all right, thanks for your concern. RTR cancelled bet?
Interesting, but why did it happen in the first place?*

Kevin said, ☺ *We had too many beers. No excuses, Ani. I
apologize.*

Your apology accepted, Kevin. Ani hesitated, then wrote, *Am
continuing work on 3P.*

Before she'd finished her entire message to Kevin, her laptop
beeped, warning her that an emergency encoded instant message was coming in from the U.S.S.A.

Her heart jumped. Maybe she already had a new assignment.
That would be great. It would take her mind off slimeball Richard Rexford and his betrayal.

She clicked keys, immediately recognizing that the I.M. came
from Lewis.

Next she saw the code that meant that an agent had been
captured.

Nauseous and ill, Linda Wing sat in a chair in a cold, dark
room. The space was so lightless that she couldn't see any of its
features, so quiet that not even the slightest sound betrayed her
location. Only a low-decibel hum revealed that an H.V.A.C.
system was working, cleansing the air so that no trace of scent
or aroma gave her a clue as to her whereabouts.

Nor could she explore her environment to discover anything.
Her hands were strapped with duct tape to the arms of a plain
wooden chair, so she couldn't reach for a shuriken for protection if the need arose, or use its sharp points to free herself.
More tape wrapped around her waist, securing her to the back
of the chair so tightly that she couldn't draw a proper breath.
Like the impenetrable darkness, the bone-chilling cold, and the
incapacitating drugs, she assumed it was a tactic to weaken her.

Worse, the tape's adhesive would surely ruin the fine wool of the vintage Chanel she wore. "This suit is trashed," she said aloud, crossing her right leg over her left.

A deep, soft voice came from behind her, speaking in Cantonese. "Your concern about your clothing is misplaced."

She tried to control her fear and surprise, but she hadn't known that anyone was in the room with her. Probably the drugs used to knock her out had diminished her perceptions.

It was of no importance.

She wondered what tack to take. Given that she was likely the captive of the Chinese, calm and confident would be best. Later she could segue into outraged American citizen.

"This is a unique garment," she replied in the same language. "The viscose trim is a fabric that is no longer manufactured. You are obviously a peasant with no respect for fine art." She selected the word "peasant," knowing that to many Chinese males, the label was an insult.

Laughter in that same deep, soft, very masculine voice. "I am not surprised by your courage, Ms. Wing, but startled that you aren't curious as to how you became our guest."

"Whose guest am I?" she asked, pretending ignorance.

A subtle illumination began to rise from recessed lighting.

A dim form clad in black took shape. He leaned against a wall perhaps ten feet away, arms crossed over his torso. His face remained in shadow, but he continued to speak in the same measured, good-humored tone. "As you have already surmised, you are the honored guest of the Chinese Consulate."

How had she been discovered? Perhaps someone at the office had seen her photographing her old-fashioned boss's old-fashioned Rolodex cards. She'd been careful, using a tiny camera concealed in her lipstick when she was alone.

That would be just her luck. She'd only made it through the C's.

"Charmed, I'm sure," she said. "But why? Let us not mince

words. I believe that one of the jealous women in the law firm at which I work has been spreading vicious rumors about me. But because I am an American citizen, I feel confident that I will be released shortly."

While her captor chuckled, Linda slid her right leg down her left until she felt her stiletto heel slip inside the anklet she always wore. A little push, and she sensed that the links had parted. A tiny clink told her that the chain had fallen away. For good measure, she ground her heel into the clasp, then leaned back into the chair to resume the verbal sparring.

"You are not an ordinary American citizen," he said. "You are Korean born, but you understand several Asian languages. Most Koreans are insular, ignorant pigs."

Linda's jaw tightened involuntarily though she surmised that the insult had been a goad, with no true malice behind it.

Her captor went on, "No Korean would learn Cantonese without a gun held to his or her head."

"I'm an American," Linda said. "None of that applies to me."

"That is correct. You are a most unusual woman. Very beautiful, very clever." Did she detect respect? He continued, "You also know your way around computers."

Aha, she thought. "Not really."

"You hacked into our system," he said, smiling. "We traced the incursion to your laptop via its electronic signature."

Damn it. Ani must have failed to cover her tracks properly. But where did the Chinese get the tracing technology? It had been developed quite recently . . . by Richard Rexford's company.

Now Linda was sure there was a spy at Rexford.com. Hoping she covered her anger, she shrugged. "Really? I must have taken a wrong turn on the information highway. So sorry if I have caused inconvenience."

"We have a proposition for you."

She raised her brows. "It is far too soon in our acquaintance for you to proposition me. I don't even know your name."

"You can call me . . . Darkness."

"How melodramatic." She had to admit to herself that the name suited him. Despite the increased level of light in the room, she couldn't see her captor clearly. A lean, muscular shadow clad in formfitting black, he remained a mystery.

"Spies like us, Linda Wing, never have ordinary names."

Damn, damn, damn. She'd been made. She'd never work undercover again. Sweat oozed from her armpits, wetting her silk blouse. "My name is quite ordinary for an American."

"As you say, let us not mince words. If your handlers discover that your, er, employment by the U.S.S.A. has been uncovered, your usefulness to the Americans is over." He came closer and knelt before her. "But you can work with us."

His eyes were dark, unfathomable, boring into hers without a flinch. She told herself she wouldn't be the first to blink.

His lips were less than an inch away.

She smelled ginseng and incense and man.

She wouldn't let him get to her.

She said evenly, "I don't know what you're talking about."

He shifted position so he whispered in her ear, "Help us out. It can be our little secret."

His breath stirred the tiny hairs on her neck, and she couldn't stop her flesh from quivering with a purely female response.

No, she thought. No. I will not want this creature.

With a wiggle, she settled her bottom more deeply into the chair and straightened her back as best she could. "I have no secrets, but I do have demands. If you believe that I have broken the law by hacking into your computer, why don't you contact the police?"

Before she knew what was going on, a knife appeared in his hand. With the tip, he flicked off the button securing her jacket.

It fell open to the tape at her waist.

In an entirely reflexive action, she head-butted him, hitting his nose with her forehead.

"Ahh!" He clapped a hand to his face. Blood ran through his fingers. "You bitch!"

The door burst open, and a voice she recognized shouted, "Drop the knife!"

Linda almost fainted with relief, sagging in her bonds as Ani released her. Lewis sprinted to the open window, but all that remained of Linda's captor was a swirl of curtains whipped to a wild froth by Darkness's flight.

With shaky limbs, Linda rose and paced the U.S.S.A. office, stopping at the coffee pot. Seated in front of Lewis Anglesey's desk, Ani watched her, worried. She'd seen her foster sister in many moods, but never one so distressed.

Linda still wore the same suit in which she'd been discovered, bound by duct tape in an empty apartment near the Chinese Consulate. Remnants of the tape and adhesive still clung to her clothing.

She poured coffee into a mug and sipped.

"Goddammit!" She flung the mug across the room. It smacked the wall a foot from Lewis' head. "Goddammit, Lewis, after all these years can't you make a decent cup of coffee?"

Lewis leaned back into his chair, appearing unruffled by Linda's outburst or the events of the night. "Apparently not."

"I've been made." Linda's voice was so soft that Ani wasn't sure what Linda had said.

"What?" Ani asked.

"I've been made, damn it, and it's all your fault!" Whirling, Linda pointed a finger at Ani.

"*What?*"

"Your head is so far up your ass about that guy, you can't see straight, let alone do your job."

Ani jumped to her feet. "You get made and it's my fault? The almighty Linda Wing screws up and it's someone else's fault. Can't you take responsibility? How is this my fault?"

"When you hacked into the Chinese Consulate, you didn't cover your tracks. They traced the hack back to my laptop."

"That's impossible! That's technology we just developed at Rexford.com. No one is supposed to have it!"

"I don't know. All I know is what that joker calling himself Darkness said that the hack had been traced to me."

"Perhaps through the cable line." Ani mused. "That's easy enough."

"He said that they knew its electronic signature."

Ani glared at Lewis. "Why isn't her laptop clean? It should be totally untraceable!"

"Stop it, both of you." Lewis stepped in. "We already know there's a traitor at Rexford.com. That person passed the technology to the Chinese."

Ani continued to scrutinize her handler. "What did you find from the downloads of Richard Rexford's laptop?"

He shook his head. "It isn't him, Sharif. You have to get back into that company and find out who it is."

"I can't! I broke up with Rexford, as you instructed, and resigned."

He rubbed the back of his head. "That instruction was in error. We're trying to place someone else there, but—"

"I can't go back," Ani said with emphasis. "I had a huge fight with Rexford. I alleged sexual harassment. I'll have no credibility if I return. They'll wonder why I'm back, because it won't make any sense to them."

"Can you hack in?"

"There isn't a computer on this planet I can't hack."

"All right. You, Wing," he said.

Linda glowered at him, arms folded.

"Your cover's blown. I don't know exactly who Darkness is, but clearly the Chinese are onto you. Get outta here. Go to the safe house in San Mateo for now. We'll pack up your apartment and put everything in storage until you're reassigned."

Shrugging, Linda walked out, her gait radiating fury and contempt.

Lewis turned to Ani. "What did she mean about 'that guy?' Did she mean Richard Rexford?"

Ani pursed her lips. "Nothing happened to compromise the mission. I got in, got the information, and got out." She raised a stony gaze to Lewis. "That's all."

"The Chinese might have gotten the software from another source."

"Who?"

"There are numerous connections between Rexford.com and his father's firm, CompLine."

"There's a traitor at CompLine?"

"Could be. We're not sure."

She rose and began to pace. "Silicon Valley is like an anthill. There's so much moving around that it could be anyone, anywhere. Programmers go from job to job, to whichever company's the hottest."

"That's true." Lewis steepled his fingers and stared at them. "At the same time, I have a feeling that Richard Rexford will come knocking at your door."

"Why?"

"His software's been stolen. You just left his company after an argument that obviously became personal."

She refused to meet Lewis' gaze.

He continued, "He's going to want to find out if you're the thief."

"No," she said. "That can't be." She couldn't believe that

after everything that had happened between them, Richard would think she was a thief.

"Yes, I know it's ridiculous and a little ironic." Lewis smiled. "But it's an opportunity. Make yourself accessible to him. Find out what you can. In the meantime, we'll get you another office from which you'll conduct offsite investigations into CompLine."

Using the speakerphone, Richard was deep in conversation with one of the new guys in Marketing and Sales when the double doors to his suite burst open. One banged against the wall behind as Kevin Wilson hurried in. More disheveled than usual, his glasses were askew, his hair rumpled. He bore a sheaf of printouts. "Look at these." He thrust them in Richard's face.

Richard raised his eyebrows at Kevin and said, "Later, Mike," ending the phone call.

Then he looked. The top sheet, a press release from Comp-Line, his father's company, bore that morning's date. Richard's jaw tensed as he read that CompLine planned to market a revolutionary password protection system that not only blocked a series of false passwords, but acted like a virus, turning on the electronic signal of an invader and disabling the attacker's system. Tracing technology enabled the attacker's computer to be identified, and the perpetrator prosecuted.

He met Kevin's worried gaze. "This has elements of—"

"Ani Sharif's work."

Richard's gut churned. He clenched a fist. "If she's turned on us—"

"How can we find out?"

"The old-fashioned way." Richard reached for the phone. After punching a few buttons, he connected with the same private investigator who had initially checked out Ani Sharif.

CHAPTER TWENTY

It's deja vu all over again.

Ani didn't understand how her handler had figured out what Rexford would do, but Lewis had been right, because Richard Rexford had contacted her and asked her out to dinner. Preparing for her date with him on Saturday evening, she stared into the cottage's bathroom mirror and played with the shorter tendrils of hair curling around her face.

"Still not sure about the bangs?" Linda stuck her head around the open door.

"Nope."

"I think they're cute." Linda entered, dressed in her new persona as Punk Asian Chick, with loose camouflage cargo pants topped by a sleek black sweater. She'd received permission to leave the San Mateo safe house to stay with Ani, since the U.S.S.A. had reviewed Linda's status and decided that she wasn't at risk.

"You needed a change," Linda continued. "So did I." Both women had spent the day at Elizabeth Arden, getting massages, facials, and haircuts.

"Something to unsettle Richard," Ani said. "Since he threw my feelings into chaos, why not return the favor?"

"Exactly." Looking into the mirror, Linda swung her head. The short, shiny strands of her chin-length bob caught the light, its red and gold streaks gleaming. "And I needed to change my appearance."

"Think you'll get out into the field again?"

"Yes, but not around here. Maybe back in D.C. or in Canada. Vancouver has a lot of Pacific Rim action where my skills would be useful."

"Linda, I'm sorry. If anything I did—"

Linda held up a hand. "No, I'm sorry. In the heat of the moment, I said some things I shouldn't have. In the meantime . . ." She fiddled with the ends of Ani's hair. "How about a French twist?"

Despite Linda's light tone of voice, Ani sensed that her foster sister was deeply perturbed about this setback in her career, but didn't want to discuss the issue. "Okay," Ani said. "A French twist. Yes, that will set the tone I want to achieve. Formal and a little distant."

Linda picked up a brush and began to sweep Ani's mane back and up. "Sexy but elegant."

"Yes. Nothing slutty." Ani believed that having sex with Richard had created all the problems. Opening her unguarded heart had been a big mistake, and their physical intimacy had deepened her emotions.

The bondage had intensified everything, she realized. As Celeste had implied, allowing your lover to bind you created not only physical ties, but emotional ties as well. Richard, with his issues about intimacy and trust, couldn't understand. Celeste was right.

She sighed. Evidently he'd viewed their erotic explorations as merely sexual fun and games, without an emotional dimension. How could he be so dim?

Well, there'd be no more bedroom adventures for Ani Sharif, not for a long time.

Linda shoved a last bobby pin into Ani's updo. "How much make-up?"

Ani considered. "Quite a lot. I need to play the femme fatale tonight, find out as much as I can while maintaining my distance."

"You'll be fine, and remember, I'll be near. Hey, look at the bright side! At least you know he's not a traitor."

"Lewis thinks that Richard believes that I'm a thief."

Linda took Ani by the shoulders. "That shouldn't matter to you."

"But it does," she whispered.

"Stop." Linda gave her a little shake. "I told you before. Sex yes, love no."

Ani sighed.

After Linda made up Ani's face, giving her enormous, smoky eyes and ruby lips, they selected her outfit: a Chanel dinner suit with a severe, sophisticated cut, to contrast with the sultry makeup. Ani added her locket, to remind herself of who she was. A last deep breath, and she was prepared to meet with her adversary.

Ani's eyes widened as she scrutinized the gentleman at the door of her cottage. Richard wore immaculate charcoal gabardine, perfectly tailored, with a starched shirt and a colorful, silken tie. His trousers bore knife-sharp pleats, and his face, a grim expression that lightened when he saw her. "Ani." He reached for her.

Avoiding his embrace, she took both his hands instead. "Richard." She turned and smiled at Linda. "I'll be home before midnight, I'm sure." She kept her voice pitched so Richard could hear her plans, and, hopefully, cooperate. Despite his apparent sincerity, there was no question about spending the night with him.

"Did you like the flowers?" Richard nodded to the bouquet of red roses he'd sent with an equally flowery and eloquent card, begging for her forgiveness. They adorned the kitchen table.

Ani stepped through the door onto the porch. "Linda liked them."

So she was going to be difficult. Great, thought Richard as he took her arm.

Ani didn't look much like a motorcycle mama or a bytehead geek tonight. Heaven knew where she'd found her ivory suit, which looked like an outfit his stick-up-the-butt step-cousin Evelyn Kehoe might wear. The jacket's militaristic epaulets and brass buttons gave it a martial air. He hauled at the tie constricting his throat, fearing that Ani's attire and attitude had already set the tone of the evening.

So much rode on this night. Though a risk-taker, Richard didn't like the high stakes. If he played his cards perfectly, he'd get the girl back and protect his company. If he blew it, no Ani and no Rexford.com. The theft of the anti-virus software could cost him the queuing program, the tracing technology, and 3P. Richard's company had precious little to peddle on the software market other than those programs. Their loss gutted his inventory.

The prototype of the anti-virus software, after debugging, had been distributed to very few, highly trusted people for testing. Even so, the rumor of its existence had jetted shares in Rexford.com to stellar heights. Reports of its acquisition by a competitor would plunge his stock into a black hole. Having sunk his fortune into Rexford.com, Richard would have nothing if he couldn't recover from this setback; he couldn't sell his shares without getting into serious trouble with the S.E.C. for insider trading.

If Ani admitted the theft, he'd have something with which to bargain when he confronted his father and his uncle, the guiding lights of CompLine. Tired of his family's manipulations, Richard decided he'd sue them if he had to.

But heaven only knew who else had the technology. The

investigator he hired had found that keeping Ani under surveillance was nearly impossible. Apparently she'd been living away from her cottage.

One day, she'd returned briefly, and the investigator had followed her to a strip mall in Cupertino. What she'd been doing there was a mystery. The mall's tenants included a Mailboxes Etc., a real estate agency, and a dog groomer. The other two offices appeared empty, but the investigator swore that he saw Ani go into one of them.

The owner and the property manager of the mall were interviewed. Neither had admitted anything of note, but a clandestine search of the manager's files had revealed that the "empty" offices were rented by the United States government. Richard had assigned more personnel to the problem and begun to milk his many government contacts, finding information that increased his suspicions about the ever-more-mysterious Ani Sharif.

On the other hand, maybe she'd been mailing a package or looking to sell her home. Who knew?

He led her to the 'Vette, then opened the door for her. She accepted his courtesy with a softly murmured, "Thanks."

Richard had no doubt that she was the culprit who'd sold the software. It certainly hadn't been written by anyone at Comp-Line. Kevin, who'd somehow acquired a copy from CompLine, had explained the situation to him. As individualistic as any other creative venture, software written by a particular programmer bore his or her own "voice." In the same way that a novel by Stephen King or Nora Roberts reflected its author, the pirated software screamed Ani Sharif.

She'd been infuriated by the bet. Between whacks at his cousin Mark, Richard had caught a glimpse of her face when she'd cornered Kevin. Her pale cheeks, trembling lips, and blazing eyes betrayed her reaction to the news that three men with whom she worked had bet on possession of her body.

That she'd been inexperienced worsened his transgression. Richard winced, eyeing Ani's still, set profile, silhouetted by the shifting highway lights.

How the hell could he make amends? He patted his jacket pocket. A gift might help. Presents always satisfied the mercenary hearts of females. But women of the new millennium also liked to communicate. Though he'd rather kiss a shark than have a relationship chat, he cleared his throat and said, "We have to talk."

She fiddled with a brass button. "Yes. I suppose that's why I agreed to this dinner." She sighed. "Why did you do it, Richard?"

Plaintive and needy, her voice betrayed her. Good. "Do what?" he asked. "I bet on you because I was drunk and stupid. I made love with you because I wanted to."

"And that's all that matters, huh? What Richard wants?" Anger sharpened her tone.

"I hope I'm not so selfish. You wanted it, too, and I showed you a damn good time."

"Please don't be so blunt and crude about it."

"Okay, I'll admit it. It wasn't just wanting. I needed you very badly, Ani." He deliberately gentled his voice, dropping it several registers. "I still do."

"Really?"

Hearing sarcasm in her voice, he groaned. "You're still mad at me."

"I have a right."

"Yeah, you do." He turned off the highway onto a slick, wet surface street. "But if you don't get over it, this is going to be a very unpleasant evening for both of us."

Typical of a woman, she gave him the silent treatment until he'd parked the car near the Matsuhana Restaurant.

The white stucco facade of the Matsuhana concealed an opulent, modern Japanese restaurant, gleaming with polished granite counters and chrome trim. Its sleek, well-dressed patrons matched the place. Richard eschewed the crowded sushi bar in favor of the privacy of an enclosed booth. Once in the tiny room, surrounded by shoji screens, he and Ani removed their shoes to step down into a well beneath a shining wooden table.

They sat next to each other on a padded bench, exactly as he'd planned. He wanted to get close to her. After they'd been seated, a kimono-clad hostess slid open the screen in front of them.

"Would you like something to drink?" he asked Ani.

"Uh, all right." Ani hoped her thin, high voice wouldn't reveal her uncertainty.

Richard ordered in Japanese, increasing her unease. On what seemed to be familiar ground for him, he'd regained complete control over the situation.

How had she allowed that to happen again? Hadn't she learned from her past mistakes? Apparently not, she thought gloomily, since she longed for the return of the man who'd taken her body and her heart. She wanted Richard back.

Intuition told her that one defense was that he didn't know how much she loved him. And he'd admitted he needed her. Not the "L" word, but if he'd spoken the truth, that was good, wasn't it? Her other shield was her mission, but now that she was alone with Richard, she wasn't quite sure how to start. Although he wasn't a traitor, she didn't want to be obvious.

The hostess returned. She carried a tray with two small porcelain cups and a tall, slim porcelain pitcher from which steam curled. She slid the tray onto the table.

Richard said something to the hostess, who nodded and withdrew, closing the screen with a snap. He lifted the pale green vessel.

"Celadon ware." He looked at the porcelain, then at Ani. "Almost as beautiful a green as your eyes."

"Hmmm. Really?" Ani asked, secretly delighted by his compliment.

He poured for both of them. Raising the small cup, she sniffed. The steamy, pale liquid emanated the ephemeral scent of apple blossoms.

"Have you drunk sake before?" Richard asked.

"Yes, of course." She'd enjoyed many sushi meals with Linda, an expert on Asian cuisines.

His eyes gleamed in the dim light from wood and paper lanterns. "To the evening."

A safe and innocuous toast, she thought. "The evening." She sniffed, sipped, and swallowed.

"You like?"

"I've always loved sake. It reminds me of winter sunshine." Ani drained her cup. "May I have more?"

"Sure." Richard poured.

The hostess entered. "What kind of sushi would you prefer?" she asked in stilted, accented English. Japanese-born, Ani concluded.

She hesitated, scrutinizing the menu, which bore colorful pictures of the food available. Linda usually ordered for them; half-toasted on sake, Ani had never really taken note of the details. Eying the menu again, she randomly poked at a photo that looked vaguely familiar, a cylinder of rice covered by tiny orange dots, topped by something yellowish. An egg?

Richard looked impressed. "*Uni* rolled in *masago*. An interesting choice. Pick a few more."

Emboldened, she selected *ika*, *tago*, and *anago*, all of which appeared unexceptional. He ordered, and after the hostess left, he settled down to watch Ani again.

His steady gaze, potent as a laser, both attracted and

frightened her. The tiny hairs on her nape prickled. What was his agenda for the evening?

"I want you back," he said, his voice husky. Reaching for her, he drew her into his arms.

With effort, she resisted. Though Richard could spark her soul, render her feverish with want, she pulled back to look into his eyes. They twinkled with pleasure, but she couldn't read his mood. A sensualist, he could delight in situations that caused her distress and pain. Had he enjoyed the bet, the hunt, the chase? Had taking her lent their sex—she'd never call it love-making again—a spice unattainable any other way?

Ani loathed being used, abused, manipulated or dominated. What Richard had done made her feel small and betrayed. She'd thought she could trust him, but she'd been wrong. Now, she couldn't trust herself or her judgments.

But he was so beautiful. What harm could a little hug do? If he relaxed, he might tell her a little more about what was going on at Rexford.com. Maybe she'd be able to figure out who had sold the technology to the Chinese.

She slipped into the circle of his arms and tipped back her head to scrutinize him again. The sensual droop of his eyelids didn't quite hide the predatory glint in his gaze.

"You want me back? Why?" she asked.

"This is why." Richard slid his mouth over hers in a long, deep kiss that flew her straight to heaven.

The screen slid open, and the hostess entered bearing a black lacquered tray with small oblongs of fish and rice.

Ani jerked out of Richard's arms. The woman had entered just in time. Relieved to be free of Richard's ardent embrace, she watched the hostess serve their food, then leave.

Crossing her arms in front of her chest, Ani rubbed her forearms. He hadn't felt bad. No, he'd felt too good, too tempt-ing. She told herself that playing tonsil hockey was not going to get her closer to her goals. She needed a little distance and took it, sidling several inches away along the bench.

Richard sidled with her, then roped an arm around her shoulders as though nothing was amiss. "Let's eat dinner."

She checked out the sushi, pastel rectangles in golden yellow and orange, white fringed with brown, pink with a band of dark matter, probably seaweed, wrapped around the middle. "Umm, where should we start?"

Grinning at her, he asked, "You were just guessing when you ordered, weren't you?"

"Well, yeah." She resented the situation. Somehow, he had become the teacher again, in control.

"You should have mentioned it before. There's no shame in beginner's mind."

"Beginner's mind?"

"It's a concept in keeping with the culture that created sushi. Zen masters extol beginner's mind, that state of openness that promotes creativity and learning." He smiled at her. "I almost called my company Beginner's Mind. That would really have messed you up, huh?"

She huffed. "Someone would have bought a name somewhere, sometime, and made my purchases worthwhile."

"You got lucky. The powers that be are cracking down on that particular game. You moved on at the right moment."

"Why did you not call your company something fanciful, like Apple or Beginner's Mind?"

He shrugged. "Many investors have been attracted to the firm because of the family name. It's just promotions."

"Beginner's mind," she repeated. "I like the sound of that."

"So, let's begin." Richard mixed the pale green wasabi mustard with soy sauce, creating a dip for the sushi.

Using chopsticks, she pointed at a flat, white substance with a brown edge, sitting atop a pillow of rice. "What's that?"

"Something you ordered." He leaned his elbows on the table, plainly enjoying her discomfiture.

"Smart ass," she muttered in Arabic.

Her first bite, half the piece of sushi dipped in the wasabi sauce, cleared her sinuses and seemingly shot through the back of her head. Dropping the other half on the tray, she chewed and choked at the same time. Somehow, she managed to swallow her mouthful rather than spew it out over the table, the room, and Richard.

Laughing, he put her sake cup to her lips. She gratefully gulped the spirits to wash out the strong Japanese mustard.

"How much wasabi did you put in this?" The dipping sauce that Linda had prepared for them had never blown off the top of Ani's skull. Blinking away tears, she fixed him with what she hoped was a baleful gaze. "You did that on purpose."

His chest still shook with mirth. "Guilty as charged."

"Why?"

"Have some more sake."

"Are you trying to get me drunk?"

"Honey, I don't need to get you drunk."

Aware he was right, she flinched with chagrin. "Son of a camel," she muttered in Arabic.

He gestured at the other half of the sushi she'd started. "By the way, that was *tako*. Octopus."

Her stomach roiled. "What else did I order?"

"Squid, eel, and here's your most adventurous selection." He winked at her. "Sea urchin rolled in fish eggs."

"Not caviar, I take it."

"No. You picked flying fish roe, I think."

She eyed her meal, wondering how she could avoid eating foods best used as bait.

"I don't know what your problem is." Leaning back, he still had that insufferable smirk on his face. "On your father's side, you come from a culture that regards sheep's eyes as a delicacy. And your mother's people eat snails."

"True."

"I rest my case. So go for it. Here." Reaching for the soy sauce, he mixed a liberal splash with the wasabi. "This should be better. Try it with my *tamago*. Egg," he explained.

She couldn't help her suspicions. "What kind of egg?"

He laughed again. "Nothing weird, but that's a good question. If you ask, you can get everything from salmon roe to hundred-year-old quail eggs. But this is just compressed scrambled chicken's eggs. Here." He swished one end of the yellow oblong in the milder dipping sauce and held it to her lips.

She hesitated, fearing the intimacy of allowing him to feed her. But the sauce could drip onto the skirt of Linda's elegant ivory suit, so Ani opened her mouth.

He thrust in the sushi. A flavor explosion burst on her tongue, sweet, salty, and spicy at the same time. After she swallowed, he followed up the food with his tongue in another deep, demanding kiss.

CHAPTER TWENTY-ONE

Two hours and three pitchers of sake later, they'd eaten their way through most of the sushi menu. Using more liberal amounts of soy sauce with the wasabi had helped, and lots of sake smoothed out the evening, Ani reflected.

Feeding each other little bites, which Richard had instigated, had led to deep kisses. Both had discarded their jackets. She'd tugged his tie loose and opened three buttons, revealing a V of soft golden hair. He'd rucked her skirt up to her hips and tucked his hand securely between her thighs.

Soon she'd have him drunk and happy enough to get some answers. After that she could relax and have some real fun with him.

The palm on her leg inched up toward her crotch, bringing both pleasure and wariness, and she slapped his forearm. "Stop right there. I'm not giving it up in one of the back booths of the Matsuhana."

"Aw, come on, babe. I can make you feel real good."

"You can also make me feel real bad."

"Maybe this'll help make things better." After reaching for his jacket, he removed a gift-wrapped package from a side pocket.

A twirl of excitement threaded up her spine at the sight of the ribboned box. A present. She wanted to go slow after their recent misunderstanding, but he made it tough. Who didn't like gifts? "Thank you, Richard." She twined her arms around his neck to give him a big smacky one before she ripped the paper and ribbon off the box.

"What on earth?" She lifted what appeared to be a cluster of red satin strings and scraps out of the box.

"Thong panties." He untangled the web work. "Model them for me, would you, honey?" His blue eyes held a hungry male gleam.

"Right here, right now? You're delusional."

"No one'll come in. I told the hostess to leave us alone."

She examined them, dubious. The panties consisted of a very small triangle of red satin and a tangle of strings, some of which evidently were meant to drape over the hips on each side and one to fit between the wearer's buttocks. Mission or not, there was no way. "I will have to shave up to, up to . . ."

"Up to here." His index finger drew an arc well above the crease of her thigh.

Ani repressed a shiver. "Ouch. Why should I not shave it all off?"

His brow quirked. "Now, that would be very interesting."

The bizarre thought made her mouth fall open. As far as she knew not even Linda had done such a thing.

"Some wild child you are." He flicked the tattoo on her thigh. "Shocked at the idea of shaving your pubes. You, Ani Sharif, are a phony."

"You're a, you're a, you're a perv!"

"Yeah, and you love it." His fingertip slid across the fabric of her panties, probing.

She pushed against his hand, unable to stop the bursts of desire zipping through her body, jagged forks of summer lightning.

"Now, who's the perv?" He purred in her ear. "Are you going to take it all off for me?"

"Not a chance."

"Not ever?"

"I didn't say that." She stuffed the thong panties into her purse.

He pulled her onto his lap to nuzzle the back of her neck while his hands crept around, cupping her breasts. "I miss you."

Triumph surged through her. *Yes! Yes! Yes!*

"But why were you so mean to me?" he asked.

"I was mean to you?" She turned so she could see his face. How dare he try to twist the facts? She was the injured party!

His eyes widened, full of hurt innocence. "Those damn birds. And the popcorn brought rats and mice."

"Mice? Like Mickey and Minnie?" Sliding off his lap, she sat next to him on the bench seat.

He snorted. "No, not like Mickey and Minnie. Nasty little vermin infesting my home."

She giggled.

"Traps don't work on them. I had to get a cat."

"A kitty!" Ani clapped her hands.

"Not a kitty. A big, mean Manx cat with a reputation as a mouser." Richard rolled up his sleeves. "A big, mean cat that hates me and makes me sneeze." His forearms bore several vicious scratches, swollen and red.

"Ooh, those look painful. I'm sorry, Richard."

"What are you going to do to make it better?"

Moving closer, she stroked the chest exposed by his open shirt, then licked the hollow of his throat, feeling delightfully tipsy and reckless. Perhaps Linda was right. Agents could have fun and work at the same time. "What would you like me to do, big boy?" She'd make him very happy, then go in for the kill.

"For starters, you can tell me what's at 30791 Stevens Creek Boulevard in Cupertino."

Ani's mind dipped and spun, dizzy with shock and sake. The U.S.S.A. office was at 30971 Stevens Creek, but she couldn't tell Richard that. Why did he know that address?

She pressed the heel of her hand to her forehead, trying to dispel the effects of the alcohol. "I don't know." Lame, she thought. Truly weak. Some agent you are, Sharif!

"You were seen going into an office suite there," he said.

She stared at him. His voice had dropped, growing darker, angrier, shattering her good mood and shoving her back into sobriety. His blue eyes had chilled. His mouth was set and tight.

"You're mistaken. I have no knowledge of that address." She eased away.

"I have photos."

She shrugged. "Not possible." Had he made her, pierced her cover stories? No. Her career would die, stillborn.

"Quite possible. In fact, it's the truth. There's a Mailboxes Etc., a real estate office, and a dog groomer. The other offices are rented by the feds, specifically by an obscure entity called the United States Security Agency. I called in every government favor I'm owed to find out about it. What's the U.S.S.A., Ani, and what were you doing there?"

"I don't know anything about that. Maybe I mailed a letter at the M.B.E. I don't remember."

"That M.B.E. isn't open at eleven o'clock at night."

"You know I keep odd hours."

"You do a lot of unusual things."

She narrowed her eyes at him. "Why were you following me?"

"Are you a government spy? Did you sell corporate secrets to CompLine?"

She went limp from sheer stress. "Are . . . are you serious?"

"Someone sold or gave the anti-virus programming to Comp-Line, and you're suspect number one."

Collecting her wits, she realized she had to go on the offensive if she was going to ever work undercover again. "How dare you? Having me followed, accusing me of crimes—" She tried to rise, but he grabbed her, holding her firmly.

Rage flared. She didn't like to be manhandled, and Richard had grabbed her one too many times. Twisting her arms, she broke his hold. When she jumped up, her stockinged feet slipped on the wood floor. He snared her with one arm behind the backs of her knees.

Down she went, cocking one elbow behind her head to protect herself from a bump.

He was on top of her in a flash, pressing her to the floor with his big, strong body. The glare of his laser-bright eyes burned everything extraneous away, leaving the harsh truth.

He hadn't sent her flowers or asked her out because he cared about her, missed her, or even wanted her. Oh, no. He'd always kept his own selfish agenda, and consideration for her wasn't part of his game plan.

He'd plotted against her as effectively as any U.S.S.A. operative. He'd gotten her drunk, sweet-talked her, then confronted her, hoping she'd slip up and divulge her plans.

She'd been outclassed and just plain trapped by an expert. Richard Rexford had missed his calling. He should have been a spy.

His erection stabbed brutally into her thigh. He was still as willing to use her as much as she'd been ready to use him . . . maybe more.

She deserved what had happened. She'd plotted to trap him, but he'd acted first.

But she couldn't admit the truth. To keep her career, she had to continue the farce.

"Tonight wasn't about us, was it? You rat." Raising a knee and gripping one of his arms, she used a wrestling technique to flip him over. She jammed an elbow into his side, forcing him to release her with an "oof." After struggling to her feet, she stood for a moment, staring down at him.

"You rat. Someone passed along the anti-virus software and you think . . . you think *I* did it? Based on what?" Lewis had been right. She'd refused to believe it, but he'd been right. Rexford thought she was a thief.

And Linda, also, had spoken the truth, when she'd said that letting sex blossom into love was a mistake.

"It's your programming. You're mad at me."

"That's not evidence. That's just . . . just a set of suspicions." She hated the way her voice wobbled with angry tears.

"You're a cyber-pirate from the word go. Remember how we met?" he taunted.

"I did what I had to do." She shoved her feet into her pumps. "How dare you judge me, after that bet?"

Face hard, eyes slitted, he shrugged his shoulders, seemingly unconcerned.

She grabbed her purse, resisting the impulse to swat him with it. "Relationships should be based on trust. You don't know how to trust. You never did. You never will. Why don't you think about this rationally? Are you saying that no one else who had access to the programming could have done it?"

He hesitated, and she pressed her point, wanting to get the information Lewis needed and finish this horrible evening.

"Who, Richard? Who?"

He shook his head. "Just you, Ani."

"Bastard."

"You're calling me names?" He leaped to his feet. "You're a spy. Nothing you've told me has been true, has it?"

Trembling with shock, she somehow stayed upright.

"You're a spy." He shook a finger in her face. "A fuckin' spy. You deceived me from the get-go, didn't you? And I thought I was in love with you. Ha, ha. What a joke. You were laughing at me all the time, weren't you? You and your U.S.S.A. friends."

"Th-that's not true!"

"Typical woman. A deceptive, manipulative bitch."

Her open hand smacked his cheek as hard as she could. Jerking on her jacket, she walked out of his life for the second and final time.

Great job, Rexford. Really slick and suave. Richard cursed himself as Ani, leaving, slammed the shoji screen closed behind her.

He'd intended to give her a Big O or two before gently probing about her government job and the loss of the software. Instead, his hurt and betrayal had led him to blurting out his angry accusations.

Lord. He'd called her a thief, a spy, and a bitch. She'd never forgive him.

Rubbing his head, he realized he'd have one hell of a sake-induced hangover in the morning, but none of his problems would be solved. No girl, no software, and no company.

He was now sure that Ani was a government agent. She had the self-defense techniques of an expert. Plus, her denials sounded hollow and false. If a U.S.S.A. operative was passing Rexford.com technology to his competitors, something was seriously wrong.

Why had the government slipped a spy into Rexford.com? He thought he was on good terms with the Defense Department and the other agencies with which he did business. The feds were his major customers. Without those contracts, his company would fail.

Of all his losses, the business was the most important, Richard told himself. He could live without Ani Sharif.

But even as he tried to persuade himself he'd get over her, he remembered how she'd come in his arms, helpless with passion. Passion meant only for him. Passion only he had aroused.

Ani.

Seductive and compelling.

Courtesan mouth and witch-green eyes.

And the biggest heart . . .

He didn't care if she was an agent, a spy, or a thief. How could he let her go?

CHAPTER TWENTY-TWO

The growl of the Corvette's engine still rattled around Linda's ears when she locked the door of Ani's cottage. Shrugging on a leather motorcycle jacket, she sprinted toward the hog.

She followed Richard along Skyline, remaining a couple of curves behind him. She gunned the engine, speeding up to see him turn left at the intersection with Highway 17, toward Silicon Valley, rather than right in the direction of Santa Laura.

The roar of the well-tuned engine and its vibration between her thighs was sexy, daring. Though she wasn't an experienced motorcycle rider, she pushed the bike up to seventy-five, weaving in and out of the Saturday evening traffic.

She tailed the 'Vette to the Matsuhana, circling the block while Richard escorted Ani into the busy restaurant. After parking the bike, Linda entered. Rather than choose a seat right away, she ambled toward the women's restroom, casing the interior of the Matsuhana.

Tables surrounded the sushi bar, which dominated the center of the restaurant. She couldn't see either Richard or Ani, which meant that they were in a back room, near the lavatories. A small stage was stuck in one corner, near the far end of the main dining room, which meant that perhaps there'd be live music or karaoke later.

She used the toilet, then washed her hands and tinkered with her hair and makeup. When she left the lavatory, she again examined her surroundings, noting two rooms in the back concealed by sliding shoji screens. Kimono-clad hostesses bustled in and out of the rooms, bearing sushi, sake, and beer. Richard and Ani had to be inside one of them.

Linda tucked herself into an inconspicuous corner of the sushi bar, picking a spot with a view of the back rooms and the front door. Tugging off her jacket, she draped it over the chair next to hers, claiming it. She wanted plenty of space if it became necessary to move quickly.

Then she turned her attention to the food. The Matsuhana's sushi bar had one of those corny water features that allowed the sushi chefs to place plates on little boats that floated around an artificial canal to the diners. Hostesses served drinks, so Linda ordered an Asahi beer and took a serving of *hamachi*, raw yellowtail sushi, from one of the little boats.

Eying the screened, private rooms, she contemplated the changes in her life. Their roles had reversed, hers and Ani's. Six months before, Ani had covered Linda's back at a sumptuous Chinese dinner with the enforcer of a Shanghai tong. Held in a curtained booth in the back of a restaurant off Stockton in San Francisco, the dinner had yielded rich fruit when several of the enforcer's associates had stopped by to pay their respects. Ani had snapped photos of each while Linda had played the stupid American girl, concealing her knowledge of Shanghainese dialect.

On the basis of information she'd gathered, shipments of Chinese knock-offs of American pharmaceuticals were intercepted by customs officials at the port of Oakland. They hadn't exactly saved the free world, but no sick Americans purchased substandard, fake drugs.

Now Ani was the spy, and Linda played back-up. She mixed wasabi into soy sauce, deciding that she liked back-up just fine. She lingered over her meal, guessing that Ani, less experienced, would need to take her time to calm down and focus on her assignment. The poor child had been thrown into a complete tizzy by Richard Rexford, which didn't augur well for her future as a spy. Hopefully Ani's next mission would be completed more smoothly.

With an occasional glance toward the back rooms, Linda nibbled her way through five of the little boats, feeling a trifle lonely. She dated regularly, but hadn't become involved in a relationship since she discovered her confused feelings about her handler.

Still fit and active, Lewis, an attractive older man with influence in the U.S.S.A., was temptation in a six-foot-four package. She knew he was divorced; knew he had teenaged children somewhere; knew he was trouble. Loving Lewis would be insane.

Somehow, she'd managed to keep her emotions under control, never allowing the slightest overt act to reveal her heart, not even a smile or a wink. She knew she was naturally flirtatious, and her restraint regarding Lewis was incredible, she mused, especially since every female instinct she owned told her that her interest was returned.

Then she'd been captured by Darkness, and everything had changed.

She didn't like to admit it, but she was haunted by that man. The frightening sexual allure Darkness radiated had intrigued her to the extent that she couldn't focus on any other male. His aura of danger both thrilled and alarmed her.

The entire matter infuriated Linda. She'd considered herself a better than competent agent, but she'd been exposed and captured. If she allowed herself to contemplate what she now called The Darkness Debacle, anger and shame, two useless emotions, re-emerged.

So she refused to think about it, or him.

At about nine p.m., the restaurant employees set up a microphone and screen for karaoke. Someone would have to put a gun to her head to get her up there, but she loved watching half-soused Japanese perform karaoke. A couple of businessmen amused her with their renditions of old pop songs before a young girl took the microphone to wail about love, loss, and daring to love again.

Linda wondered if she'd ever love, even once. She'd told herself over and over, until it had become her personal mantra, that spies couldn't love. The only agents she knew with a successful marriage were Tommy and Kate Forrester, her foster parents, and they lasted not only because they loved each other, but because they worked at the same company. They didn't need to keep secrets from each other. And they weren't really agents anymore. They were administrators, probably Linda's fate if she played the spy game long enough.

She was thinking about another beer when someone pulled out the chair next to her. "I'm sorry," she said without looking up. "I'm saving that place for someone."

"He's arrived," said a soft, deep voice, speaking in Japanese.

Linda's hands tightened around her chopsticks, splintering the flimsy wood pull-aparts.

Darkness removed the snapped bits from her fingers. "Sharp edges, very dangerous," he murmured. His eyes met hers. "I wouldn't want you to hurt yourself."

A hostess fluttered by and asked, "What may I serve you?"

"I'll have whatever the lady's having," Darkness said. "And bring her another."

Linda breathed deeply, scenting ginseng, danger, and man. Excitement flickered deep in her belly. Was it coincidence that had brought Darkness to her side? She doubted it.

Fury clenched her muscles. She'd been made. Again.

Without looking at him, she said, "I probably shouldn't have another. I won't be able to get home."

"I will ensure you get home safely."

"Since you apparently know where I live, I'll have to move. I won't be stalked." She glanced at him.

He wore a slight smile and black leather. "I don't need to stalk you. You'll come to me."

She chuckled. "And why is that?"

The drinks arrived, and Darkness paid with a C-note, opening his wallet so she could see a hefty wad of bills. For the first time, he repelled Linda. Men who flashed cash disgusted her. For Darkness, the act seemed incongruous. Linda said, "If you're implying that I'll seek you out for money, dream on. Money doesn't interest me."

"Not interested in money, eh? We shall have to work harder." He lifted his glass. "To temptation."

Raising her brows, she sipped.

He asked, "What tempts you, Linda Wing? My friends will provide whatever you desire."

She set her glass onto the bar. The crooner continued to sing about love and loss. Darkness' thigh pressed against hers. Warm, tingly, good. Too good. All over.

Then his booted foot sought her ankle.

Covered tonight by a Doc Marten, her replacement ankle chain couldn't be broken. But she wouldn't play footsie with an enemy agent, even if he made her tingle in all the right places, and in a few she hadn't known she had.

Linda placed her ankle onto the opposite thigh, purposely jabbing him in the leg with her knee. She didn't apologize, but said, "I don't want anything from you."

He leaned toward her, bypassing her outthrust knee. "Liar," he whispered in her ear, nipping the lobe.

She turned to face him. "So you make me hot. Big deal. You and ten thousand other men. Accepting your offer would put my life into chaos."

"But you've always been disappointed by men, haven't you?"

Dropping her foot, Linda pressed a hand to her stomach. How could he have known that? She breathed deeply, seeking, then recapturing her equilibrium.

A guess, nothing more. She was single. It stood to reason that if she hadn't been disappointed by man after man, she'd have married. A simple set of deductions. Darkness didn't know anything about her and certainly couldn't look inside her heart.

He played with a lock of her hair, bleached golden. "Meet me halfway. Sample my wares. You won't be disappointed."

"Nobody will ever accuse you of low self-esteem. By the way, how's your nose?"

His rueful smile surprised her. She thought he'd be mad. "It's okay." He touched it with the tip of a finger. "I'm sorry I called you a bitch. But you, umm, startled me."

"You were torturing me. You deserved what you got."

"Oh, I would not have hurt you with the knife. I simply wanted to see what you look like naked."

Her jaw dropped, and he laughed. "Perhaps we should start over."

Recovering herself again, she snapped, "Start over? How? Hi, Darkness, I'm Linda."

"Yes, I see what you mean."

She leaned toward him. "Who are you?"

He moved closer to her. Now his lips were only a breath away from hers. "Someone who wants you. You game?"

"I can't do this."

"Of course you can." Closing the gap, he pressed his mouth onto hers, kissing her firmly, letting her feel how good it was, how good it could be between them.

Darkness knew how to kiss. A lot of men didn't, rushing in with demanding tongues before she was ready to receive them. Darkness seemed to understand that kissing was an analog for sex, and that foreplay was important.

He used his lips to caress hers, to entice her into opening to him and exploring his mouth. Time, space, and even a sense of her own identity drifted off, and she became just a woman enjoying a kiss with an exciting new man.

Before she was ready to stop, he pulled away, creating a cold gap between them where there had been warmth, promise, even the heat of desire.

Reality returned, and with it, the hostess. While she refilled their beers, Linda cast a quick look toward the back rooms. All quiet on the Ani front.

Darkness caressed the back of her hand. With an indrawn breath, she savored the flame of desire he traced. She wanted him back, but she wouldn't ask or beg. Never.

He smiled. "It's just a little kiss, right? Nothing serious. And if it were to go further . . ." He trailed a finger down her bare arm.

She swallowed. She wouldn't let this man see how he got to her. "It wouldn't be anything serious."

"Nothing serious. So why not?"

"So you are offering yourself, money, whatever I want if I join your friends?"

"Put crudely, yes."

She smiled and flipped her hair back. "I have all the money I need." She leaned forward, letting her lips brush his, hearing him suck in a breath. She whispered, "And I can have you any time I want."

He drew back, visibly offended. His injured masculine pride, no doubt.

Linda laughed.

Darkness reached into the inner pocket of his jacket and took out an envelope. "Perhaps you will be interested in these."

"I doubt it." But she slid one finger beneath the flap, tearing the seal away from the heavy paper before shaking out the contents onto her lap.

Two photographs. One, in shades of fading gray, was yellow and crumbling around the edges. The other was a recent shot, in sharp, crisp color.

She picked up the older photo, the black and white image of a woman and a small child. With an effort, she restrained herself from clenching her fingers around it. She hadn't seen either the woman or the rickety little house in the picture for over twenty years, but she recognized them immediately. She knew the child, because an older version of the same face stared at her from every mirror.

"Th-that's my mother. And me," she whispered. "When we lived in Korea." Her heart began to pound, and she pressed her free hand to her chest.

She closed her eyes, allowing herself to sink into the memories, cloudy and shadowed by time. The scent of her mother, an aroma really, of the spicy, grilled food she'd prepared; her round, shiny, loving face. Her father had smelled like the forest and the woods. Strong, he used to pick her up to cradle her in one arm while he tucked her baby brother under the other.

All three had been killed in a border skirmish about a year after the photo was taken. She still didn't understand why or how it had happened. She'd survived only because she'd been in school that day.

She shook her shoulders, banishing the past, and took the other photo from Darkness' hand. It depicted a forty-something woman standing in front of what Linda recognized as the Forbidden City.

Her brain blanked out as if every brain cell had overloaded and misfired at the same time. Her hand shook, and she dropped the photo in her lap. "This can't be possible," she whispered. Her mother had lived in the same little town all her life, had never been to Beijing or anywhere else. She'd been killed when Linda was seven.

She pulled herself together and said, "Faked, of course."

"Can you be sure?" Darkness's voice was smooth, low, enticing.

She cut him a hard glance. "I saw the car, with all the, umm, all the bullet holes. I saw her purse open, her things scattered on the roadside. I saw the coffins. I went to the funeral. My family is dead. My mother never vacationed in Beijing, thanks to your friends."

"The Chinese didn't kill your family," Darkness said. "The Americans did."

She clenched her hands around the counter. "You lie."

"The truth. Why do you think the Americans took such good care of you, an orphaned Korean peasant girl?"

She'd had the same questions herself, but said, "They found me useful."

He shook his head. "You're clever and bright, but not unusually so."

"Don't flatter me too much. I might get conceited."

"Guilt," he said. "The Americans felt guilty because their inexperienced border guards sprayed your family's car with bullets when your father strayed close to the barbed wire at a checkpoint."

Her insides twisted into gnarls and knots. "How do you know so much?"

The snap of a shoji screen, opening violently, grabbed her attention. The staccato clatter of high heels cut through the music and the chatter of diners. Ani strode toward the exit, her face stormy.

Linda ripped a fifty out of her wallet and dropped it by her beer glass. "It's been great, gotta go." Tugging her jacket out from behind Darkness's back, she raised her voice. "Hey!"

Ani stopped, scanning the room before her face broke into a smile. She hurried toward Linda. "I'm really glad you're here." She reached for Darkness's now-empty chair. "Huh!" she said to Darkness, who edged away. "What are you doing here?"

Linda seized him by his forearms and held on tight. "You know this guy? Ani, this is Darkness!"

"The hell you say." Ani glared at Darkness. "Linda, this is Michael!"

"That Michael?" Linda looked at Ani's stricken face, then turned and socked him on the side of the jaw.

Michael bounced off another patron's chair. She reacted with a squeal and a push as he slid to the floor. Her date jumped to his feet, a fist cocked.

"Fuck this!" Scrambling to his feet, Michael scrabbled for a gold bracelet at his wrist. He tore open its clasp, breaking it. When it dropped to the floor, he stomped on it with a booted heel.

Other diners began to shout and clap, cheering on the brawl. Richard Rexford stumbled out of the back room, walking like a victim of too much sake and too much Ani Sharif. He hurried in their direction, bumping elbows with a sharp-featured Japanese woman. Muscling past her, he reached the group at the sushi bar first.

"Well, shit," he said. "If it isn't Mike Han, in cozy with the U.S.S.A. girls."

Three heads turned. "Shut up!" they hissed.

Rexford planted his hands on his hips. "Isn't this interesting? I bet I could mess ya up real good."

Linda raised a fist, but the Japanese woman scurried between the combatants. A badge on her black uniform lapel identified her as the manager. "No, no! All of you out, now. Or I'll call the police."

CHAPTER TWENTY-THREE

Kate Forrester sat behind a desk in the penthouse suite of the Peninsula Hotel, high atop San Francisco's Nob Hill. The cherry-wood desk was an antique, polished and rare. The thick, full rugs and drapes were ivory, an elegant setting for the woman, completely at ease in her luxurious surroundings. Not for Kate the rundown strip mall in Cupertino, Ani thought. Whatever Kate did, she did with unmistakable style, befitting the head of the U.S.S.A.'s domestic branch.

Rising, she poured tea from a porcelain service set on a credenza behind her. She didn't offer Ani anything, which didn't portend well. Ani straightened her back, sitting erect in a carved cherry-wood chair. Having completed her mission, she told herself not to worry, even though the scene felt like being called on the carpet.

Kate continued to regard Ani with steady gray eyes. Her dark brown hair and unlined skin belied both her age of fifty-four and her stressful profession. Though she'd traveled all night from D.C. to reach the west coast by morning, Kate's dove-gray suit remained crisp, her white blouse starched, and her expression calm, giving nothing away.

She didn't say anything and Ani, familiar with Kate's routine, didn't either. Ani was reminded of similar events years before, when Kate and Tommy had confronted her with evidence of her teenage misdeeds. She'd learned that the best tactic was to hold her tongue and let others talk, so the room was entirely quiet.

Ani knew that Linda Wing, Michael Han and Lewis Anglesey waited in an anteroom for their debriefings, but no sounds of conversation penetrated the closed door.

The mess at the Matsuhana had the potential to wreck all four agents' careers. Linda's attack on a fellow operative couldn't go unpunished, and Lewis Anglesey would probably bear the brunt of the responsibility for Rexford's public unmasking of three U.S.S.A. spies. That Rexford was uncommonly clever wouldn't enter into the equation, nor would his loyalty to the U.S.A. Even though his trustworthiness had been established, the fact remained that a civilian had not only uncovered the existence of the U.S.S.A. but had identified three of its undercover operatives. Besides, the mole inside Rexford.com was still hidden.

Finally Kate said, "We could sit here forever without talking, or you could explain yourself, Agent Sharif."

Agent Sharif, not Ani. That was bad. She said, "There's nothing to explain. I completed my mission inside Rexford.com about a week ago, and was reassigned to surveillance of Comp-Line, another software company. I was recontacted by the previous target, Richard Rexford. In obedience to Supervising Agent Anglesey's orders, I met with the target last night."

"Explain to me how and why a civilian exposed three of my agents in public."

Ani flinched. "Apparently a software program was pirated from Rexford.com and sold to CompLine. When Rexford discovered the theft, he suspected me, since I had just left the firm."

Kate's gaze raked her. "Inconspicuously, I hope?"

Ani hoped she wasn't blushing. "No, but I was in character."

"What character?" Kate sipped tea.

"Outraged girlfriend." She adjusted the lapel of her olive-drab trouser suit.

A pause. "I see."

Another pause. I will not be ashamed, Ani told herself. I won't. I won't. She said, "I think that Rexford or an employee followed me to headquarters. I suspect a professional. Believe me, I was careful."

"Not careful enough."

Ani's gut twisted. Nevertheless, she met Kate's gaze. "And at the restaurant, Rexford saw me with Agents Wing and Han. Agent Wing was acting as back-up. Neither of us had any prior knowledge that Agent Han was involved in either my assignment or Agent Wing's."

"I don't know what to do with you, Sharif, or with the other two." Kate's lips tightened. "The Matsuhana has video surveillance of its interior. They gave the tape to local law enforcement."

Ani's mouth went dry.

"Of course we've retrieved the tape, but still, the local police have seen the three of you. All of you will have to be reassigned."

"Oh, no," Ani said. "We haven't found the spy. Someone at Rexford.com or CompLine is selling secrets, and I want to complete the mission."

"How?" Kate asked.

"I'm close to getting into CompLine's internal systems, and I've been surveilling their campus. Plus, Thomas Rexford, the head of CompLine, once offered me a job. I could get in there easily."

Kate pursed her lips. "That's a possibility. Richard is Thomas's son, isn't he?"

"Yeah. He owns Rexford.com."

"Both firms have a number of government contracts," Kate said. "Important ones. Either company could be a cozy nest for a spy. What about Richard Rexford?"

"No," Ani said with certainty. "We've cleared him."

"But there could be someone else in there. What can be done? Haven't you burned your bridges with Richard Rexford?"

"That's true, but we now know that he's not a traitor." Ani rose to pace. "I can't go back in there, but it's my understanding that Agent Han is still implanted. If you talk with Rexford, he might be persuaded to cooperate. If he wants to continue working for the feds, he'll play ball."

Kate stood to pour tea, then offered it to Ani. "Okay, let's get him on the phone."

Linda had spent the night with Ani putting the pieces together. They'd realized that the kidnapping was a fake, and that the assignment with the law firm was probably also a sham. Linda wondered what, if anything, was real, other than betrayal.

They'd talked about the men involved, concluding that not a one of them could be trusted. Quite possibly, Lewis, Michael, and Richard all felt the same way about them. Given her "spies can't love" philosophy, Linda could handle that, but she was concerned about Ani. First Michael Han had treated her like a disposable sex toy, then Richard Rexford, after showing her how great lovemaking could be, had ruthlessly torn away every one of her defenses.

Linda wasn't a violent person, but her major regrets were that she hadn't broken Michael's jaw, and had then hesitated, losing her opportunity to punch Richard's lights out. For Ani.

Linda adjusted the waistband of her sober black suit, fondling a concealed blade. She occupied the exact but narrow center of a small sofa in the anteroom on Kate's suite. About five feet to her left, Michael Han slouched in a wing chair, in a navy pin-striped suit and serious shoes. Five feet to her right, Lewis Anglesey sat ruler straight, wearing a gray three-piece and a somber expression.

The trio remained absolutely silent until Ani emerged from

her interview with Kate. Even to Linda's trained eye, Ani betrayed no hint of emotion. She said, "Linda, she wants to see you."

Linda stood and stalked toward the door, setting down each high-heeled foot with confidence, walking tall with her shoulders squared. She might be getting her head chopped off, but she'd hold it high. She'd already decided that in this situation the best defense would be a good offense. Otherwise, she'd lose her career, which at the moment looked as though it was headed straight for the nearest sewer.

She closed the door behind her with a click. Not a slam, for that would be immature, but an audible and definite click and advanced on Kate, seated behind a cherry-wood desk. Slapping both palms onto its polished surface, Linda snapped, "You set me up."

"I was also tested." Kate stirred her tea. "So was Tommy. So was Lewis Anglesey."

"Tested? Lewis?" Linda's jaw tensed. So Lewis had known, just as Ani and she had surmised. She'd trusted Lewis, even thought she was a little in love with him, and he'd set her up. "What of Michael Han?" She spat out the name.

"Code named Darkness. Yes, and Michael also. All of us, at a certain point in our careers."

Linda sank onto the nearest chair, willing herself to calm. "So, to get to the next level, the agency had to—"

"Test your trustworthiness, by the most severe means possible."

"I'm trying hard not to feel insulted."

"In the general scheme of things, your feelings about this aren't important."

Linda stuck her chin into the air and stared at her foster mother. "Why aren't you offended? You raised me from childhood. Any slight on my character is a slap in your face."

"No. Policy and procedure bind all of us, with no exceptions." She stood and turned to a credenza behind her upon which rested a china tea service. One used teacup already sat nearby; Ani's, Linda guessed. "Would you like some tea?" Kate asked.

"Umm, yes." Linda was surprised, but pleased. Maybe, just maybe, that punch to another agent's jaw hadn't drawn Kate's wrath.

Kate lifted the top of the teapot. "I don't know if this is still hot enough for you."

Linda relaxed a little more. Her foster mother knew that Linda hated weak coffee and lukewarm tea. If Kate were truly angry, she wouldn't worry about whether or not Linda liked the tea.

Kate poured, and steam rose from the surface of the liquid.

"It looks fine, thank you." Linda said, accepting the cup of pale, fragrant oolong. "You were tested . . . how?"

"The usual ways, like what Agent Han did to you. The threat, the enticing man, the implied promise of cash, the use of family pressure."

Linda stirred her tea, frowning. "He . . . he showed me a photo of my mother in China."

"Faked, as you must have guessed. Your mother died. You saw her coffin." Kate's voice was flat.

"Is what he said true? Did the Americans kill my family?"

Kate sighed. "No one knows."

Linda's body jerked involuntarily, and Kate said, "Truly. No one knows. There was a shootout when your father mistakenly drove into the demilitarized zone. No one knows who fired the first shot, and we don't know which bullets killed your family."

Linda dropped her head into her hands. A few seconds later, she felt the warmth of Kate squeezing her shoulder. "I'm sorry, darling."

Leaning back into her chair, Linda sighed some more. "It doesn't really matter, does it?"

"If you say so." Kate's tone was dry.

Linda wanted to change the subject. Fast. "What happened to you during your test?"

Kate returned to her chair and fiddled with the teacup. "After the stud-boy and the bucks didn't work, they tempted me with Tommy."

"How?"

"The agency faked his kidnapping. My tester told me that if I turned, he'd live."

"What did you do?"

Kate set down her cup. "I held a gun to my tester's head and demanded to know where Tommy was being held." Linda's mouth dropped open.

"He refused to tell me, of course, until I'd shot him."

Linda found her voice. "You . . . you killed him?"

"Oh, no," Kate said. "Then I wouldn't get any information. I shot him in the hand, and told him that I'd work my way up his arm, then move onto the other arm, then to his legs . . . he had to admit what was going on." She smiled at Linda.

She hung her head. "I didn't do nearly as well. I cracked like a leaky teapot."

"You were fine. I was somewhat unconventional, but you performed exactly as we'd hoped. We don't want our agents getting hurt or killed during the testing process. But I'll tell you that my reaction prompted a number of changes in the procedure. We're now more careful to keep matters from getting out of hand." Kate sipped her tea.

Linda raised her head and smirked. "I broke his nose."

"Yes, Lewis had to intervene at that point. Michael is too valuable a commodity for you to injure."

"Then I socked him in the jaw. In public."

"He shouldn't have approached you at the restaurant. He was overconfident and lost control. And you also blew it. Don't let it happen again." Kate crossed her arms over her torso.

"He knows every one of my weak spots."

"You don't have any weak spots."

Linda remembered Michael's kiss, and her reaction to it. She'd wanted sex with someone she'd thought was an enemy agent. "I nearly broke, Kate." She chewed on a fingertip.

"But you didn't."

"Was . . . was anything real? My assignment at the law firm—"

"Oh, yes," Kate said. "You're too valuable to waste on weeks of busywork. But when it appeared as though someone suspected you, Lewis and I set up the testing process. You completed your assignment admirably, getting us all the information we needed before the faked kidnapping took place." She rose and extended a hand. "Congratulations, Agent Wing. You're ready for the next level."

Linda walked out of the room considerably more relieved than when she entered. Michael then talked with Kate, emerging about ten minutes later, looking chastened but not particularly upset. Linda figured that Kate had dressed him down, but not suspended him. Damn. Though attracted to Michael, Linda didn't like him. He might be sexy, but she knew from her own experience as well as talking with Ani that Michael was selfish in the bedroom and a jerk outside it.

Lewis Anglesey's interview was the longest of all. During his debriefing, a knock on the door preceded none other than Richard Rexford, attired in an even nattier suit than the one he wore to seduce and trap Ani the previous evening, in navy gabardine with a subtly colored tie.

Ani shifted her position on the sofa next to Linda, occupying as much space as she could. She did not want Rexford on the snug little love seat with them. Apparently getting the message, he took the chair that Lewis had vacated.

"What are you doing here?" Linda asked him, with no effort to conceal her contempt.

"I asked him here." Kate's voice sounded from the doorway to her office. She strode into the room, hand extended to shake with Richard. "Mr. Rexford, I'm Kate Forrester of the United States Security Agency. Thank you for coming to talk with us on such short notice. If you can give me five more minutes, we'll meet as a group. It's time to break this one wide open." The door closed behind her.

Richard sat back down. "She doesn't waste time, does she?" he asked no one in particular.

Both women ignored him. Linda, seated on the sofa, edged closer to Ani. "What do you think is up?" she asked quietly.

Ani whispered, "I told Kate to bring him in."

Linda raised her brow. "And she did? A civilian?"

"Why not? We know he's trustworthy, for a rat."

"If you're going to gossip about me," Richard said, sounding testy, "the least you could do is talk outside of my presence."

Ani turned. "Oh, don't flatter yourself. You're not worth the sustained attention."

Michael laughed, and both women nailed him with frosty glares.

"Don't you start," Linda snapped.

"You really ought to be nicer to me," Michael said.

"What for?" she asked.

"What if we end up on the same assignment?"

"I suppose that's possible." Linda considered. "In that case, I'll refrain from breaking any more bones. But only because I'd be damaging government property."

The door opened again, and Kate said briskly, "All right, everybody, get in here. It's time to put this case to bed."

As Richard filed into the room after the women, he wondered what the hell was going on. He'd been inclined to believe that Kate Forrester's phone call was a fake, like everything else about the U.S.S.A., including Ani Sharif. But a couple of calls to his other government contacts convinced him that Kate Forrester was the real deal, a straight shooter who, with her husband, ran the entire secret show.

So he'd hotfooted it to San Francisco, hoping to find some answers as well as resurrect his company. Forrester had assured him that his help at this juncture would lead to some lucrative deals down the road.

He glanced at Ani, who sat in one of the chairs surrounding Forrester's desk. She returned his gaze, her green eyes colder than a dead penguin's nuts. The other seats were occupied by Linda Wing, his "employee" Mike Han, hired by Rexford.com in Marketing and Sales, and an older man Richard didn't recognize.

Kate Forrester tapped her fingers on the surface of the desk. Her nails were cut short, buffed rather than polished, in keeping with what he'd already seen about her no-nonsense personality. She said, "Mr. Rexford, I believe you know everyone here with the exception of Lewis Anglesey, our local station chief."

"Anglesey." Richard extended a hand in the older agent's direction.

Lewis Anglesey shook his hand, giving Richard a tight nod before sitting in a chair near Forrester, tacitly acknowledging her dominance. Richard took the last remaining chair, between Wing and Han.

Forrester said, "I believe we've been approaching this from the wrong direction."

"Wait." Richard held up a hand. "I'm at sea here without any nav charts."

"There's a spy at Rexford.com or possibly at CompLine,"

Ani said bluntly.

"No," Richard said. "I know everyone in my company, except for you and Han. It's not possible."

"Agent Sharif is correct," Anglesey said. "We're sure that there's a mole in one of the two firms passing secrets to foreign governments. We initially thought it was you—"

"What did you just say?" Richard was outraged by the suggestion that he was a traitor.

"—and assigned Sharif to find out." Anglesey had continued as though Richard hadn't interrupted. "You've been cleared, but we learned that software she developed for your firm under a government contract has ended up with the Chinese."

"There's definitely more to all this than meets the eye," Richard said, his jaw clenching. He had been right. Ani was a spy, a liar, and a betrayer. "Has anything you've told me been the truth?" he asked her.

"Request permission to respond," Ani said to Forrester.

"Permission denied. Let's get back on track. I realize that there's been some, um, volatile interactions during this operation," Forrester said, eying Linda and Mike. "I have to ask all of you to put your personal interests aside for the next few days while we trap the mole."

Richard leaned forward. "How can we do that when we don't know who it is?"

"Perhaps we've been going after this all wrong," Forrester said. "If we treat this like an old-fashioned whodunit, we'd be asking different questions."

"What would Jessica Fletcher or Sherlock Holmes do?" Lewis Anglesey grinned at Forrester. Evidently the woman liked cozy mysteries.

She smiled. "Jessica Fletcher would look at motive. Discover why, and who and how may fall into place."

"Perhaps we're not dealing with terrorists or traditional

spies," Ani said. "What does that leave?"

"Greed. Filthy lucre." Mike Han turned to Richard. "I don't know everyone in your firm yet. Is there anyone constantly in debt, maybe has a gambling problem or always needs money?"

"I don't know," Richard said. "I don't like to poke my nose into my employees' private lives."

"In this case, we'll ask you to give us access to your company's personnel files," Forrester said. "Someone may have recently come into unusual amounts of money, purchased a large house or expensive cars. Agents Sharif and Han can use the information to find out."

"In addition to my investigation of CompLine." Ani eyed Forrester. "I want to go in there. Thomas Rexford said he'd hire me."

Forrester tapped the point of a pencil on the blotter. "Permission granted, Sharif. Infiltrate CompLine."

CompLine. Richard rubbed his chin. Family loyalty warred with self-preservation, as well as with his bedrock sense of right and wrong. Should he say what he thought? What he feared?

Closing his eyes, he sighed.

Forrester said, "If there's something you need to tell us, Mr. Rexford, I recommend you do so right now."

He looked up to encounter a flinty gray stare, steady and calm. Colder even than Ani's, Kate Forrester's stony eyes no doubt reflected her nature. Nothing would wear her down or deter her.

Richard accepted the inevitable and said, feeling sick to his stomach, "I know someone who's always in debt and always needs money."

CHAPTER TWENTY-FOUR

For this gig, Ani had decided to alter her previous personal style. At CompLine, her task wasn't to attract male attention, but to sneak, to spy, to learn. A classic assignment, one she relished after the emotional tumult of her affair with Richard Rexford. So she and Linda, in effect, traded wardrobes. Heading for a vacation on Maui, Linda borrowed Ani's cutoff shorts and crop tops, while Ani wore Linda's beautifully cut suits, subdued makeup, and restrained hairstyles.

Thomas Rexford had welcomed her with arms as open as old T-Rex could spread them. Triumphant at what he viewed as another score won over his son, he installed her in a dandy corner office with a window overlooking the parking lot, not a featureless cubicle. Ani exulted, not due to the corporate flattery, but because she could easily watch comings and goings.

Telling T-Rex and security that she customarily kept unusual hours, Ani frequently stayed late, spending evenings breaking into CompLine's internal security system while pretending to work on company projects. Hijacking the signals from their array of surveillance cameras in and around the building gave her views of the entire place.

Her industry paid off within two weeks. One evening, as she labored to break into the telephone lines in Thomas's office, she saw Mark Rexford walk into the building from the back door rather than the front, bypassing nighttime security's skeleton staff, which manned a lobby desk. Using the internal video system, she watched him go to Sundeen Rexford's office suite. How odd was that?

She frowned. Mark was one of Sundeen's many children, but why would he meet his father at CompLine? This was potentially more than "take your child to work" day. Sundeen Rexford had been fingered by Richard as a possible mole.

When Mark left, she kicked off her heels and sprinted down two flights of stairs and along a hall, then waited. She ambushed an astonished Mark as he tried to stealthily leave the building the way he'd come in.

Ani body-slammed him against the nearest wall. "We need to talk."

He gasped for breath, tearing at his constricting tie. "What are you doing here?"

"I might ask you the same thing." She grabbed his throat and dug in her nails just enough to warn him, keeping control of his stocky body with an elbow in his chest. "Somehow I think you're here for more than a little cozy father-son bonding. You work for Rexford.com. Merely being here could be a serious ethical breach and a conflict of interest. It could affect your license to steal, er, practice law."

She tightened her grip, remembering that he'd deliberately set her up for complete public humiliation. "Ten seconds, Rexford, or it's lights out."

He kicked her knee with a loafer-clad foot. She laughed.

"Italian leather doesn't hurt very much." She pressed closer, denying him the use of his knees and feet.

He scrabbled for her head, grabbing her updo, pulling hard. With a cry of pain, she let go of his throat to smash a palm into his nose. Blood spurted, and Mark screamed. She seized his wrist, twisting it hard behind his back, then shoved him face down onto the cold linoleum.

He broke faster than Seabiscuit ran.

CHAPTER TWENTY-FIVE

Maui, Hawaii
Three weeks later; mid-afternoon

Ani stretched out on a lounge on the beach near Wailea Point, reflecting that December in Maui had been a fine idea. After she'd completed her assignment, she'd joined Linda for a little vacation prior to reassignment. An ocean away from their hassles, Maui had been a haven from the stresses and strains of the Bay Area.

Too bad Ani couldn't relax. Erotic dreams of Richard Rexford disturbed her sleep. But at the end of each sexual encounter, his penis turned into a giant snake and threatened to devour her with foot-long sharp fangs, dripping with poison. Ani shuddered. She didn't need a psychotherapist to interpret those nightmares.

She sipped a piña colada, leaned her head back, and contemplated the lapis-blue Hawaiian sky. Though she'd had a rocky and difficult autumn, life was definitely improving. Her work, at least, was back on track, or so she hoped.

After the confrontation with Mark Rexford, during which he'd confessed that he'd given his father Sundeen several C.D.s with Rexford.com software, Ani had rifled CompLine's accounting records, finding recent payments to Mark for unspecified services. The hack into Sundeen Rexford's bank accounts had been even more fruitful. She'd discovered deposits that didn't match his CompLine paycheck, suggesting that he'd been paid from another source. She suspected the Chinese but didn't know how to prove it. Though she could break into the local consulate's system, she doubted that they maintained a computer file of payments to American traitors. She left further investigation and prosecution of Mark and Sundeen to Justice Department attorneys.

She prayed that her successful completion of the mission would win her another undercover assignment. Otherwise, her career was stalled, stillborn, dead in the water. Over.

She'd emailed the information and evidence to Lewis and, with his permission, to Richard Rexford, suggesting that perhaps Mark was responsible for the theft, since he'd been paid. In fact, she'd emailed the entire payments file to Richard, just to show him she'd never received anything from CompLine.

And then nothing. Zip. Zero. Not the tiniest response from Richard Rexford, that ungrateful goat's spawn. She thought at least she deserved an acknowledgment, but had to admit that because she'd ignored several of Richard's emails, she couldn't be surprised if he ignored hers. Her romance with Richard was probably irreparably damaged, even destroyed. Perhaps that was for the best. Though deeply attracted to each other, neither could trust. Richard didn't know how, and, at this point, Ani knew better.

So she had one last task: getting over Richard Rexford. Problem was that she didn't know how. She'd never fallen in love before, been dumped on before, betrayed before.

She picked up the latest issue of a women's magazine she'd laid on the sand nearby. Its cover featured a model and various captions, one of which read *How to Get Over Him*. Despite the capital on "Him," Ani doubted *Cosmo* intended its readers to forsake religion. The article surely contained advice for the lovelorn. And she was lovelorn, all right. Richard Rexford had ripped out her heart with a meat hook, leaving a gaping emotional wound.

Still, she hoped that one day she'd mend, becoming able to open herself to another man. Having tasted the delights of romance, she wanted more. But next time around, she'd insist upon commitment. She remembered that her birth mother had once pointed out that no man will pay for milk if his cow will give it for free.

Though Richard had claimed her heart, she'd take it back. Ani Sharif would be her own woman.

The whisper of sand shifted by feet drew her attention. Lifting her gaze from the magazine, Ani saw Linda, dripping from her swim, stroll to a nearby lounge, then recline.

"Can I get you something?" Ani asked.

"No, thank you, darling." Linda gestured to a waiter attired in shorts and a Hawaiian shirt. "That lovely boy will bring me another mai tai." She and the bronzed beach boy eyed each other with obvious hunger on their faces.

Ani smiled to herself. Yes, Maui had been a great idea. Finally out of her snit after the testing process was revealed, Linda was herself again: slim, sleek and on the prowl. Envying her friend, Ani sighed. She dropped the magazine and scanned Wailea Bay's shifting shades of blue. Pale in the shallows, aquamarine farther out, deepening to cobalt and indigo where turtles swam and dolphins leaped.

While she'd been absorbed in her thoughts, a lovely yacht, like a white cloud borne on the wind, had entered the bay. Though she couldn't read the boat's name, Ani's heart jolted in recognition. But surely it couldn't be the *Trophy Wife*. That was just wishful thinking, or, perhaps, fear. Lots of boats are white, she told herself. Nevertheless, she continued to watch the yacht. She caught the glitter of a spyglass as its captain surveyed the shoreline. Then its anchors clattered out of their ports, and a tanned, blond man, clad in a black Speedo, dove off the back of the boat into the bay.

She resolutely pushed aside her hopes. Dreamer! she admonished herself.

The warm waters of Wailea Bay slid pleasantly past Richard's skin as he swam to the beach to claim Ani. He'd spotted her from the *Trophy Wife,* her red bathing suit a flag for his attention even on the crowded beach.

His pulse pounded in his ears, the product of both exercise and tension. He'd enjoyed these last days on the sea. If he couldn't win Ani's love, he'd just chuck it all and again make the ocean his home. He knew he'd be running in a vain attempt to escape his problems, but so what? He couldn't bear to return to Santa Laura, where reminders of his failure would confront him every day. Without Ani by his side, nothing meant much.

He'd swum close enough to the beach that his feet touched the sandy bottom. Ignoring the waves, which were perfect for bodysurfing, he emerged from the ocean and strode toward Ani's lounge.

Her frown could sour a lemon. "What are you doing here?"

He gingerly sat on an empty corner of her chaise. "To see you."

"Bad idea. I came here to get away from you."

"Not possible."

She blinked. "How did you find me?"

"Lewis told me where you're staying."

Her glower darkened, if that were possible. "Go away. You're dripping on my magazine." She moved it aside.

He didn't leave, but picked up a nearby towel and began drying his head, torso, and arms.

"Please don't use my towel."

He glanced at the embroidered logo. "It's not yours, it's the hotel's."

She eyed him, but the look wasn't a glare. A spark of carnal interest flared in her gaze as she glanced at his body, then lowered her lids demurely.

Aha. He had a chance. Richard sucked in a deep breath. He'd practiced this moment at least fifty times aboard the *Trophy Wife* during the trip from the mainland. "Ani, I'm sorry. What I did was horribly wrong. I've treated you badly from when we met till . . . well, till right now. Is there any way you can forgive me? Can we possibly start over?" He accompanied this speech with one of his most winning smiles.

She gave him a brief, cold scowl. "No."

He was taken aback. He'd expected a confrontation with her at least, an argument that would clear the air. "That's all, just 'no?' "

"Yes." Picking up the magazine, she flipped through its pages.

Intrigued, he examined the *Cosmo*'s front cover. " 'How to get over him'?" he asked. "Don't tell me that the brilliant Ani Sharif has been reduced to seeking advice from Helen Gurley Brown?"

Green eyes blazing, Ani slapped the magazine onto his thigh. "What I read is not your business. Nothing about me is your business. Am I clear?"

He leaned closer, willing her to feel his nearness, his want, his love. "I got to you."

"That's no secret."

"I'm still getting to you."

"That's in the past. I can't change what happened, but I can decide how I'm going to live my life in the future. And you're not going to be in it. So why don't you leave?" She pushed him, gaining a few inches of space.

He scooted back toward her. "Leave? I just got here. I'm not leaving you for a very long time."

"I don't think so." Carrying her towel, Ani stood, then walked away toward the hotel.

He followed for a few steps. "There's too much between us to avoid. You may run now, but sooner or later, you'll hear me out."

"How about later?" She continued walking.

He dropped his arms to his sides in temporary defeat. If she kept up this defiant, angry attitude, then all was lost. He had a lot to say, but he couldn't tell her anything else now. In her temper, he knew she'd reject him, and if she did, he couldn't stand it. Rejection by the only woman he'd ever loved would forever destroy him. He'd exposed parts of himself to Ani no other woman had seen. Though his former fiancée, Celeste, had introduced him to the notion of bondage, he'd refused to let her cuff him, and he'd had no particular desire to assert control over her. Ani had been the first woman he needed to bind, possibly because he'd fallen in love with her.

Celeste had once explained that sexual bondage was a metaphor, with the chains representing emotional ties. At the time, Richard had thought they symbolized control. But his experience with Ani had blindsided him with new knowledge. The moment he'd deprived her of physical freedom, she became his responsibility, a heart delivered into his keeping. He'd committed to fulfilling her every need, not just physical but emotional. He bound her hands with ropes; she'd bound his soul with unbreakable ties of love.

Celeste was right. He'd fallen for Ani harder than before, but at the time, he couldn't face that reality. He hadn't been ready to change his self-centered existence for a woman. He'd wanted everything his way.

Then control had slipped out of his grasp, resulting in the loss of Ani's love.

The loss of the only woman he'd ever really trusted.

Ironically enough, events had transpired such that neither

could completely trust the other, adding a layer of complexity to an already messy emotional mix. Ani's complicity in the software theft had seemed logical, but logic had misled him. He should have listened to his heart.

Shouldn't he trust an agent of the U.S. government? From what he'd observed, she was one of the government's best-trained, most highly trusted agents.

As for Ani ever trusting him . . . Richard grimaced. Why should she? He'd betrayed her not once, but twice. From her standpoint, perhaps she'd never trusted him. Her mission had been to discover if he was a traitor. Even though he'd been cleared, that he'd ever been suspected was the ultimate humiliation.

But he needed Ani more than his life, and if she wasn't part of it, he'd just dump it all: Santa Laura, Rexford.com, and the whole sorry mess.

The idea of such emotional dependence on another person, especially a woman, frightened Richard to his core. His mother had abandoned him when he'd been a toddler. And wasn't the maternal tie supposed to be the strongest of all? If his mother could leave, anyone could, he reasoned. He wondered what would have happened if fate had granted more time for his mother. Maybe they would have repaired their relationship.

Richard knew his father was impossible to live with in some of his moods. Maybe she would have discussed why she'd left. With her dead, no one would ever know.

A chuckle emanating from another lounge caught his attention. Turning, he beheld a slender, lovely Asian woman, with short, damp hair and a skimpy, leopard-print bikini. Linda Wing.

He walked over to her, then slumped down beside her chaise. "I've ruined everything with Ani. What am I going to do?"

Linda leaned back into her lounge with an exaggeratedly casual air. "Well, you really screwed up, you know."

"Yeah, I know."

"Ani's a fine person and a really sweet girl. You broke her heart."

"I know. I was totally wrong."

"You were a heartless bastard."

"That's enough," he said with irritation. "I'm not going to pay for this forever."

She laughed. "But if you can't get her back, you will, right? And so will Ani. And you saw through her cover. That's bad. Rexford.com was her first job. She might never work undercover again."

"What about you? What do you do?"

She winked. "If I told you, I'd have to kill you."

Richard wasn't sure if she was joking or not. He decided not to push it. "Since Ani can't work undercover anymore, why not help me out? It's not as though I'm compromising her."

"Yeah, you already did that. You took out three of us. Fortunately, I have more experience, and I'll be reassigned. Ani's another question." Linda stood and stretched, a lithe, cat-like creature. "You don't deserve her, but she loves you, the fool. And you've admitted that you blew it, which shows that maybe you'll learn from your mistakes."

"I'll try," he said, hoping he sounded humble. If he had to eat a little crow to get Ani back, he would.

"She enjoys Kihei town," Linda said. "Suggest an outing. She'll want to go."

"Okay!"

"But you're going to do the right thing, aren't you?" Leaning forward, Linda fixed him with a direct, dark glare. "She's not like me. Ani needs and deserves total commitment. Everything, including white lace and wedding cake."

Damn, these U.S.S.A. women were tough. Richard had a vision of Linda, armed with an Uzi, chasing him to the doors of a chapel where a white-clad Ani waited.

Except for the Uzi, the image didn't look so bad. Hell, Ani looked pretty good in white.

Clearing his throat, he said, "Yes, I'll do the right thing."

In a state of turmoil, Ani returned to the hotel suite she shared with Linda. Seeing Richard Rexford again had shaken her to her soul. She'd consciously suppressed her love for him, pushed aside her memories of him so completely that she'd almost forgotten how good he looked, smelled, felt by her side.

Less than five minutes of contact had brought everything rushing back. The way her heart leaped when he was near. His unique scent, oceanic but not fishy, freshened today by his swim. He'd emerged from the waves like a sea god, the sun glistening off every wet, tanned plane and toned muscle. More handsome than ever, he didn't appear to have suffered weeks of sleepless nights tossing and turning.

Ani frowned. Some people have all the luck.

A tap at the door heralded Linda, with Richard in tow. "We're going into Kihei town," Linda said. "Richard says he knows a local massage therapist with magic hands."

Miffed, Ani narrowed her eyes. She didn't like this new development. Was Richard Rexford trying to get to her through Linda?

Ani decided she'd better watch the situation. "I'll come along." She reached for her black flowered sarong and began to knot it around her body.

"Are you sure?" Richard shot her a sharp glance. "After all, you'll be with me."

She glowered back. "It can't be helped."

Chapter Twenty-Six

Somehow, Richard stopped himself from dancing a jig as he let Ani lead the way to a rental car. He exchanged a wink with Linda Wing when he helped her into the front passenger seat. She'd been right about Ani.

Linda responded with a coolly raised brow and a frown, reminding him of his promise.

Ani drove along South Kihei Road between Wailea and Kihei, a route that had become familiar since their arrival four days before. "Where do I need to go?" she asked.

"I know the way." Richard smirked at her from the back seat. "You should have let me drive."

She bit her lip. Perhaps her approach was childish, but she'd wanted to retain control, so she drove. "Just tell me where to go," she said through gritted teeth.

"Now, children," Linda interposed.

"How do you know your friend is still there?" Ani asked.

"I phoned," Richard said with exasperation.

"Fast work," Ani grumbled. Typical of Richard Rexford, always bulling ahead at laser-speed.

With Richard's help, Ani easily found the office building where the massage therapist was located. Oliver, a thin, shaggy-haired Hawaiian who shared Richard's beach-bum demeanor, showed Ani and Linda around his spa.

Ani hadn't wanted to like Richard's friend or his facility, but despite herself, she was impressed. Oliver's spa, which comprised an entire floor of the building, included a locker room, showers, hot tubs, and several massage rooms. Everything was beautifully furnished, with rattan, tropical plants, and ceiling fans giving the place an open, airy feel.

When they returned to the waiting room, Richard said, "See you for dinner."

Oliver answered, "Wailea Bay? Okay, six p.m."

"It's a date." Linda beamed at Richard.

Faster than Ani liked, she found herself alone with Richard, wondering if she'd been set up by both her ex-boyfriend and her sister. "I'll take you back to your boat," she told him.

He grinned at her, opening the door to usher her outside. "Okay, after we go shopping. Oliver and Linda expect dinner aboard the *Trophy Wife*. You're invited, too."

Dumbfounded, Ani stared at him. "What did you say to Linda? Why is she doing this?"

"Maybe she knows I'm good for you."

"You're the worst thing that ever happened to me."

He raised his brows. "The very worst?"

An image of Daoud and Renée flashed through her mind. "No, not the worst," Ani admitted, riven by guilt. How could she have forgotten, even for a moment? "But you're absolutely not good for me."

"I can make you happy, Ani." He caught and held her gaze, certainty in his eyes. "Let me try."

She became absorbed in the blue depths. He seemed so earnest, so sincere. But how could she trust him?

After a brief fight over the car keys, she drove to Star Market. "You're going to shop like that?" She nodded at Richard's Speedo, covered only by a Hawaiian shirt borrowed from Oliver, with Oliver's spare thongs on his feet.

"You're not wearing much more, and a delightful sight you are," he murmured into her ear.

Ani had to admit that most of the shoppers were dressed with equal casualness. Even in December, Maui's weather continued mild and sultry. Heavy clothing wasn't practical.

Despite her resentment toward Richard, Ani became impressed by his care and preparation for the dinner. He picked out the best food in the store, sniffing both the fish and the pineapple to find the perfect pitch of freshness and ripeness. He even bought local, organic kim chee for Linda.

After returning to Wailea Point, they carried the sacks of groceries to the beach. Richard again stripped down to his Speedo and swam to the boat, then returned in the Zodiac for Ani. With trepidation, she watched the *Trophy Wife*'s hull loom larger in her vision as the Zodiac approached the yacht. How on earth had this happened? She'd flown half an ocean away to forget Richard Rexford, but here she was again, climbing aboard his boat.

Cursing herself, she helped him secure the Zodiac, then unload groceries. At six o'clock, when Linda and Oliver showed up on the beach, Richard would pick them up for dinner. Until then, a whole three hours, she estimated, she was alone on the boat with Richard. Pushing aside her memories of what they'd done on this vessel, she busied herself carrying food to the galley and putting it away.

A skittering sound, like tiny claws, came from behind one of the cabinets. She grinned, realizing that at least one of her little allies had survived the ocean voyage.

Richard entered the galley. At his heels trod one of the biggest cats Ani had ever seen. A tailless gray tiger—a Manx?—he had to weigh at least twenty pounds, Ani guessed.

"Oh, your kitty!" She bent, hoping to pet the cat. "Here, kitty, kitty."

The Manx purred.

"What's his name?" she asked.

He glared at the Manx, whose purr increased to a growl. "I don't know what its previous owner called him. I call him Psycho Killer. He's clawed me, bitten me, even peed on my bed. He hates me."

"Why did you get him?"

He shot her a nasty grin. "He's a good mouser. Every day, he brings me another furry little varmint. He usually leaves them on my pillow in the mornings."

"Ewww!"

"Ew is right. And this is all your fault."

"You deserved it," she said, defiant. "A small price to pay for what you did."

Purring loudly, the cat stalked toward Ani and wrapped around her legs in a figure eight pattern. Kneeling, she ruffled the cat's ears and stroked his soft, furry neck. "Psycho likes me."

"He would." He cast her a bitter glower. "Look at what he and your avian friends did to my lovely decks and railings."

She stepped outside and let her gaze follow his pointing finger. The formerly flawless, varnished wood had been defaced by scores of cat scratches and bird claws. Eying Psycho Killer, she resolved to stay very friendly with the feline.

She glanced at Richard. The old scratches on his arms had healed, and he appeared to have reached a truce with the cat. She wouldn't waste any pity on Richard Rexford. Just remember that, Ani, she told herself. No mercy!

Ani slipped into her old habits as though they were comfortable, broken-in shoes. In the galley, she prepared salad while Richard grilled ahi tuna steaks and pineapple on his hibachi after Linda and Oliver showed up. They enjoyed the sunset, then a wonderful fish dinner. After dessert, they sipped wine, talked, and watched an enormous moon ignite the night sea with silver.

And Richard . . . *boy, is he pouring it on!* He didn't miss a chance to touch her in passing, flatter her, show her in a million ways he wanted her back. She realized she remained susceptible. Even a fleeting caress on her shoulder made her quiver with need. She wanted to touch him back so badly her shoulders were tense with the strain of keeping her hands to herself.

Finally the evening came to an end, and Richard loaded them all into the Zodiac for the short return trip to the beach. Oliver stepped out of the Zodiac first, then turned to help Linda, leaving Richard and Ani alone in the boat.

Richard resisted the impulse to gun the engine and abduct Ani, take her back to the *Trophy Wife* to ravish her until she came to her senses. Instead, he brushed his lips along her hairline, enjoying her flowery scent melded with sea and sand.

"I had a wonderful time." He stroked her shoulder, left bare by the sarong. He watched the tiny hairs on her arm lift and tried not to grin.

"Thank you for dinner."

"I liked seeing you back in my boat, where you belong."

Ani stiffened. "I don't belong there."

"You do, and someday soon, you'll realize it."

She stuck her defiant little chin in the air. "No. I belong with Linda, at this hotel."

"Better make sure that Linda agrees." Richard climbed out of the Zodiac and offered his hand. Ani took it, and he helped her to shore.

"What do you mean?" she asked.

Richard nodded in the direction of Oliver and Linda, who stood closer to each other than mere conversation required. Ani couldn't help overhearing Oliver, who asked her sister to breakfast the next morning. She wasn't surprised to hear Linda accept.

"Well, I guess it's just you and me tomorrow," Richard said to Ani.

She raised a brow. "Or just me."

"Oh, come on. You're not going to sit in your room alone when Linda's out having fun. Let me take you snorkeling."

"Hmm." Every morning, Ani had seen swimmers floating slowly in the waters outside of Wailea Point. Later she'd overheard them excitedly discussing the beautiful tropical fish and turtles they'd seen in the ocean. She hadn't tried it yet, but with Linda busy, why shouldn't she?

When Oliver called their room the next morning, Linda left for her breakfast date in an excited swirl of French perfume and gauzy skirts. After braiding her hair, Ani dressed in her bathing suit and a sarong cover-up before walking to the beach. She settled down on a lounge to wait for Richard.

Normally Ani wouldn't see the light of day until mid-afternoon. But the best snorkeling was in the morning, she'd heard, before the trade winds blew, churning the waves. Tender and pearly, the early light had just touched the water when Richard made his appearance. But instead of diving into the water with snorkeling gear, he piloted the Zodiac to shore.

"Hop in," he said.

She eyed him suspiciously. Again, control emerged as an issue. She didn't trust Richard to take her anywhere. "Why?"

"The snorkeling is pretty good here, but I can take you to a place where it's even better. Come on. I have espresso on the boat," he coaxed.

She perked up. She'd wanted coffee, but the beachside vendors weren't open at this early hour. Perhaps she shouldn't be a pushover. But espresso . . . "All right."

Richard's blood sang in his veins as he navigated the *Trophy Wife* southward. Though a slight breeze rattled the rigging, the sea was flat and calm, excellent for snorkeling. Better, the woman he loved stood by his side in the wheelhouse.

He wondered if he prayed hard enough, he could make this perfect moment last forever.

He took the boat around La Perouse, a spit of hardened lava, and pointed. "These are the youngest lava fields on Maui, a mere couple of centuries old, or so."

"A wink of time, geologically," Ani murmured. She seemed fascinated by the mysterious landscape. "This is what the moon must look like." She shivered.

"Desolate and barren."

"So lonely." She wrapped her arms around herself.

"Hey." He roped an arm around her shoulders. "I'm here. None of that."

She snuggled into his embrace for the slightest moment, then, as though remembering her anger, moved away. Though he would have preferred her to stay, his heart lightened. She'd allowed his touch, however briefly. This was the beginning of trust, he hoped. By the end of the swim, he believed she'd learn to trust him some more. The ocean was as alien a world as Mars, with all kinds of dangers. If she'd let him guide her underwater, maybe she'd allow him more latitude above it.

Chapter Twenty-Seven

Richard anchored close to the point so that the reef was an easy swim, but far out enough so that the yacht would be safe. Then he found the snorkeling gear, stored under one of the bench seats rimming the deck. "Let me show you how to do this." He disentangled a facemask with a snorkel attached and fitted it to Ani's head. "I'm glad you braided your hair. Good move. It stays out of the way."

She visibly blossomed from the compliment. He managed to stop himself from kissing her, though he didn't know how, since she looked adorable and sexy at the same time. Though a one-piece, the red bathing suit she wore didn't conceal very much. Cut high on the hip and low over her breasts, it covered just enough to make his imagination work overtime and his memories run on overdrive.

If he tweaked the top just a bit, he'd see the nipples he'd loved so well. And if he tugged at the crotch, he could probably get to her in the water. The thought made him start to harden.

The red suit reminded him of the thong panties he'd bought for her. He wondered if she'd ever worn them, how she solved her shaving dilemma, and if he'd find out.

Pulling the mask off, he handed it to her, then leaned over into storage to find matching swim fins. The move gave his hard-on time to shrink. He took his gear and walked to the back of the boat. "We're gonna put our mask and fins on here, and just drop backwards over the transom."

"Like on T.V.?"

"Exactly. But first . . . " He spat into his facemask.

"Richard!"

"Hey, I'm not just being gross. Saliva is the best thing for keeping the interior of your mask from fogging up. Spit, swish it around a little, then wash it out with seawater."

With a dainty little wince, she did as he asked, then set the mask over her face and followed him over the back of the boat.

The turquoise, liquid world beneath the waves immediately fascinated Ani. Everything shimmered with a luminous, magical light. The temperate ocean buoyed her, suspending her in a weightless state. Her land-based concerns washed away, left behind the moment her body hit the water.

She stuck her head above the waves. "Wow."

"Yeah." He smiled at her. "Now let's practice breathing through the snorkel. Stay relaxed and breathe through your mouth. If you get tense, just stop what you're doing, relax, and breathe."

She floated on her stomach for a few seconds, then raised her head. "I think I'm ready to go."

Taking her hand, he swam with her toward the reef. The warmth of the sea didn't compare to his grip. Amazing that the ocean separating them didn't crackle with sexual electricity. Energy traveled up her arm from his fingers, flowed through her body, and centered at her sensitive female core. The current sliding past her skin heightened her excitement; even her bathing suit, snugly clasping her delta, conspired to arouse her all the more, as did the slight sting of salt water in the tiny nicks her razor had left.

To top it all off, Richard in the water was sleek and glorious, as though he were half-dolphin. His sinuous body seemed to be one with the ocean as he led her to the reef. If she'd known how sensuous an experience this would be, would she have backed out? Never, she thought. Whatever the risk, this was worth it. She knew she'd be underwater again and again.

Three enormous, silvery-blue fish flashed past her, causing her to gasp in water and choke. Raising her head above the waves, she spat out her mouthpiece, coughed, and asked, "What were they?"

Richard's shoulders shook with laughter. "Dinner."

"What?"

"Those were ahi, sweetheart. The same fish we ate last night."

"They were huge! They won't attack us, will they?"

He laughed harder. "No, they won't. The only animal that would hurt you here would be a moray eel, and they're easily avoided. Just don't put your hands into crevices in the reef. Actually, don't touch anything. The coral is very delicate."

"I have read that it's composed of millions of tiny animals."

"Yeah, and the slightest touch kills them."

"So it's look, but don't touch. Are there sharks?"

He frowned. "They're around, but rarely seen. They feed at night, so don't worry about them. C'mon, let's go."

Replacing her mouthpiece, she followed him closer to the reef. A school of round, bright yellow fish zipped past. Below her, hardened dark lava flows interrupted fields of pale sand, sporting numerous stationary creatures: red, spiky sea urchins, ghastly-looking brain corals, and strange animals completely outside her education.

The varied life astounded her. Fish of all sizes and colors of the rainbow, even striped and spotted fish. Most amazing of all were fish she recognized from tourists' t-shirts, the humu-humu, Hawaii's state fish. She immediately understood why its nickname was the Picasso fish. Their markings were random, crazy to the eye.

He grabbed her hand again, seizing her attention, and pointed. Bigger than a platter, a massive sea turtle hovered majestically below them, slow and serene. She floated, her hand in Richard's, watching. The turtle had to be old, she thought, trying to count the number of plates on its green-brown shell. It occasionally sculled with two leathery, scaly flippers on either side of its squared-off head, but otherwise seemed contented to drift, calm and unhurried, through its quiet world.

Every once in a while it poked its snout at something on the reef or in the sand. Then, with a flick of flippers, it shot through the water to the other side of the reef, without apparent effort, remaining suspended and at ease.

Effortless motion, she thought. Amazing. And the turtle seemed so content, at one with everything around it, at peace with its journey.

Her hand still in Richard's, Ani watched the turtle for a long time. Gradually her breathing slowed and evened. She swayed up and down on the ocean's breast, riding the gentle swells. Her world narrowed until it contained only the sea, the turtle, and Richard.

She was at peace.

Richard squeezed her hand and, as one, they surfaced. She pulled off her mask, aware of a slight ache beneath her nose where the mask had pressed. After swimming quietly back to the boat, he served her coffee and rolls on deck. She examined him as he relaxed, at ease in his environment. He seemed different, somehow, more centered and calm than in Santa Laura.

Ani realized he really didn't belong in that high-tech world. At heart, he was a simple person who appeared content to sail his boat and stare at the horizon where sea and sky met.

But where did that leave her?

She cleared her throat. "I wondered why I hadn't heard from you for so long."

He tipped back his chair, balancing on its two back legs. "I've been here." He gestured to the wide Pacific. "Before that, I had to straighten some things out."

"Like what?"

"After I got your email I had a lot of thinking to do." He looked at her. "I don't know if I can ever apologize enough."

She shrugged. "I don't know if you can, either," she joked. "But what else did you do about it?"

"Nothing."

"Nothing?"

"Like I said, I thought a lot, and came to some decisions."

"Ummm?"

He stared out to sea, his profile limned by the ocean waves in the background. "I've decided that not one of my relatives will ever work with me again." He turned his head to look at her. "Except for my wife."

"Your . . . wife?" she faltered. If he was talking about someone else, she'd kill both of them. If he meant her, he was deluded.

"Mmm. It happens that the woman I love is the most talented programmer I've ever met. It would be a shame to limit her to motherhood."

She stared at him. "Who, exactly, are you talking about?"

"You, of course."

"Me? You're crazy. I'm not ready to have your baby or anyone else's. But I do feel the loss of my parents. How can you cut off your father, your uncle, and your cousins, just like that?" Ani made a chopping motion with the side of her hand.

"When I followed up on the files you sent me, I discovered that my cousins Evelyn and Mark have always been in Comp-Line's pay, with specific orders to trash Rexford.com." He shook his head. "I should have seen it coming, but I wanted to prove myself to my father and uncle."

"That's only natural."

His jaw tightened. "I kept doing them favors, like hiring family members, as though that would earn their respect or approval." He gave a grim little laugh. "What a joke that was. They've been undercutting us from day one."

"I wondered about that bet," she said. "Mark's a lawyer. Shouldn't he have stopped you?"

"Stopped us? Ha. He suggested it."

"Ohhh . . . and he stole the software and passed it to Comp-Line."

"He sure did, under Sundeen's orders. Sundeen, the traitor." Richard's laugh was bitter, more like a choke. "I saw him on T.V., doing the perp walk into federal court in San Francisco. Then I came here."

"Did Thomas know?"

"I'm not sure yet. He denies it, but I don't know." Richard looked at her, his eyes dark and tortured. "He met you, you see, and could tell there was something very special between us. But he's always wanted me to marry money rather than brains."

Ani couldn't help smiling.

"Anyway, I hope I can reconcile with my family once I've eliminated the rivalries between us." He rubbed the blond stubble on his chin, lit golden by the mid-morning sun. "I'm selling Rexford.com."

She gasped. "But you've worked so hard."

"I'll be amply rewarded for it, I'm sure." He grinned at her. "To the tune of many millions. How'd you like to be a rich man's wife, Ani Sharif?"

She lifted her chin into the air. "You can't buy me. I don't care about money."

"I know that."

"I can't marry you, or anyone. Spies can't love."

"So don't be a spy."

"It's all I know."

"Honey, if the first target on your first undercover mission saw through you, how long do you think you're going to survive playing the spy game?" he asked, with great gentleness.

She looked down at her plate. "Maybe not very long."

"You could get hurt, even killed. Wanna play games with me, instead?"

"Play games? You've been playing games with me from the day we met."

"Cute, very cute. A new company called Game Systems has asked me to create a second, more sophisticated version of Mega-Bet. One that can be downloaded onto cell phones and P.D.A.s."

Ani's mind began to race. "You want to work with me?"

"You betcha. I'll dump Rexford.com and its problems. You quit playing Bond girl. We'll live on the boat, get rich, and have fun writing game programs."

She wrung her hands together. How could she decide right away? She'd be giving up everything she'd built her life around for the last ten years.

She looked at Richard. His blue eyes were earnest, maybe even a little desperate.

He touched her body, mind, heart, and soul in ways no one ever had, or ever would again. How could she let him go?

What did she really want?

She wanted to trust him. She wanted him to love her forever, and to love him back.

But how could she know? Taking a deep breath, she said, "I'm game to play."

"Good." He made a grab for her.

She dodged him with ease, slipping around the foremast. "Not that kind of game. We have a lot to work out."

He stopped, his expression solemn. "I know we do. I know I've behaved shamefully."

"Shamelessly, too."

"And that I don't deserve you."

"No, you don't."

"But you're so wonderful, I can't stay away." He cocked his head. "In fact, is there any man alive who's worthy of the wonderful Ani Sharif?"

She aimed a barefooted kick at his shin, leaving a damp print.

"Ow. I suppose I deserved that, also."

"Yes, you did."

"You're acting as though I suggested bungee jumping without the cord."

She gave her sarcastic little laugh. "Something like that."

He heaved a sigh. "All I can tell you is that I screwed up. I probably will again, though I hope not as monumentally as I did this time. Most people do screw up, Ani. If you want perfection, you'll end up a pretty lonely lady."

She paused, then said, "There's something we could do that would show you have really changed."

"Beyond offering you marriage and commitment?"

"I never asked for marriage and commitment. I don't want a silly ring. I want you. All of you. Your love and your trust."

He hesitated. "You're a smart lady, and I'm sure you've already figured out that trusting . . . well, it's hard for me."

"Yes, but I know a way to, how would you say it? Jump-start the process." She smiled at him, feeling daring and bold and very, very wicked. Then she took his hand and led him below, to his bedroom.

"Are we gonna fool around? Cool!" Richard bounced on the bed, a roguish glint in his eye.

Ani submerged her smile. He needed to be tested. Trust would be forged, or all would be lost. "Take off your clothes." Turning to the closet, she removed his robe. She wondered if Richard remembered the day he'd worn it with her as vividly as did she.

Compelling as ever, he securely held her attention while he stripped. Her gaze trailed over his fit torso, the muscles, tense and corded; the long, tanned legs; and in between, his penis, jutting from its golden lair.

When he was naked, and she still clothed, she pulled the sash from the loops of his robe with a snap. "Lie down, please."

He swallowed. "Oh, Lord. I think I know what's coming."

CHAPTER TWENTY-EIGHT

Ani let herself smile. She could empathize with Richard's predicament. But she had no choice. If he didn't give himself to her completely, without reservation, she'd never know if he truly trusted or loved her. "Can you handle this?"

His jaw clenched. "With you, yes. Anything."

"Good." She drew out the word, made it into a caress to match the one she smoothed over his tanned chest. "Good." Pressing a palm into his sternum, she pushed, forcing him to lie on the bed.

Straddling his hips, she kissed him, thrusting in her tongue as forcefully as he'd ever taken her mouth. Beneath her swimsuit, his arousal swelled against her, his need feeding hers. Sweat glistened on his pecs.

"Good," she murmured against his mouth. Reaching for the silken sash, she bound it around his right wrist, looped it over his headboard, then pulled it tight.

Richard gripped the headboard with his bound hand. Somewhere deep in his soul, he'd known what she'd demand as proof of his love and trust. He believed she'd kill herself rather than hurt him. So why was he afraid?

As she secured his second wrist next to the first, the realization burst upon him. The bonds around his hands symbolized the chains around his heart, tying him forever to Ani. The silken sash would drag him into their shared future, from the empty pleasures of bachelorhood to the fullness and security of commitment.

"Together always," he said to Ani.

"Yes, forever and always." She grinned at him, white teeth flashing against amber skin. Damn, but she was beautiful and oh, so sexy, as she dipped toward him. Tugging down the top of her suit, she treated his mouth to the tiniest taste of a nipple.

Bobbing and weaving, she teased him without a shred of mercy, and his mind went blank with need. "Please," he begged, his voice raw.

Ani slid down his body, caressing his aching hard-on with the slick, damp fabric of her bathing suit before suckling him once, hard and fast. She popped him out of her mouth and he yelled with frustration, writhing against the bonds.

She laughed. Laughed!

"You little witch!" He yanked hard against the sash, but she'd bound him tight.

"Watch, Richard," she taunted. Standing close, so he could smell her sultry fragrance, but not near enough to reach with his mouth, she slid one red, satiny strap off her shoulder. Its elastic left a narrow red line on her golden skin. He longed to run his tongue along that line, kiss it and make it all better. A shame that such perfection should ever be marred.

He caught the merest glimpse of one nipple, a dusky crescent. He sucked in a frantic breath. He thought he was going to explode. He'd never been so hard in his life. He didn't know if he could stand it much longer.

Slipping a finger under the other strap, Ani tugged it down, baring herself to the waist. She cupped her erect breasts and smiled at him.

"Please. Please hurry. Lord, Ani, you have no idea what you're doing to me."

"Does it . . . hurt?" She trailed one finger along his length.

"It will if something doesn't happen soon." His entire body vibrated with unfulfilled want.

"Oh, poor Richard." She stood, placed both hands on her hips, and slowly rolled her bathing suit off, letting it drop to the floor. Stepping out of it, she draped it over him. The damp, cool cloth calmed him down a little, until he noticed that something was different about her body.

"Oh, Ani." He laughed. "So this is how you solved the shaving dilemma."

She looked down, blushing. "I started to shave so nothing would hang out of this suit, and I just couldn't get the sides even. One thing led to another, I guess."

"Until it all came off. Oh, baby. You look like a porno queen. Come over here and let me have a taste."

She gave him a frown. "Hey, I'm the one in control."

"So you are. But don't you want to have a good time?"

Her brows contracted. "Good point. Sorry if I'm not doing this the right way. I've never done this before."

"I haven't either." If he really tried, could he reach her thigh and get a nibble? He strained against the bonds.

"Really?"

"Yeah. I couldn't stand the idea of being tied up, until now."

"But you wanted to tie me up."

"Very much." He smiled at her, heat running through his veins as he remembered. It had been one hell of a turn-on.

"What was that about?"

He shifted. "Everything happened so fast between us. I needed to keep control."

"You were the person who initiated everything." She sounded surprised.

"I couldn't help myself. I had to have you. I still feel the same way." Maybe she needed to hear it again. "Ani, I love you. Nothing—*nothing*—will stop me from having you in my life."

"What if I say no?"

He closed his eyes. "Don't play with me, please. I have to know. Now."

She looked at him, really looked, and saw him opened to her completely for the first time. Richard had never before revealed himself so entirely, hadn't given himself so utterly.

Ani knew she held his fate, and hers, in her hands.

She rubbed her body over his, lying full length. She opened her legs, and his erection slid between her thighs, cradled by her flesh. She murmured into his ear, "I'm yours," before she took him.

CHAPTER TWENTY-NINE

Five days later, as the sun set amid swirls of coral and gold, Richard waited for Ani beneath a white-painted gazebo near the beach. He wore the local equivalent of formal wear: a bleached linen suit with an aloha shirt, open at the collar. He wondered what kind of dress Ani had selected for their special day.

The hotel had been marvelous. The concierge had assured him that weddings were their specialty and had taken all the arrangements out of their hands. "Just show up with the rings," she'd said. Slipping a hand into his pocket, he ran a finger around the chased filigree band he'd selected for Ani. Delicate and strong, like her, it would complement the locket she frequently wore.

Though the hotel staff seemed competent, Richard still worried. Ani had taken a lot of persuasion to agree to marriage. She was young, just twenty-three. Maybe too young to tie herself down to an old sea dog like him.

What if she backed out? An icy hand clutched his heart at the thought.

He looked at his watch. She was twenty minutes late. And where was Linda? He paced back and forth across the narrow confines of the gazebo.

Oliver entered. "Don't worry, man, they'll be here. Linda went upstairs to do something different with her hair. She told me that Ani had an errand to run in Kahului."

"Kahului?" Richard was confused. Ani hadn't previously

shown interest in visiting Kahului, the county seat. "Why Kahu-lui?"

Oliver shrugged. "Beats me. Maybe she's getting a special outfit or something. There's more shops there."

"What's Linda doing?"

"Probably putting more streaks in her hair."

Both men laughed.

"I dunno what's up with her," Oliver said. "She's been acting a little weird lately."

"I thought you and she were getting along great." Richard didn't tell Oliver what he knew: that Linda, dedicated to the spy life, would never commit to any man.

"I did, too, but . . . Who knows about women?" Oliver shrugged. "Hey, they did a nice job on the flowers, didn't they?"

Good. Oliver didn't want to discuss Linda, so Richard was spared the awkwardness of deceiving his friend. Relieved, he nodded, then tried to show interest in the setting. The latticework gazebo had been entwined with tropical vines and flowers, so the scents of tuber-rose and plumeria hung in the sultry air. He and Ani didn't expect many guests, so only a few white chairs had been set up. At one side, tables draped in white held silver ice buckets chilling bottles of his favorite champagne.

Everything was perfect, except for the absent bride and her tardy maid-of-honor.

"Do you know what you'll say in the ceremony?" he asked Oliver, an ordained minister.

"Sure. I do this for tourists all the time. They like having a native Hawaiian conduct wedding ceremonies."

Richard grinned. Oliver was typical of locals. Jacks of all trades, they did whatever they needed to do, letting the tourist industry support them.

Oliver continued, "A little hula, a little native hokey-pokey, then everyone drinks champagne and toasts the happy couple."

"It's legal, isn't it?"

"Oh, sure." Oliver took a folded piece of paper out of his pocket. "Here's the marriage license, ready for you and Ani to sign. I'll take it to Kahului tomorrow and record it, and then you're married."

Richard nodded. "Good. But where is she?"

"Here I am." Ani appeared at the doorway of the gazebo. She wore an ankle-length white sheath, flowers in her hair, and a big smile. She held the arm of someone familiar.

His father.

So that had been Ani's errand . . . picking up his father at the airport in Kahului.

The creeping fear of rejection that had always nagged at the edges and corners of Richard's life reappeared deep in his belly, twisting his gut. He'd never been able to trust his father to react predictably. What would Thomas Rexford, the original T-Rex, say now?

After what his father had done, Richard wanted to throw out his old man on his butt. But Ani had gone to a lot of trouble to get Thomas Rexford to Maui for this ceremony.

Richard wouldn't disappoint her. He swallowed his pride and advanced, holding out his right hand. "Father."

"Richie." Instead of shaking his hand, the old boy hugged him. "Congratulations, son. I never thought I'd see this day."

"Uh, thanks." Over his father's shoulder, Richard caught Ani's glance. She had a sentimental smile on her face and, he suspected, a tear or two misted her eyes. He pulled away from his father. "I take it I have your blessing?"

"You do."

"I'm surprised. I thought you didn't approve of marriage."

"Everyone's different, son. I approve of your marriage."

Richard shook his head. "I'm confused. Did you sell secrets

to the Chinese? And why did you try to torpedo Rexford.com?"

"I didn't. I didn't do any of that. It was Sundeen, all of it. I'm afraid your uncle's gone off the deep end," Thomas said heavily. "After planting Evelyn and Mark in your company, he's been plotting to destroy you."

Ani's brows contracted. "Why does he hate Richard so much?"

"It's more like jealousy," Thomas said. "Look, Mark's never been much in the brains department. Sundeen had to give Harvard a huge endowment to get him into their law school. He hated your successes."

"I thought it was all about needing money," Ani said.

"That's another factor. His ex-wives have sucked him dry. Deep down, he loathes women." Thomas squeezed Ani's elbow, cackling. "Just wait 'til he gets a load of this little lady!"

Ani gave him a frown from beneath her dark eyelashes. "We will not be your tools, Thomas. Remember what we discussed?"

"Yes, I do. Your plans sound great to me. Richard has a natural talent for game creation. Shame to waste it."

Will wonders ever cease? A compliment from T-Rex. Must be a historic occasion. "Thank you." Richard's brain buzzed with the implications. Acceptance and affection from his father; along with Ani's love, the last, missing pieces of Richard's life had fallen into place.

"I won't go back on my word, Ani, but I expect you to keep yours." His father beetled his brows at Richard. "Just make sure you perform your part, young man."

Richard's heart accelerated. "And what part might that be?"

"Just do what comes naturally." Thomas cackled again before ambling over to Oliver, who had taken his place in front of a massive bouquet arranged in one corner of the gazebo.

"What's he talking about?" Richard asked Ani.

"I think he wants grandchildren." Tipping back her head, she kissed the hollow of his throat.

Richard's eyes widened as he envisioned Ani ripe and round with his daughter while he played with their son on the swings near their cottage in the Santa Laura Hills. He slid his arms around his bride to hold her close.

Linda appeared at the door of the gazebo, looking superb in a plain slip-dress painted with pale pink flowers. The streaks in her hair had been subdued.

Ani went to her foster sister and hugged her fiercely. She whispered into Linda's ear, "You look wonderful."

"I do? Oh, good. I toned down the streaks in my hair. I didn't want them to distract people from you." Linda smiled. "You're a beautiful bride."

A break in Linda's voice caught Ani's attention. Linda Wing, turning into a sentimental slob? Uh-oh. What would take Linda out of her funk? "I have a surprise for you," Ani told Linda. "It followed me from the airport, and it should be here shortly. Right now, in fact."

Linda turned. Entering the gazebo were a couple that she recognized instantly and greeted with hugs. "Tommy and Kate!"

After a few seconds, she let Kate go so Ani could introduce the Forresters to everyone else. As Linda stepped away, allowing greetings to take place, she jostled the arm of a dark young man who'd slipped in behind Tommy Forrester.

"Oh, it's you," she said with irritation. "What are you doing here?"

"Ani thought you needed a date." Michael Han smiled. Suave as ever, he wore a black linen suit and a collarless shirt.

"Liar," Ani said without animosity. "Linda's with Oliver."

Michael looked in the direction of her gesturing hand and frowned. "I'm actually here to give you your new assignment," he told Linda.

Oh, shit, she thought. Don't tell me . . .

Michael smirked, but his tone was matter-of-fact. "I'm the new Honolulu station chief. Kate and Tommy asked me to fly here because you'll be transferred to Hawaii."

She didn't want to disrupt Ani's special day, so Linda grabbed his upper arm to drag him out of the gazebo. "The hell you say!"

"There's no need for you to become so upset." Brown, calm eyes surveyed her. "Listen, I pulled every string I had in D.C. to get you for this mission."

She glared. "I don't want to work for you."

"It's done. You're mine."

"What did you say?"

"After your vacation, report to the station office in Honolulu. There are some very interesting matters developing there." He slid one hand behind her elbow, as if he wanted to escort her inside.

Despite her helpless fury and rage, the touch of his hand reminded her of his kiss. Damn, damn, damn.

Turning her mind to business, she decided to nuzzle at the bait he dangled. "What interesting matters?"

He stopped at the doorway. "As you know, Honolulu Harbor is one of the biggest, busiest ports in the world."

She pulled away. "I know. I'm not an idiot."

"I know you're not. The I.C.E. is a great organization, but they can't inspect every cargo container that comes through there."

"Neither can we."

"We suspect that there's a terrorist cell, Taliban or Al-Qaida, smuggling in nuclear material in order to detonate a dirty bomb somewhere, maybe in a tourist section like Waikiki or at an event like the Pro Bowl."

Linda sucked in a breath. "Thousands could be hurt or killed."

"And widespread panic could ensue. It's our job to intercept the nuclear materials and capture the bad guys."

"What's the Honolulu U.S.S.A. office like?"

He shrugged. "Moribund. We have to get it going. On top of that, we have to infiltrate the terrorist cell, deal with the I.C.E. and the local authorities. This is a very sensitive mission, and I want you to be my main troubleshooter. Interested?"

Linda bit her lower lip, thinking, then met his gaze. "I'll do it, under one condition."

"Name it."

She leaned into him, letting him smell her perfume, bringing her lips close to his, exulting at the return of her feminine power.

A light flared in his eyes, and she knew he was hers.

She'd torture him for years. She whispered, "Never, ever touch me again."

Smiling, she turned on her high heel and walked into the gazebo, deliberately swinging her hips a little more than necessary, then turned to see what he was doing.

He hadn't taken his eyes off her. He said, "I won't have to. You'll come to me."

She huffed. "When angels dance in hell."

"I bet it'll be more like devils doing the watusi in heaven." He grinned at her, following as she sashayed toward the rest of the bridal party.

"Hey," she said to Oliver. "Don't you have a wedding to perform?"

"I sure do," he said. His glance found Richard and Ani. "If these two folks are still game."

"Call me a bunny," Richard said. "I don't care if anyone, ever again, calls me T-Rex."

"I hope not," Thomas rumbled. "That's my nickname, and I'm not ready to give it up."

Smiling, Ani gazed at Richard. "I believe it's time, then." She felt her heartbeat quicken.

Richard took her hand and raised it to his mouth, nipping gently at her soft skin. "Long past time, my love." He turned her wrist over, rubbing the pulse point with his lips.

"Do you feel that?" she asked. "My heart beats faster, just because you're near. I feel like a dopey teenager in a silly love song."

"If you're dopey and silly, I'm goofy and loopy." He winked. "And, I'm ready. Are you?"

"Always. Forever."

Together, they turned to face the minister.

ABOUT THE AUTHOR

After dumping a brutal career as a trial attorney, **Sue Swift** turned her attention to writing. Using two pseudonyms, she has sold eleven novels, plus several short stories and articles. Her previous Five Star books are *Walk Like a Man* and *Triangle.*

Her hobbies are hockey, world travel, and Asian martial arts, in which she's earned a second-degree black belt. She can be contacted through her website, sue-swift.com.